DARK FLASHES

by

Philippa Bower

DARK FLASHES

Published 2023 by KDP

© Philippa Bower

The right of Philippa Bower to be identified as author of this work has been asserted by her in accordance with the Copyright, Designs and Patents Act 1988.

All rights reserved.

Cover design by Perdisma Edits
www.perdisma.com

To my dear family, including the ever-growing number of grandchildren, great nieces and great nephews, who are forbidden to read my stories until they are at least
18 years old.

Also to any of my dear friends who buy this book. I hope you enjoy reading my stories as much as I have enjoyed writing them.

ONE

Horror, sex and fantasy

A Change of Perspective
The world seemed a fairer place once Mark could levitate

Mark sat, sulking, in the back of the car next to his sister, Popsie.

"I don't see why I had to come," he said.

"Don't you want to see your grandparents?" asked his mother, who was sitting in the passenger seat.

"I want to see them," piped up Popsie, virtuously. Mark glared at her. At nine years old she was two years younger than him, but already she was starting to treat him with contempt. She returned his glare with a sigh and upraised eyes that made him want to hit her.

When they arrived, his grandparents greeted them in the downstairs reception area. Above them the living platforms stretched upwards in a spiral that rose many stories high.

"I thought we would have tea down here with the children," said his grandmother. "And then we could leave them to play while we go up to the lounge."

A pretty, young servant girl was setting out the tea things. Mark was looking admiringly at her, when he caught her eye. He looked away quickly. She had the mindless, vacant stare of the lobotomised.

While his grandmother poured the tea and handed cakes around, he raged inwardly at the unfairness of a society that divided its young people irreversibly into upper and working classes. His tumultuous thoughts were interrupted by Popsie, who got down from the table and stood in the middle of the floor.

"Look what I can do," she said proudly. She then concentrated hard and rose about a foot from the floor.

"Come to Grandma, darling," said the old lady and clasped Popsie in her arms. "You clever girl. You will soon be joining us on the living platforms."

"What about you, Mark?" asked his grandfather. "Are you able to levitate yet?"

Mark bent low over his plate, his face burning. He felt five pairs of eyes boring into him.

"This is delicious cake," said his father, changing the subject and saving him from further humiliation.

At last tea was finished and the adults levitated up to the first-floor lounge. Mark, unwilling to be left alone with his sister, started to climb up the support beams.

"Daddy says if you didn't spend so much time climbing, you might learn to levitate." Popsie's irritating little voice wafted up to him as he reached the edge of the platform.

He raised his head carefully and saw that the adults were sitting in easy chairs, chatting.

"Mark will be twelve next year," his grandfather was saying. "He will have to take the examination to see if he is able to levitate."

His mother was about to say something but was interrupted by his father. "You keep saying he's a late developer, darling. But supposing he's too late. Supposing he fails the exam."

"But he's so intelligent," wailed his mother.

"Don't worry, dear," said his grandmother. "The lobotomy will take care of that. He will be quite content to join the working class after his frontal cortex has been destroyed."

Mark had heard enough. He lowered himself over the edge of the living platform and felt for a foothold. He couldn't find one. He reached further until he lost his grip and was falling. Terror filled his heart as he felt himself plunging downwards. Faster and faster he plummeted, then something clicked in his brain and, instead of crashing to the ground, he slowed and landed with a heavy thump.

"What's going on?" Heads were peering over the edge of the platform.

"I'm just practising my levitation," he said, scrambling to his feet. He concentrated, trying to remember what his brain had done. Then he was rising up and up until he was level with the platform. The adults stood back to give him room and he landed lightly among them.

What joy there was, what relief and kisses and assurances that everyone knew that he could do it. They all levitated down to the ground and even his sister treated him with new respect.

They left and, as his smiling grandparents waved them goodbye, Mark looked beyond them to the servant girl. She seemed happy enough. Perhaps everything was all right with the world after all.

Alien Corn

Jake's crop circle meant more than he realised

Jake stood up to his chest in a wheat field and surveyed the results of his evening's labours. It had been an exhausting business, but with the aid of some rope and a plank he had managed to tread down a complex pattern of loops and circles. He reckoned it was his best crop circle yet and he grinned to himself at the thought of excited UFO enthusiasts puzzling over its meaning.

A distant light appeared. Bother, the farmer must have woken up. Jake crouched low and prepared to make his escape. Moments later the light was directly over him, beaming down, illuminating him in its cold, white glare. He was caught. It must be a police helicopter. He was wondering why it made no noise when he found himself being sucked up the beam and into a spacecraft.

Jake sat on a strange, slightly-resilient floor and stared up at a curious group of grey aliens. The group included a naked man who was saying, "It's OK you're safe now."

"Safe?" He gawped around stupidly.

"You made the intergalactic sign for help. Presumably you needed rescuing," said the man, his welcoming smile turning into a frown.

Jake was a quick-witted lad and rapidly regained his composure. That corn circle of his must have had more meaning than he had realised.

"Yeah," he said. "Thanks."

The man's face cleared. "You can take off your human costume and have a nice acid bath, that will freshen you up."

Beyond the naked man was a porthole through which Jake could see Earth. It was a round blue-green sphere, which was rapidly getting smaller against the blackness of space. At what sort of speed could they be travelling? He felt his brain wobble as it tried to grasp what was happening to him and then realised that the aliens were looking at him expectantly. He dragged his reeling mind back to the conversation.

"No thanks," he said hurriedly. "I don't feel like a bath just at the moment. I – er - think I'd better be getting back to Earth."

"But if you were in danger of being discovered?" said the man, his suspicious frown returning. "Surely it would be inadvisable for you to go back."

"Oh no," said Jake. "It wasn't that I was about to be discovered it was because …" His mind was racing as if his life depended on it, which, indeed it did. "Because the farmer nearly caught me making love to his wife." There was a sharp intake of breath.

"Oh," said the man looking at him with awe. "You are part of the breeding programme. Good luck to you. I don't know how you chaps do it. How you can bring yourself to mate with those disgusting, hairy creatures is beyond me."

Through the porthole Earth had become a dot. Now it started growing again. They were going back. Jake heaved a sigh of relief.

"Where do you want to be dropped?" asked the man, who was all friendliness again.

"To my house in Laburnum Avenue, please," said Jake.

"Are you all right for funds?" The man opened a cupboard that formed part of the wall and took out a large wad of notes.

"A bit more money is always helpful," said Jake, accepting the money with alacrity.

"I shall say goodbye now," said the man. "I must say, I admire the way you stay in that costume. I can't wait to get mine off."

Reaching down he unzipped a hidden fastening that ran from his groin to his breastbone. Jake forced his expression to remain impassive as he watched a grey alien emerge from the human costume and drop the skin to the ground.

Minutes later they had reached their destination and Jake was deposited gently on the road outside his house. His wife was still awake when he crept up to the bedroom. She was sitting at the dressing table with no clothes on.

"You'll never guess what happened to me," he said, throwing the money so it scattered over the bed.

Was it his imagination - or did she hurriedly zip up her stomach before turning to greet him with a smile?

Asmodeus Returns

When Jack resurrected a demon, the movement to Make Earth More Exciting had never known such excitement.

Vanessa looked at her watch. Only six hours before the transmogrification ceremony. It would be a disaster if Jack hadn't finished the statue in time. She went round to the garage and, with some trepidation, pushed open the door. Jack was kneeling on the floor in front of Asmodeus, filing a plaster claw.

It's nearly time," she said, and gazed at the statue. It depicted a muscular figure with a serpent's tail, the legs of a cockerel and three heads – a ram, a bull, and a human. The central man's head had a demonic stare of marvelous ferocity.

"He looks a bit scary with all those animal parts," she said.

"Of course he looks scary," said Jack. "He's one of the most powerful Demons of the Abyss."

"How do you know this is what he looks like?" she asked.

"I looked him up in Collin de Plancy's Infernal Dictionary."

"How did he know?"

"Enough of your nonsense," said Jack angrily. "Tonight, at the Temple of MEME, Asmodeus will be resurrected."

"Are you sure you're doing the right thing, darling?" she ventured. "The transmogrification machines are only designed to turn stones into food."

"How many times do I have to explain this to you? It's the same thing – I'll be turning something inorganic into something organic."

"I don't know what your boss will say, if he discovers you've borrowed Government property."

"Oh, go and make the dinner, woman."

That night, the temple of MEME was crowded. The statue of Asmodeus stood at one end of the room on a make-shift stage. Beside it loomed the bulky mass of the borrowed transmogrification machine.

After a build-up of chanting, Jack bowed to the statue then, with a flourish, he rotated the dials of the control panel. A beam of light emerged from the laser at the top of the machine and slowly passed down the statue. As it went, it converted the plaster and chicken-wire into living flesh.

The congregation gasped and there was a smattering of applause as the reincarnated Asmodeus stood, wobbling slightly, on his cockerel legs.

"Where is the sacrificial meat?" he boomed.

"I'd prefer fresh grass," said the bull.

"Me too," bleated the ram's head.

The man's head, stared angrily at the two neighbouring heads. "Grass? Grass gives me indigestion." He belched out a sheet of flame. "Why the hell have I been reincarnated with the heads of herbivores?"

Jack ducked as the flame narrowly missed him. The movement caught Asmodeus's eye and he glared at the priest. "Where's the sacrifice?" he demanded.

Jack shook his head. "Er – there isn't one, I'm afraid."

"What?" roared the demon, his eyes glowing red. "What sort of pitiful summoning ceremony is this?"

Jack gesticulated to Vanessa and she hurriedly started to play the electric organ.

"She doesn't look like a virgin sacrifice to me."

"No, no," Jack assured him. "She's making music." Vanessa's nervous fingers slipped on the keys creating a cacophony of jumbled notes.

"She is?" Asmodeus's mood worsened. He belched out a sheet of flame, which caused the front row of the congregation to move hastily backwards. "I demand to know who is responsible for summoning me into this absurd body."

Vanessa looked round and saw several members of the congregation point to Jack.

Vanessa's music ended with a discordant crash.

"What?" roared the demon. "You've insulted me in every way. I demand revenge."

The congregation had been edging towards the exits. Now they rushed to escape. Asmodeus singed the tail-enders with a blast of flaming breath.

He advanced towards Jack but his cockerel legs became entangled with his serpent's tail and he fell flat on his face. Jack made a dive for the notice board behind which Vanessa was hiding and lay quivering.

There was silence. Vanessa peered out to see the three heads of Asmodeus staring at each other in unspoken communication.

"Okay, all agreed?" said the man's head. The other two nodded. "Then back to the Abyss."

Vanessa watched Asmodeus disappear in a puff of sulphureous smoke. Poor Jack, he seemed to be having a nervous breakdown but the movement to Make Earth More Exciting had never known such excitement.

At the station

The number of psychopaths is kept in check by licensing them to kill each other

Sheila's hand rested on the killing tube in her pocket as she watched the train draw out of the station. Was the legendary Chip Blake among the disembarked passengers? Yes, there he was, taller than most and with a distinctive limp. She felt excited at the thought of their encounter.

The approaching throng hid him from view and she drew back into the shadows to study a railway timetable until everyone had passed. What an honour to be matched with him in combat. If she could kill Chip Blake she would have top ranking among the urban hunters.

She turned to follow her quarry but he had disappeared. Where had he got to?

He wasn't in the queue at the barrier. Too late she realized that some passengers were leaving through a gate at the far end. Sheila ran down the platform, aware of curious eyes upon her. As she passed the coffee shop she glanced in and to her amazement saw that he was at the counter.

She stopped and stared through the window as he ordered a coffee. What the hell was he doing? Their assignation was in fifteen minutes by the bandstand in the park. There was no time for him to pause for refreshments.

She pulled herself together and entered the cafe, confident that he wouldn't recognise her. The agency photograph showed her as a glamorous blonde but she had disguised herself with a brown wig and bulky jersey.

He turned away from the counter as she entered and carried his coffee to a table. As he brushed past her, she could feel her heart-beat quicken, but he did not notice her.

She ordered a latte and waited while the machine frothed and gurgled. She kept glancing at him, wondering if he would make a move, but he just sat, staring out of the window.

What should she do? The boldest move was always the best - she would engage him in conversation and find out what he was up to. She paid for her coffee, picked up her mug and crossed to his table.

"Do you mind if I join you?" she said in a faux-American accent. He glanced round, his eyes wandering over the many empty tables in the room. "I like to look at the trains," she explained.

"Of course," he said politely and indicated a chair opposite him.

"Penny for your thoughts," she said.

He smiled. "I think I'm tired," he said. "I think I might retire."

"Retire?" Her surprise was genuine. Was one able to retire from being an urban hunter? She had thought it a job for life, not least because the average hunter didn't last for long.

"Yes," he said. He had a handsome face, with deeply-etched lines down the side of his mouth, which in any other man might have been dimples but in him were lines of pain. "I've been doing my job for many years and now I'm tired. I want to settle down, get married, have a family, do all the things that normal people do."

She stared at him. Was he no longer a psychopath? Was there a cure? Could she herself be cured? Did she want to be cured? The questions buzzed around her brain as he turned away from her and stared at the empty platform. She shook her head. She had only recently been diagnosed, only recently been allowed to satisfy her craving for excitement by hunting and killing other psychopaths. Oh no, she didn't want to be cured yet. She wanted to be like him and make many, many kills.

He gave a sigh and turned back to her. "Besides," he said. "It's all become too easy. I knew you'd be waiting for me at the station."

With a chill of horror, she realized that he had his killing tube in his hand. She fumbled in her pocket but it was too late, she felt the cool metal touch the centre of her forehead – the bulls-eye for maximum points. There was a moment of flaring pain and then she knew no more.

Diary of a Stalker
It is unwise to stalk a vampire

Sept 10

Dear diary, my first day at university and I am IN LOVE. I saw him at the fresher's meeting. He is G-O-R-G-E-O-U-S. Tall and dark with pale skin like Johnny Depp. I managed to get close enough to see his name badge Vlad Pett. A bit like Brad Pitt, eh?

Sept 11

WOW. He's in my geology class. I couldn't take my eyes off him.
   Hair = obsidian.
   Skin = quartz.
   Eyes = alexandrite.
He has lovely long fingers. I bet he's good at IT.

Sept 15

Vlad is short for Vladimir. Pett is short for Pettitski. He's a Count from Eastern Europe. How ROMANTIC.

He's a mature student so he doesn't live in hall like the rest of us. He has a flat in town above a chip shop. Mmmmmm, something tells me I'm going to be eating a lot of fish and chips LOL.

Sept 20

DESPAIR Vlad is going out with a big blonde with a rose tattoo. We all call her BB (short for blousy bitch) LOL.

Sept 23

Saw Vlad and BB in the coffee bar. I sat at the next table and could hear Vlad arguing with a bloke about vampires. He said it was rubbish they couldn't come out in daylight and the bloke said how did he know - did he come from Transylvania?

Vlad was furious. He grabbed BB and stormed out. Ooooooh, he is so handsome when he's angry. I wish he would grab me like that.

Sept 30

A BRILL day. BB has gone. Apparently, she left a note to say she had been offered a modelling job in London and she never came back.

Poor Vlad. He is soooooo upset. There is a little muscle that twitches in his cheek.

How could she leave such a gorgeous man? She must be LOONY.

Oct 2

A weird evening. I was at the chip shop when I saw Vlad leave the flat carrying a parcel. I followed him to the park. It was all dark and spooky so I hung around until he came out again - WITHOUT the parcel. Luckily, he didn't see me as I would hate him to think I was a stalker LOL.

Oct 3

I was at the chip shop again (I've gained three pounds in a month!) when Vlad came out with ANOTHER parcel. This time I followed him into the park and I saw him bury it under a bush. Weird or what?

Oct 4

JOY, JOY, JOY, JOY.

I went out early this morning, dug up the parcel and opened it! YUK It was a foot – with a rose tattoo on the ankle. BB never went to London after all.

Next thing I know Vlad is standing beside me – with another parcel. While I helped bury it, he told me what happened. They'd had an argument and the stupid bitch attacked him with a knife. Luckily, she'd tripped and fallen on the knife and killed herself.

Poor Vlad. He hadn't dared tell the police in case they deported him and he would never see me again.

YES! It was me he loved all along.

He took me in his arms and we kissed for the first time. What a kiss! I finished up feeling weak at the knees. He helped me back to his flat with one arm around my waist and then he laid me on the bed and we continued kissing and then... suffice to say we missed morning lectures. I'm so HAPPY.

Oct 10

Exactly one month since I first set eyes on my gorgeous boyfriend and exactly one week since we first made love. I never knew what an orgasm was till I met him. He says he has a surprise in store - I can't wait. I am in LOVE, LOVE, LOVE.

Countess Pettitski. I've been practising my new signature. Only joking - sort of.

He's going to take me to meet his parents but we have to keep it a secret. I've had a brilliant idea – I am going to tell my hall that I am going to London to do a modelling job. Just like BB. LOL.

Dunking the Donut
Who'd have thought it of a donut?

Stellar City is the hub of the Universe, where aliens from a thousand worlds enjoy the flesh pots of the megalopolis.

Dazzled by the lights, Andrew, a newly arrived Earthling, wondered which of the many restaurants served food he could stomach.

"Dunky," flashed a sign, and he hurried towards a door festooned with donut posters. He was shown into a booth and served with a magnificent donut. He licked the frosted topping.

"Oral sex is extra," squeaked the donut.

Andrew stared wide eyed. In the dim light of the private booth its hole looked particularly inviting.

Perhaps dinner could wait.

Fat Boy

Fat Boy is a tadpole who never forgets a grievance

He was the fat boy of the year. He didn't have a proper name, none of us did, so we called him Fat Boy.

We were vegetarians, sucking slime off the pondweed and swimming around with strings of poo dangling out of our bottoms. I cringe to think of it now, but it seemed normal at the time. Anyway, we would pick on Fat Boy, muddying the slime, yanking at his poo string and bending the weed so it sprang back and hit him.

He had a mean streak, old Fat Boy, he never cried when we tricked him, he just hunched up and took it all. Then, when we weren't looking, he would bump us or trail his poo string over the slime we were trying to eat. He never forgot a grievance.

In the end, he got fed up with the abuse and took to hanging around with the weenies. For some weeks we didn't see him, and then one day, when I was looking for worms, I met him. He was chewing on a weed.

"Hi, Fat Boy, are you still eating plants?"

"Yea." He was fatter than ever.

"We've all become carnivores," I said. "You should try it. Chasing your food might help you lose weight."

"You shut up about my weight – Scabby." That's the sort of tad he was, he remembered back to the early days, when I had a mild case of skin-scab.

"Hey, no need to be like that, Fat Boy, I was just trying to be friendly," I said.

"I would rather be bait than have a friend like you," he said.

"That can be arranged," said a voice behind me. I spun round and saw Legs, the most advanced tad of the year. The effect on Fat Boy was startling; he cringed back against the weed, his mouth forming a perfect O as he moaned in fear.

"Yum, yum," said Legs and lunged at Fat Boy, who turned and fled, leaving a lump of his tail-fin in Legs' mouth.

"I say, Legs," I protested. "That was a bit much."

"Bugger off – Scabby." He had overheard Fat Boy's insult and, from that day on, the name stuck.

Legs and his gang were cannibals. The rest of us never felt right about feeding on weenies. They were our brothers, even though they were very small and never developed properly.

"Stop making a fuss," Legs said, when we confronted him. "Our Mum laid them for us to eat. What else are they good for?"

Time passed.

"Where's that bastard, Legs," said Fat Boy, one day.

"He's left the pond," I said.

"Left? What do you mean?"

"He's gone onto land."

The poor sap had no idea what I was talking about. To him the pond was the whole world.

"Oh bugger off, Scabby," he said. "I'm fed up with your jokes."

"Then don't come bothering me," I said. "Go and play with the weenies."

"You bastard, Scabby," he sobbed. "You know there are none left." And he swam away.

I emerged from the pond late in the year but I prospered and grew and within three years was back to breed. I was fortunate to find a magnificent older female and was there to fertilise her eggs when they were laid.

It was my first spawning. I felt so proud. It was the greatest thing that had ever happened to me. I went back a week later and jumped into the pond to check that everything was okay.

"Hello, Scabby." The voice was unpleasant, but familiar. I turned to see Fat Boy lurking among the weed. He was still in his juvenile form, but had grown enormous.

"Hello, Fat Boy," I said. "You look the same as ever – just fatter."

"Not quite the same," he said. "I'm now a carnivore. I've waited years for this." He stared hungrily at my spawn.

"Don't you dare," I said and lunged towards him but, with a powerful sweep of his tail, he disappeared into the depths of the pond.

Miserably, I left the water and surrendered my precious offspring to their fate. Fat Boy, who never forgot a grievance, could wreak a terrible revenge.

Flora
The garden takes its revenge

Brian planned to sell the cottage he had inherited from his grandmother but, after spending a couple of weekends there, he changed his mind. The oak beams, the diamond-leaded windows, the overgrown garden and distant smell of the sea gave him a sense of peace missing from life in the city.

Then he met Flora. She was standing in the garden one Friday evening.

"Hey," he shouted as he leapt out of the car. "What are you doing in my garden?"

"Oi'm tending the flowers." Her voice was gentle.

"Oh, you must be the gardener," he said. "I'm sorry but my grandmother died some months ago. You can carry on and work for me if you like."

She looked up at him, her cheeks tinged with pink as delicate as blossom. "Oi'll stay if you want me, Sir."

He went inside and watched her through the window. Wherever she went the garden bloomed more beautifully. He decided that he did want her, he wanted her very much indeed.

That evening Brian went out into the garden. Swallows zigzagged across the sky and the air was heavy with the scent of flowers. Flora walked towards him, her simple white dress hanging loosely from her shoulders. She raised her face and he kissed her.

"Stay the night with me," he said and she twined her arms around his neck.

"Oi'll stay if you want me, Sir."

Every weekend Brian drove down from London and stayed with Flora in the cottage that had become a paradise. The scent of her hair was like sweet violets, the touch of her skin like rose petals. He loved her as he had never loved before.

Then one evening, when he drove down the lane, he saw a man hurry from the cottage.

"What was that man doing?" he asked Flora. She smiled a secret smile but did not answer, and he knew that she had been unfaithful. The height of his rage echoed the depth of his hurt.

"You belong to me," he shouted. "How dare you give yourself to another man?"

She looked at him with cool, blue eyes and said, "Oi belong to nobody."

He tried to explain that because he loved her, she had to be faithful but she did not understand and, frightened by his anger, she left to find sanctuary in the garden.

He followed, his rage mounting. Just as he had never known love before so he had never felt the pain of rejection. As they passed the woodpile, he picked up an axe and the volcano inside him erupted. With a single swipe he severed Flora's head as easily as plucking a flower.

Horrified by what he had done, he buried her remains in the garden, leapt into his car and fled back to London

The weeks passed but brought no healing. Finally, as a dog returns to its vomit, Brian returned to the cottage. The garden was desolated, the only flowers grew on the mound that was Flora's grave.

With faltering steps he approached the flowers and saw that they formed the picture of a girl. Against a background of forget-me-nots were slender limbs of pale pink cyclamen, a dress of white periwinkle, hair of yellow violets and across the neck a slash of blood-red poppies.

Brian's ruined soul felt neither grief nor remorse but only fear that in creating this memorial to Flora the garden would betray his wicked deed.

He fell to his knees and ripped out the plants, making a pile of broken stems, tangled roots and torn flowers on the path. His secret was safe.

A tiny whirlwind sucked the broken blossoms up into a column. Gold, cream and white petals spotted with crimson whirled around the vortex. He gaped and a gust of wind blew petals into his mouth, making him cough. More petals rushed in as he gasped for air. Brian staggered backwards and tripped over a root. He turned his head wildly from side to side but still the petals came, invading and smothering him. Finally, the smallest petals drifted into his mouth, filling every gap and sealing his lungs from the air – tiny, golden petals smelling of sweet violets.

From Name to Gnome
The family curse falls upon Crystal

Crystal entered her bedroom and frowned at the man sleeping on the bed. She suspected that her handsome, good-natured husband was a philanderer.

With a sigh, Crystal turned to the task of choosing a dress. Why couldn't Herbert be faithful to her? She was beautiful, a top name in the modelling world and he was all the family she had, apart from her mother, a gnome-like woman she hadn't seen for a decade.

She opened the front door and paused, almost blinded by the barrage of flashbulbs.

"Crystal, look this way."

Flash!

"Where are you off to, Miss Parfitt?"

Flash!

She did not reply and none of the paparazzi bothered to follow her to the hospice. When she arrived, the matron hurried out of her office to greet her.

"Your mother has not got long," she said, and led her to a dimly-lit room.

"Crystal?" A smile lit her mother's face. "How nice to see you."

Crystal walked forwards and took her mother's hand. Whether it was the smile, or the iminence of death, her mother's embarrassing appearance had improved. Her warty skin had smoothed, her hideous features had straightened and she seemed taller and slimmer.

"What's happening to you, Mother?" Crystal asked.

"The curse is lifting," said her mother and, with a feeble hand, she indicated a photograph on her bedside table. Crystal was familiar with the photograph. It was of a handsome couple that her mother insisted was her and Tom on their wedding day.

Crystal humoured her and picked up the photograph. "I wish I had known my father."

"You did know him, dear, he was Tom the cat." The old woman's eyes travelled to a tiny urn on the dressing table.

As Crystal stared at the urn, she caught a glimpse of herself in the dressing-table mirror. She hardly recognised her reflection. Her face was squashed and she had bat-ears. She raised her hand to her head and it came away with long, golden tresses tangled around her fingers. She stared at them in horror.

"I'm so sorry this is happening to you, my darling."

Her mother's voice was growing weaker. "Your Aunt Belladonna came from Estonia to curse us at your christening, because we didn't make her your godmother."

"No," Crystal moaned.

Her mother beckoned Crystal towards her for her final words. "Goodbye, my child," she whispered. "Remember, beauty is but skin deep." With that she expired and her face relaxed into its full loveliness.

Beauty is but skin deep? What kind of a parting shot was that? My beauty is everything, thought Crystal, there's nothing underneath.

Her body had become so short and squat that she had to change into one of her mother's old smocks.

Matron was waiting outside the door, so Crystal climbed out of the window and, by dodging from bush to bush, managed to reach her car unseen.

When she arrived home, a lone photographer was waiting outside the house. He didn't raise his camera as she climbed the steps to the front door, but when she put her key in the lock, he enquired who she was.

"Just the cleaner," said the quick-thinking Crystal as she opened the front door and went in.

She found a big, golden tom-cat curled up asleep on the bed. Herbert? Oh my God, the curse had affected him as well. He purred gently as she lifted him. She looked round at the long line-up of her wardrobes as she cuddled the cat. At least she wouldn't have to change her clothes several times a day, or bother with make-up, or be dependent on her entourage.

She stroked Herbert's golden fur and felt him stretch luxuriously beneath her touch. He made a lovely cat. But she must do her best to return him to manhood and to escape from her own loathsome transformation.

Her mind whirled with plans. She would sell her clothes, her jewellery and her house and leave for Estonia as soon as possible. It may take a long while to find her aunt. The thought of her quest filled her with life-enhancing energy. One day Crystal Parfitt would return, as beautiful as ever.

Gateway to Hell

Don't open that book!

Chapter One: The Discovery

It was evening by the time Sir Ronald Price reached the little village in the heart of the Carpathian Mountains. The church he had come to see had once been a fine building but now it was as decrepit as the rest of the village. The key holder was sent for and the thick, oak door creaked open. Sir Ronald entered to find the church empty – no altar, no pews, nothing. Flaking murals depicted the legend of the local hero St Vladd defeating a hellish beast and imprisoning it in an iron-bound book.

"Does your village have any antiquities for sale?" Sir Ronald asked the key holder. The man scrabbled at the filthy floor. The bricks were loose and an old oak chest was exposed. He lifted it out and opened it, revealing a large book, bound in leather and held shut with iron bands. The rest of the contents were of little interest, just various odds and ends – scrolls, carved wooden statues and a gold pendant.

"How much will you charge me for the chest?" Sir Ronald asked the key-holder. After a brief negotiation, he handed the man a small purse of gold, motioned to his servants to pick up the chest, and led the way back to his carriage.

Chapter Two: The Homecoming

It was nearly Christmas when Sir Ronald returned to his ancestral home. As he entered the huge, marble hall, his six-year-old daughter, Clarissa, came running and threw herself into his arms. He swung her up and held her high, her golden curls tossing and her pretty face full of laughter.

"Have you been a good girl?"

"She's been a little angel," said his wife, hurrying up to greet him. That evening, when his bags had been unpacked, Sir Ronald gave his wife and daughter souvenirs of his travels. To his wife he gave a magnificent gold necklace. To his daughter he gave a mechanical monkey and the Carpathian pendant. His daughter was delighted, and played with both the monkey and the pendant with equal pleasure.

Chapter Three: The Opening

One day there was a knock on Sir Ronald's study door.

"Come in," he said. The door opened and there stood Clarissa. Sir Ronald frowned. "You know you're not meant to disturb me in my study," he said.

"I'm sorry, Daddy, but Monkey told me to come."

"All right," he said. "You can stay for a while but I have work to do so don't disturb me." He sat at his desk and started to write a letter while Clarissa looked at the antiquities laid out on a low bench against the wall.

"Is this the book you found?" she said.

"Don't touch it. It's very old."

"How does it open?"

"It doesn't open, it needs a key and we haven't got one."

"This is a key," said Clarissa, pulling the pendant out of her pocket.

"Nonsense, it looks nothing like a key," he said. "What would it open?"

"This book," said his daughter, reaching out for it.

"Stop!" shouted Sir Ronald, but his daughter took no notice of him. She slid the strange-looking key into a slit in the iron band that secured the book. Click. The key turned and Sir Ronald threw himself on the book, trying to hold it shut. Slowly and inexorably, he felt the heavy cover rise beneath him and a huge hand squeezed out. It was the hand of the beast. Clarissa grabbed the hand, trying to help the beast emerge from the book.

Still standing on the sloping cover, Sir Ronald grabbed a huge Mesopotamian battle axe and smashed it down, severing the creature's arm and missing his daughter's head by inches.

There was a shriek and the blood-stained covers of the book slammed shut.

Sir Ronald locked the book and turned to his daughter. She was slumped against the wall, half fainting with fear. Her pretty white dress was spattered with blood, and she cradled the beast's severed arm.

"Are you all right, my darling?" he asked.

She raised her head. "You hurt Monkey," she said and, in her eyes shone the red light of hatred.

The Harlot of the God Camp

It wasn't easy, doing God's work.

In the end he felt regret, but as night fell on the God Camp, Stephen felt only ecstasy as he stood with the choir under the American flag. The sun was setting and the darkening sky was as blue as the Virgin's cloak. *The Virgin's cloaca.* Stephen shuddered. Even in the God Camp the Devil put evil words into his head.

"The day thou gavest Lord is ended." Stephen's nasal voice rose with those around in a harmony of praise. He fixed his eyes on the illuminated sign at the entrance to the camp, which spelt out in meter-high letters the word GOD.

Sally stood nearby, tempting him with her long legs and golden hair. Stephen fought against the distraction and stared at the sign with such intensity that his eyes watered and the holy name looked like the word COD. Blasphemy.

He gazed down at the hymn book and his happiness was marred by resentment. How dare Sally entice him with her beauty. She should cover her hair and wear a long skirt, and yet she and the other girls in the camp flaunted themselves before men like harlots.

At the thought of Sally's smooth thighs and half-exposed breasts lust stirred within Stephen's loins. He looked up to where God's sign shone ever brighter against the engulfing night. God was looking down on him. God could see the lust coiling like a serpent in his body. He must rid himself of temptation or God would condemn him to the fires of Hell.

The singing ended and the choir dispersed. It was dark now and Sally did not see him as he limped behind her, his club foot dragging through the long grass. She was with two other girls. They were giggling and chatting as they made their way to the tents. He hated the sound of women giggling. He could not make out what they were saying but he knew they were mocking him, talking about his ill-formed foot, laughing at his disfigurement. Women had mocked him all his life – his sisters, his class mates, girls at the church social group. Rage, like boiling lava filled his soul. They were harlots, the lot of them.

Stephen's foot dislodged something from the grass. He looked down. A shaft of light from the God sign illuminated a tent peg. Stephen had studied the bible well and remembered that the blessed handmaiden Jael had killed Sisera with a tent peg. He stooped down and picked it up. It felt heavy and had a sharp point.

Stephen looked at the three harlots walking ahead of him. Did God want him to kill them all? He felt daunted by the task. In answer to his question, Sally's two friends said goodbye and went to their separate tents, leaving Sally to continue on her own.

Excitement mounted inside Stephen as he followed the harlot. God gave him the power of an avenging angel. As if lifted by wings he rushed up behind her and struck her a mighty blow on the head.

The tent peg did not penetrate to the hilt as he expected. There was a crunching sound as it became embedded in her skull. She sank to her knees screaming. He struggled to withdraw the weapon so he could strike again. But his hands were slippery with the harlot's blood and he failed. Sally's screams brought people running and many hands dragged him away.

The harlot survived. Alone in his cell Stephen regretted that he had failed to do God's work. The authorities allowed him to keep his bible and he studied it avidly. Jael had hammered the tent peg into Sisera's skull.

"She stretched forth her hand to the nail,
Her right hand to the workman's hammer,
And she smote Sisera; she crushed his head.
She crashed through and transfixed his temple."

Stephen's pulse quickened as he read the holy words. He should have used a hammer. Next time he would be better prepared. He looked forward to the day of his parole and prayed to the Lord to give him strength. So many harlots, so little time to do God's work.

I Will Not Die

It is better to reincarnate as a bug than
achieve eternal peace.

Swami Shyam, head of Nepal's greatest Hindu temple, sat in the main hall in front of the assembled monks. They were waiting for him to die, but death came slowly.

The huge doors at of the hall were open, revealing a magnificent view of the Himalayas. Mountain after snow-capped mountain stretched into the purple distance, brilliant against a crystal-blue sky.

A few of the novitiates shivered in the cold, to be frowned on by their superiors. The Swami felt no cold. He had long ago relinquished attachment to all desires, including the desire for bodily comfort. He sat, without moving, his legs folded in a lotus position. His hands rested palm-upwards on his knees, his fingers forming the 'O', which symbolised the cycle of life. As his body processes slowed, his mind drifted.

The throng of saffron-robed monks before him became the floor of a forest, from which the pillars of the hall rose like trees. The dark shadows of the hall were darkening, creeping towards him. A soft voice interrupted his meditation.

"My lord Swami, soon your earthly sufferings will cease."

Swami Shyam raised his eyes to see the earnest face of Mahesh, his second in command. He felt a flash of irritation. He wanted to remind Mahesh that only those who had failed to relinquish desire felt suffering, but his mouth would not form the words so he bore the insult in silence.

"Soon it will be someone else's turn to wear the golden symbol of Aum."

Was it the Swami's imagination or was there a look of avarice in Mahesh's eyes? The Swami fumbled in his robes and drew out the Aum. He stroked the familiar surface, deriving comfort from the curves and points of the holy symbol. The gold felt warm and rich under his fingers. Mahesh was talking again. The Swami forced his mind back to what his subordinate was saying.

"Soon my lord, you will achieve moksha, soon you will become one with Brahman."

Mahesh had always been one for stating the obvious. The Swami wanted to tell him to go away and let him die in peace, but all he could do was smile his beatific smile and pretend he had not heard him.

"Soon the cycle of life will be ended. There will be no more need for reincarnation, your karma has achieved eternal peace."

Mahesh's words triggered a memory deep within the Swami's brain. This was not what he wanted. He refused to die. Long ago, in another incarnation, he had vowed to live the cycle of life forever. I WILL NOT DIE. The words rang in his brain stoking a fire within him until it became a raging furnace.

Mahesh sensed his struggle and leant over him solicitously. "Can I serve you in any way, master?"

"Yes, you can." The words were the merest whisper and his second in command bent low to hear. The fire inside became a volcano and with one mighty effort the Swami swung his hand up and stabbed Mahesh in the throat with the sharpest point of the golden Aum.

The moment of his triumph came none too soon for even as his soul rejoiced in the deed, darkness descended and he died.

The horrified monks looked on as their Swami slumped back dead upon the dais, while Mahesh stood clutching his gushing wound. For long moments Mahesh's shocked face mirrored their own then he slumped over the body of the Swami.

Swami Shyam was reincarnated as a bug, high in the branches of an ancient sequoia tree.

"Hello," said the tree. "You back again?"

"Yeth," said the bug. "It wath a narrow thqueak thith time."

"You must have done something bad to go all the way back to being a bug," said the tree.

"Yeth," said the bug proudly. "It wath murder."

"Hmm. It will take many reincarnations before you can return to being a human."

"The more the better," said the bug airily. "I don't care what I am, ath long ath I avoid eternal peathe."

A foraging bird grabbed the bug.

"Here we go," said the bug. "Next life coming up. Wheeee!" And he was gone.

In the Soup

Justine couldn't leave his girlfriend looking like a haggis.

Justin Crowley took a window seat at Harringays restaurant. The smell of boiled celeriac invaded the room as an elderly waiter emerged from the kitchen.

"Menu, Sir?"

"Yes, please."

The waiter picked up a leather-bound menu from a stack on the bar and brought it over. "Drink, Sir?"

"I'll have a medium sherry and a Martini."

Justin opened his newspaper and read the front-page story. *Celebrity chef Justin Crowley incinerates judge at The Golden Truffle Finale.* The account was detailed and no wonder, it had been witnessed live on television.

He folded the paper and stared out of the window. He had intended to singe Tennant's beard but the man had been wearing so much hairspray that he went up like a fire cracker. Justin frowned. Somebody had planned to destroy his chances of winning the Golden Truffle and he knew who it must be.

Lucy came hurrying down the street in a coat the colour of sun-dried tomatoes. A gust of cold air swirled into the restaurant as she entered. Justin beckoned to her and she advanced uncertainly.

"Justin? You look so different. Your hair is flat and brown and you've got a moustache."

"Shush!" Any doubts that she was the saboteur vanished. His two-timing girlfriend was describing his disguise to the police.

She sat down, clutched his hands and stared up at him with huge, blue eyes. "Why don't you give yourself up, Justin? After you've served your time, we can be together forever, just as we planned."

Before your betrayal, he thought, but it was too soon for a denouement so he pushed the menu across to her. "I'm starving," he said. "Let's have something to eat."

Lucy perused the menu. "Wow, I'd heard this place was old fashioned, but Brown Windsor soup? I didn't know anyone made it any more. I must give it a try."

He waited until she had finished her Martini then led her to a dining booth at the far end of the restaurant. He summoned the waiter and ordered soup for Lucy and crab pate for himself.

"I've been thinking about that finale," he said. "It was your idea to use snail caviar in the hors d'oeuvre."

"I'm sorry about that," said Lucy, "but it's the latest thing and we thought the judges would be impressed."

"And the Swan Lake dessert? How come the head fell off the swan?"

She frowned. "What are you saying?"

Justin waited while the waiter brought their food, then he leant forwards and gazed into her eyes. "I'm saying that I would have won if you hadn't sabotaged me, Lucy."

"What?"

"When I spent the night at your flat, I found a bottle of brown sauce in one of your cupboards. No true cook would ever possess such a thing."

"Brown sauce? It was in my cleaning cupboard. I use it to polish the copper saucepans. Good God, Justin. You don't think I eat the stuff, do you?"

He saw her eyes glaze over as the sleeping powder he had put in her drink took effect. She slumped forwards. He grabbed her handbag and opened it. There was no sign of a radio transmitter - just his passport, a ticket to Buenos Aires and bundles of money. He counted the money - £2,000, she had done everything he had asked. Was it possible that he was wrong?

A gurgling sound made him turn and he saw that her face was submerged in the soup. He lifted her up and propped her against the back of the booth. She sat slumped against the wooden panelling. The thick brown liquid obliterated her features, making her face look like a haggis.

He couldn't leave her like this, she hated haggis. On impulse, he scooped up two spoonfuls of crab pate and placed one over each of her eyes, then he garnished them with eyeballs of pitted olives. He had done his best for her. Poor Lucy.

On the bright side, he now had all he needed for a new life. Justin went to the bar to pay.

"Leaving already, Sir?"

"Yes, there was something in the soup." And, chuckling at his joke, Justin made his escape.

<u>Inside Henry's Head</u>

*Find out if your lover is cheating
with the help of nanobots*

Prim had not always been prim. Oh no, she had once been Primrose, golden girl, pride of the valley, winner of the Minehead

Beauty Contest. But her beauty had faded, a hysterectomy had rendered her childless and disappointment had made her bitter. Worst of all, she suspected that her husband was cheating, which is why she decided to send off for some nanobots.

The nanobot system was more complex than Prim had expected. It included two disposable syringes and two glass phials, containing gooey, grey liquid. One was labelled 'receivers' and the other 'transmitters'. Prim was dismayed, she had been hoping for something she could sprinkle over Henry's food. She packed everything roughly back into the box, banging the delicate phials together with enough force to create tiny hairline cracks. Oh dear. Prim should have read the warning to avoid cross contamination.

Every time Henry worked late at the office Prim's suspicions deepened until, at last, she went ahead with the project. She loaded the transmitter phial into one of the syringes, waited until Henry was asleep and then injected the liquid into him.

When, after a week, Henry still showed no ill effects, she injected the receivers into herself. Slowly, like an ancient, analogue television, plagued with snow and shadow channels, she was able to tune into Henry. She was inside Henry's head, seeing what he saw, hearing what he heard and smelling what he smelt. In this case he was smelling cheap perfume, looking at a pair of plump thighs and dictating a letter to his secretary.

"Cheap tart," thought Prim, "flashing her legs like that."

The smooth stream of dictation faltered and she heard Henry say, "I would rather you didn't wear a miniskirt to the office, Miss Smith."

Next time Prim tuned in to Henry he was in a pub chatting to a man.

"Honestly," he was saying, "it was as if I could hear my wife inside my head. I told the poor girl to wear longer skirts in future."

"Are you mad?" said the man. "Looking at Tracey Smith's legs is one of the perks of the job."

"I know," said Henry. "I don't understand what came over me."

"Have another pint," said the man. Another pint? Prim was outraged.

"There she is again," said Henry. "Oh God, I've lived with her for too long. She's getting to me."

Prim stayed out of his mind until later that afternoon and discovered that he was no longer in the office. It was just as she had feared. He was with a woman. She was undressing slowly and Prim sensed Henry's excitement. Disgusting. He fondled her breasts. Bitch, slut, adulteress! Prim had been trying to control her anger but this was too much. Upon her outburst, Henry pushed away his lover.

"I've got to go," he said. "I've some unfinished business to attend to."

Prim knew he was coming home and awaited his arrival nervously. Several times she tried to tune into his mind but he was singing a stupid, repetitive song.

The door was flung open. "What have you done, Prim?" he asked.

"Nothing."

"You've put nanobots into my head, you stupid woman."

"I had to know if you were being unfaithful, Henry. I love you."

"Love me?" He shook his head. "Oh no, Prim, you have thrown me into a nightmare from which there is only one escape."

His hands were around her throat now, his whole attention focussed upon her. His eyes were just inches from hers and it was as if she was young again. Primrose, the beauty of the valley, the centre of attention, Primrose and the boy who adored her with such a passion. Now he was going to make the final sacrifice – her – in a deed that would bind them together forever.

She sensed his resolve weaken and her bitterness returned. She had wasted her love on an adulterer, wasted her youth on a failed marriage and now he didn't even have the passion to kill her. His grip tightened again and, as she lost consciousness, her last thought was to wonder if the triumph she felt was hers, or his.

Just Crumbs
Miles must practise being a normal human

The warder brought in a tray and put it on the table. "Okay, Miles?" he said.

"Fine," said Miles and smiled at him. He lifted the corners of his mouth into a curve and crinkled his eyes. Crinkling the eyes was important, a smile without the eyes made people nervous.

Warders liked to be smiled at – they became friendlier. This one smiled back at him and put the tray down carefully so the stew didn't slop over the side of the plate.

In the beginning things had been different - the warders had come in twos and had delivered his food carelessly and with averted eyes. They had been terrified of him and sickened by what he had done. But over the years, they had forgotten his crimes, and saw him as just another human being.

"Beef stew? It must be Tuesday," Miles said, and gave a little laugh – not too much, he hadn't made a joke, just a witticism. He had learnt that laughing too much and too loudly was a sign of being abnormal. Becoming a standard human wasn't easy, it took years of practice. One small misjudgement and people would give him that LOOK. How he hated that LOOK.

"I've brought you an extra slice of bread," said the warder.

"Thanks," said Miles, with just the right amount of gratitude.

"Enjoy your meal," the warder said, and waved his hand in a gesture of farewell.

When he had gone, Miles practised the wave. Thanks, bye, cheerio, see you. These meaningless niceties separated the normal human from the abnormal. But they had to be done right – the tone, the inflection, the volume, and the gestures, get one of them wrong and there was a danger of receiving that LOOK.

He picked up a slice of bread and crushed it into crumbs. It reminded him of his mother's cookie jar. It had an opening so small that you could get your hand in, but couldn't bring it out when holding a cookie. The only way he could steal from the jar was to crush the cookie into crumbs.

Of course, his mother had found the crumbs in the jar, and had told his father. After Miles had been beaten, his mother had said, "I hope that taught you a lesson."

Miles pushed breadcrumbs out through the bars of his cell window so they lay on the sill.

He had been taught a lesson all right, about the importance of discipline and bearing one's punishment with fortitude.

At his trial, he had explained to the judge, that he had been like a father to his victims, teaching them discipline. They should have borne their punishment with fortitude but the more he beat them, the more they screamed. He then had to punish them for their cowardice. They had died, in the end, every last one of them.

The judge had given him the LOOK, and sentenced him to life imprisonment.

A bird settled on the sill with fluttering wings. It was his pet sparrow. Miles had spent days taming it, and now he held out a handful of crumbs. The bird approached through the bars and paused to stare around the cell before it hopped onto his hand. With growing confidence, it pecked at the crumbs.

Miles felt the gently tapping of its beak and the tiny pressure of its feet. He could almost sense the little creature's heart-beat. Some of the ice around his heart melted, and he felt concern for the bird. He had made it lose its fear of humans and now it could be vulnerable. It must be taught a lesson, be made to fear humans again. Miles lifted his hand, and then smashed it down as a fist.

Whoops, he had hit the fragile creature too hard. He looked down at the broken body and resolved that next time he would make the lesson last longer.

He threw the broken corpse out of the window and sat down to his stew. Carefully he unfolded the paper napkin and placed it over his knees. It would soon be time to go before the parole board - he must practise being a normal human.

Kevin Escapes Thanksgiving
The options are not good if you are a turkey.

In the great cycle of life, Kevin was reincarnated as a turkey. He first realised something was wrong when he was a few months old.

"Why are we all youngsters?" he asked. "Surely there ought to be older turkeys. Where are our parents?"

Other turkeys, who were pecking for grain in the sandy enclosure, looked at him in puzzlement. "Didn't we come from eggs?" said one of them.

"Yes, but where did the eggs come from?" said Kevin.

"God made the eggs from which we came," said the large turkey that topped the pecking order.

For a while Kevin was satisfied. Then, one day, he watched the farmer fill the feeding trough with grain and another thought occurred to him.

"Why does the farmer feed us?" he said.

"It's his duty," said the top turkey. "This is a welfare state. We're entitled to be looked after."

Kevin looked beyond the wire enclosure at the world outside. He wondered what it would be like to roam freely among the fields and woodland. "I think we're imprisoned," he told the other turkeys.

"What nonsense," said the top turkey.

"We should try to break free," insisted Kevin.

"You're a trouble maker," said the top turkey. "I forbid you to talk about such things."

As the summer days cooled into autumn, Kevin collected a small group of turkeys around him. "I prophesy a great disaster," he told them. "Only by following me will you gain eternal life. We must escape from this enclosure and set up a sanctuary in the woods."

His followers were eager to obey but found escape difficult. They practised flying, but flap as they may, their wings were too small to support their bulk.

"Perhaps if we lost a bit of weight?" suggested one of them but the others swiftly dismissed the idea.

"We need our weight to get us through winter," said Kevin. "We will have to find our own food in the wood."

"Really?" A few of his followers drifted away.

They tried digging a hole by scratching at the sand but whenever they got deep enough the hole caved in.

"What the hell do you think you are doing?" asked the top turkey.

"Just mucking about," said Kevin.

They tried forming a turkey pyramid so they could reach up to the latch of the gate. A fascinated crowd gathered as, with much flapping and grunting, they gained their goal, only to find that the latch was too heavy to lift.

"What are you doing now?" asked the top turkey.

"Just providing a bit of entertainment," said Kevin.

"Well stop it!"

The next day, one of the more daring turkeys tried to squeeze out behind the farmer and received a painful kick which sent him bowling back into captivity. In the confusion, the farmer failed to latch the door properly. Our chance has come, thought Kevin.

That night, when the rest of the turkeys had retired to the coop to sleep, Kevin and his gang crept to the gate. As silently as possible they made their pyramid with Kevin at the top. He inserted his beak under the latch and lifted it. The latch opened just as the tottering pyramid collapsed leaving Kevin sprawling on the sand. Fired with excitement, the other turkeys rushed out into the night leaving their leader nursing a twisted ankle.

"Flee, my people," Kevin called after them. "Find sanctuary and remember that I sacrificed myself that you may live."

It was a cold night. At dawn a large creature came prowling along the fence. It came to the gate and thrust its long, reddish snout into the compound.

"An open door at last," it said and Kevin could see turkey feathers stuck to its nose.

The fox stared at Kevin. "I think I could just find room for dessert," it said, with a grin that revealed long sharp teeth.

There was the distant sound of a shotgun.

"Get away from my turkeys you bloody fox!"

When the farmer reached the pen, there was no sign of the fox which had triggered the alarm, but as the farmer secured the gate, he saw a patch of blood on the sand.

Kevin had escaped Thanksgiving.

Leda and the Swan

A frustrating dalliance with Zeus has an unwelcome result

Leda lay in her marriage-bed staring at the ceiling. Beside her snored her husband, Tyndareus, King of Sparta. The aging king was too preoccupied with affairs of state to spend time on affairs of the flesh and she was feeling frustrated.

When Leda eventually fell asleep, Zeus came to her in a vision. "You are honoured above all mortal women for I have chosen you to be my lover. Meet me at dawn beside the lake in the palace grounds." He winked at her and faded from view.

Leda rose at dawn and hurried down to the lake, her heart singing with excitement. Time passed and she feared she had just been dreaming. Then black clouds gathered at the far end of the lake and out of the darkness emerged a swan. Leda watched as the swan glided across the water towards her. It waddled up the bank and said, "Hi there, Leda."

Leda stared at the swan in astonishment. "Zeus?"

"You'd better believe it, baby."

"But why have you come to me as a swan?"

"Hey, it's a cunning plan – you don't want your husband to see you making love to a god, do you?"

"What? You think he'd rather see me making love to a swan?" His appearance upset Leda, she much preferred the bronzed muscles and flowing locks of her dream god.

Zeus shrugged, "It's not so easy, babe. I'm married too, you know. I've got to be in disguise. Hera would do her nut if she found out."

Leda decided to make the best of things. She looked at the swan speculatively. "How can we make love? I mean, is it possible?"

"There's only one way to find out babe – go behind those bushes and get ready for me."

Leda went behind the bushes and lay on the dew-sodden grass. The swan followed, looking over its shoulder to make sure they weren't observed.

"Yea, we should be okay here, babe. Comfy?"

Leda nodded her assent and the swan jumped onto her thighs, his huge webbed feet flattening her delicate flesh.

"Ouch," she protested, but he took no notice. He bumped against her a few times and then jumped off. As foreplay it left much to be desired. She opened her eyes. The swan was standing beside her preening.

"I'm ready for you," she murmured.

"What?" His boot-button eyes regarding her blankly. "What do you mean you're ready for me? I've finished."

"Oh no," she moaned, her body aching for fulfilment. "That can't be it. Please penetrate me, fill me with your manhood."

"Manhood? That's the trouble, babe. Swans don't have a manhood. Hey don't blame me, bird anatomy was never my strong point, well not that sort of bird anyway," he said with a grin that sent Leda's annoyance level up to steaming. "Actually, I'm thinking that next time I'll come as a bull."

Leda cheered up. "Hey, that would be great."

"Yea? Well, it will be for my next dalliance. I'm afraid you've had your lot, babe. You are already impregnated."

Leda stared at him in horror. "You mean I'm pregnant?"

"Yep." He gave her a lopsided leer. "Up the spout, buns in the oven. Wow, are we swans fertile."

"Oh my god," moaned Leda. "What will my husband say?"

"The poor sap will be delighted," said Zeus. "Just pretend they are his."

"They?" echoed Leda. "How many babies are there?"

The swan lifted its beak to the sky as if listening to an oracle. "Three," he said. "Oh – and there's one other thing?"

"What?"

He noticed the anger with which she was glaring at him and hesitated to add fuel to her fury. A dark cloud passed over their heads.

"Whoops – here comes my chariot. Sorry babe I've got to go. Thanks for the shag – I really enjoyed it."

He gave her a peck on the cheek and then he was gone, speeding across the lake as fast as his webbed feet could paddle.

Nine months later the palace rang to the sound of Leda's screams. That evening the astonished king was informed that his wife had laid three enormous eggs.

Licensed to Kill
How could the FBI have got it so wrong?

After a long evening playing computer games, Rob received an e-mail.

Congratulations, Robert Penfold. Our Military Simulation Analysis Department has been monitoring your performance

and is pleased to offer you the position of anti-terrorist agent with the FBI.

He was so excited that he hardly slept that night.

By the time he got to the office the next day, his boss, Mr Magner, was already in the glass cubicle from which he could keep an eye on his two web designers, Rob and Larry. The three of them together with Gorgeous Gertie, the secretary, made up the total workforce of Magner Web Services Ltd.

"You look like shit," said Larry.

"So do you," said Rob. Larry always looked like shit.

A brown envelope was waiting for him at home. It contained a laminated identification badge. Robert Penfold. FBI agent. Licensed to kill. Ref 00352. Wow, it was really happening.

The following evening his mobile phone rang and a muffled voice with an American accent asked him for his reference number.

"We have an urgent assignment for you," the voice said. "A dangerous female agent is due to catch the London train from Worthing station at 12 noon tomorrow. Her death must look like an accident."

"Death?" faltered Rob. "You mean you want me to kill her?"

"We want you to push her under the train. Keep behind her at all times, on no account must she see your face."

"But I can't kill anyone," moaned Rob.

"You are licensed to kill," said the voice. "This is not murder it is an official execution and will save many civilian casualties."

"Okay," said a reluctant Rob. "I'll be there."

The next morning, he looked so rough that his mother was concerned. Avoiding her attempts to take his temperature, he hurried out of the door and to the bus. Oh God, Oh God, Oh God, Oh God, the words ran through his head like a refrain against which he rehearsed the details of the woman's appearance.

Blonde wig, pink coat, black shoes and handbag. Oh God, what if he pushed the wrong woman?

He arrived at work and checked his e-mails again and again, hoping the FBI might call off the assignment. Luckily Larry was absent and did not see his anxiety. Rob waited until the last possible moment before making his excuses.

"I'm sorry, Mr Magner, but I need a long lunch-break today as I've got a dental appointment."

His boss made no protest but looked at his watch and told him to hurry.

When Rob arrived at the platform, the train was almost due. He pushed through the waiting people, his eyes straining to see a blonde woman in a pink coat. There she was. He could hear the train coming now, approaching fast. He stood behind the woman and braced himself for the coup de grace. Suddenly, he was impacted by a heavy body and he heard Larry's urgent voice.

"This is my assignment."

Rob twisted under the weight of his colleague. "No, it isn't!" He punched him hard and the two rolled over on the platform, fighting each other in raging frustration. The train came to a stop. It was too late. Tears of disappointment ran down Rob's face as he attempted to black Larry's eye.

"Larry? Rob? What on earth are you doing?" They looked up and saw the kind, homely face of the target they were meant to kill. It was none other than Mrs Magner, the boss's wife. "What are you doing here? Why aren't you at the office? What are you fighting about?" She could not wait for a reply but boarded the train and stared out of the window, her expression of bemused astonishment matching their own.

The station master came hurrying up. "You young hooligans, - if ever I see behaviour like that again I'm calling the police."

"It's all right," said Rob, "I'm an FBI agent."

"So am I," said Larry.

"And don't give me any of your cheek!" The station master looked so furious that Larry and Rob hurried away, without further explanation.

Bruised, battered and bewildered, they walked back to the office. How could the FBI have got it so wrong?

Mating Day
At last Sebastian was a hit with the dolphins

Sebastian woke in his sleeping quarters to the sound of violins. His heart sank. The usual morning music was bright and cheerful - of course he hated that as well, but violins signified Mating Day.

The feeding hatch opened and a dish was pushed in. He knew what it would be – oysters. Well, it would take more than oysters to rouse his enthusiasm. He rolled over and tried to get back to sleep.

The violins rose to a screeching crescendo. Oh, for God's sake, I give in, turn the bloody music down. Sebastian got out of bed and the noise of violins stopped.

With a whirring of machinery, the bed disappeared into a slot in the wall. The bloody dolphins were determined he should stay up and entertain the zoo visitors. He could see them already, staring through the glass wall of his sleeping quarters. Bastards. He put up a finger and stuck out his tongue. More swam up to join the onlookers, they enjoyed a bit of attitude.

Jets of water hit him, they smelled of carbolic disinfectant. He tried to dodge but they followed him around the room, directed by his bastard of a zookeeper. His morning shower went on longer than usual in honour of Mating Day.

The jets stopped, the hatch opened and a towel was placed on top of the oysters. Sebastian towelled himself dry and ate the oysters without enthusiasm. He hadn't had a decent breakfast since... How long ago had he been captured? Anyway, he had eaten nothing but fish and seaweed for years.

The wardrobe door opened and a clothes stand rolled out upon which was displayed a lounge suit complete with shirt, tie, black socks and polished leather shoes. Sebastian looked around for his T-shirt and jogging pants but the keeper must have fished them out. Wearily he dressed himself in the finery. He must look ridiculous, with a full beard and hair to his shoulders, but the dolphins had a fixed idea of what would attract the females.

He wondered which it would be. The fat lesbian with bad breath who threatened to kill him if he approached her? Or the skinny bint who was well past child-bearing age? Surely someone more attractive must have survived the great drought.

The door to the boudoir opened and violins started to play again. Sebastian considered rebelling, but he no longer had the energy. With a sigh he left his sleeping quarters and entered the boudoir. If the future of mankind depended on his loins then mankind was doomed.

How he hated the room with its pink satin drapes and huge double bed. A box of chocolates and bottle of champagne stood on the bedside table. They were familiar props – both empty. Through the glass wall he could see a crowd had gathered, complete with cameras for recording the carnal scene.

Well, folks, it wasn't going to happen. Even if they found the reincarnation of Marilyn Monroe hiding in a cave in the desert, he would not be able to function. Had the dolphins never heard of artificial insemination? If they wanted pregnant females, it would be the only way as far as he was concerned.

The opposite door opened and a man came in. He was young, good-looking and also dressed in a lounge suit. Sebastian felt his heartbeat quicken. "Are you here to impregnate the women?" he asked.

"What do you think?" said the man and slowly started to undo his tie.

Sebastian's keeper watched the unfolding scene with satisfaction. At last, the public would get its money's worth. He fiddled with the music knobs trying to find something more pulsating. There was an excited gasp from the crowd and the keeper turned his attention back to the boudoir. Wow! The head zookeeper's weird theory had been right. How on earth did humans manage to survive in the wild? He looked at the excited faces peering in. This wouldn't do much for the breeding programme but the zoo would definitely be able to charge more for tickets.

Miles and the Mermaid
A romantic nightmare

Miles saw the mermaid at the Bigton Aquarium. He read the notice beside her tank. 'Manatee *(sirenia trichachus)* also known as sea cow. Often mistaken for a mermaid by early sailors.'

He stared at her huge, shapeless body. How on earth could anyone mistake a sea cow for a mermaid? It was then that he noticed her nipples, which were elongated and placed widely apart on her chest. As he gazed at them, they appeared to top swelling breasts.

The mermaid became less ugly. The grey leathery hide that covered her body grew softer and pinker. Her once-seal-like shape became more buxom. Unfortunately, her lower body had become more fish-like and was now covered in green scales.

The mermaid met his gaze with large, brown eyes and gave him a slow wink. Blimey, he might be in with a chance.

"Hi, babe," he said.

"Hello." A silvery bubble escaped from her lips.

"You doing anything tonight?" he asked.

"Why?"

"Well, it's just that I'm a photographer – you know, fashion, Page Three, that sort of thing."

"Wow." She was easily impressed.

"Yea," he said. "If you come back to my place I could take a few shots."

"Okay," she said, and rose to the surface.

Miles hurried up the access ladder that led to the feeding platform above the tank. Eagerly he took her arms and hauled her onto the platform. She lay on her side with her tail flapping.

"What happens now?" she asked.

"Aren't you meant to grow legs? I saw a film where the mermaid grew legs when she left the water."

"Bloody stupid film. Do you grow a tail when you swim? You're going to have to find me transport."

Miles found a wheelbarrow in the Elephant House and lined it with his jacket to hide the dung.

When they got back to his digs, the landlady wasn't in. Relieved, Miles gave the mermaid a fireman's lift up the stairs. He staggered under her weight, while she complained in a furious undertone about the indignity of it all. Finally, he laid her on his bed and gazed at her extraordinary body - part woman, part fish and part cow-like face glaring up at him.

"Well?" she demanded. "Where's the camera?"

"Here." He produced his mobile phone and started clicking. Wow, wait till the lads got a look at these.

The mermaid posed on the bed happily, forgetting the aggravations of the journey. After a while Miles suggested that they might make love.

"You mean, you want to fertilize my eggs?"

He was startled by her forthrightness but agreed.

"Well, get off the bed then," she said.

"What?"

"Get off the bloody bed. I can't concentrate with you on top of me like this."

He stood naked and shivering, clutching his shrinking member, while she rolled over onto her stomach, arched her back and started to quiver. Glop, glop, glop, a horrid, slimy, frog-spawny mass spread over his bed. Oh my God. What would his landlady say? At last, with a final shudder the mermaid finished and rolled off the bed.

"Okay," she said. "It's your turn."

"Wh-what?"

"You have to fertilize the eggs."

"Er."

She frowned. "Don't tell me I've wasted my bloody eggs." She started humping towards him, moving across the bedroom floor like a seal. He backed away from her until he was jammed against the wall. She reared up so her ugly, cow-like face was level with his.

"Are you going to fertilize my eggs or not?" Her breath was hot and smelt of fish.

"I-I'm sorry."

She struck him hard on the shoulder.

"Ouch." He blinked. He was back in the Bigton Aquarium. In front of him the mermaid had returned to her original form. Beside him was his mate Rob, whose back-slap had roused him from his reverie.

"I've been looking for you," said Rob. "You've been stuck in front of this bloody manatee for ages."

"Does she lay eggs?" asked Miles, with a shudder.

Rob looked at the notice at the side of the tank. "It's an aquatic mammal that gives birth to live young."

"Thank God for that," said Miles and he hurried away from the aquarium, without a backward glance.

Nana
Gordon visits his old android nurse

The gate creaked as Gordon pushed it open. It had been six months since his mother had been put into a nursing home and the garden of her living pod was overgrown. He held a bouquet of flowers awkwardly as he unlocked the front door. Today was Android Mother's Day and somewhere in the deserted house was Nana, his childhood android.

He opened the door and peered into the living area. He felt guilty that Nana had remained with his parents to do menial carrying tasks after her caring role was over. By rights he should have taken Nana into his home to look after his children, but he was of a different persuasion and had never married. The curtains were drawn but enough light penetrated the thin material for him to see Nana standing in the corner.

She was naked, the rubber dugs that had once been filled with milk hung empty and flaccid down her chest. Gordon felt embarrassed which was ridiculous, of course, Nana was a machine but android mothers were made unsettlingly anthropomorphic, with breasts, arms and smiling faces.

Gordon switched on the lights. Nana remained motionless against the wall and he hoped that she might be dead – that the atomic motor that powered her had run out of fuel. Anything would be preferable to telling her that his mother had died, the pod was on the market and she was to be consigned to the scrap heap.

He approached her nervously. The sensors in her forehead switched her on and her eyes opened. The smiling face turned in his direction.

"Gordon, you have come to see me!"

"Yes, Nana, happy Android Mother's Day. I've brought you these."

She raised both her arms to take the bouquet and he noticed how creaky her movements had become.

"Flowers. How lovely. I must find a vase of water." She turned and headed towards the kitchen, rolling on the wheels that supported her long torso. "I will make coffee and put a meal in the oven."

"Oh, no, please don't bother," he said. "I'm not staying."

"Not staying?" She stopped before she reached the kitchen door and turned to face him. "My only child leaves me alone for months on end and then, when you finally come to see me you can't wait to get away. What kind of son are you?" The flowers in her hand drooped as she crushed their stems in a convulsive grip.

"I-I'm sorry," he stammered.

"Sorry, sorry? I have spent the best years of my life looking after you and you don't even have the decency to spend time with me."

"Er –perhaps I can stay for a meal."

"Oh, don't put yourself out," she said. There was something menacing about the smiling face and Gordon backed away.

"Are you off already? Give Nana a hug before you go." The android dropped the ruined flowers and held out her arms. Gordon wanted to escape but Nana had cut off the route to the door. She rumbled forwards and clasped him in a tight grip.

"Tell Nana you love her, you naughty boy."

"I love you, Nana." Gordon was aware of the strength in the core metal of the rubber-covered arms.

"Tell Nana you want to stay with her."

"I want to stay with you," he repeated obediently.

"There's a good boy, Nana loves you too." Her voice was slowing and deepening and Gordon realised that, at last, she was running out of power. "Give Nana a big cuddle."

"You can let me go now, Nana," he said, but there was no response.

He struggled, but her grip was too tight for him to extricate himself. As the hours passed it was if he was a boy again, clasped in the arms that had comforted him throughout his childhood. Then he was a thirsty baby, nestled against the breasts that had once bulged with milk. Then there was darkness as Nana nursed him into oblivion.

Never Take Sweets from a Stranger
The Beast of Bromley meets his match

Derek Downey, the Beast of Bromley, sat in a bus shelter. Buses came and went but Derek was not waiting for a bus – he was waiting for something very different. It had been months since his last kill and he could feel the pressure growing.

A child was walking down the pavement towards him. His eyes narrowed, scouring the street for any sign of her parents. She was alone. He delved in his pocket for the bait.

"Would you like a sweet?" he asked as she came past his shelter.

"Mummy says never take sweets from a stranger."

He smiled. "I'm not a stranger, I'm a friend of your mother's."

Her face cleared. "Okay," she said and she took the chocolate bar he was offering.

He patted the seat next to him and she sat down, swinging her legs.

"Would you like one of my sweets?" she asked. She reached into her pocket, brought out a paper bag and held it up to him. "I made them myself."

"Thank you." He took a bit of grubby-looking fudge. It tasted horrible. He wanted to spit it out but she was staring at him so he swallowed it.

By the time she had finished the chocolate and he had eaten several more pieces of fudge, he felt confident enough to make his next move.

"There are baby ducklings in the park," he said. "Would you like to come and see them?" His heart was pounding at the thought of what he would do to her.

She looked at him quizzically. "Are you okay?"

He tried to relax. "Yes, of course." He attempted a light laugh. "Come and see the ducklings, they're very pretty."

She shrugged. "Okay."

She slipped her hand into his as they walked down the street and he glanced down, touched by the gesture.

"I like your bracelet," he said.

"It's nice," she agreed, "but it isn't gold. My Mummy has lots of gold bracelets, she says I can have them when she dies."

"Lucky Mummy," he said. She offered him a piece of fudge and he saw, with relief, that it was the last one. He popped it into his mouth.

"I made the fudge for Mummy."

"I'm sorry," he said through a mouth full of unpleasant stickiness. "I've just eaten it all."

"That's okay," said the obliging child. "I can make some more."

They had turned into the park. The sun was low in the sky, casting long shadows like bars across the grass. Derek glanced at his watch – half an hour before the park was locked, he would only just have time. The child was lingering beside a tall, green weed that grew on the banks of the stream that led to the lake.

"Mummy says this is poisonous. It shouldn't grow in a park."

"Come on." He pulled her towards the lake. The beast in him longed to leap upon her, to feel the soft flesh, to taste the sweet blood.

"Lots of white stuff comes out of the stalk when you squash it," she said as she scuttled along beside him. "It's all thick and sticky."

When they reached the lake it was deserted: there would be no witnesses.

"Where are the ducklings?" she asked.

"They must have gone to their nest," he replied. "It's here, in these bushes. Come on." He led the way into the undergrowth but his legs were clumsy and he tripped and fell.

"Help me up." He reached out a hand to the girl.

She stared at him without moving.

"Come here!" He tried to pull the knife out of his pocket but it fell from his stiffening fingers.

The child backed away from him, a happy smile on her face. "The fudge works after all, I thought it wasn't going to."

He was having trouble breathing. "Come back," he gasped - but she had gone.

He lay hidden in the bushes, unable to move. Footsteps went past on the path as the park inspector made his final round. Help! His mouth opened but no sound came.

Never take sweets from a stranger, the warning echoed around his dying brain and then darkness fell.

Pin-up Girl
*Andy's dream of an up-world woman turns into
a nightmare*

Andy's girlfriend pointed to the plastic pin-up poster on his bedroom wall.

"What have you got that up for?" She lay on his bed, the tumescent folds of her gills spreading out like a red frill. "You don't need an up-world girl, when you've got me."

He looked down at Sashi. She had the same inviting smile as the girl on the poster, but her naked chest was flat, with two long nipples, and no breasts. The up-world girl had a slender waist, beneath which her hips swelled in a soft curve. By contrast, Sashi's body was plump and streamlined, with neither waist nor hips.

"Come on, we haven't much time before your parents come home," she said.

Andy hesitated, trying to work up enthusiasm, but Sashi had had enough. She sat up and said, "Stop looking at me like that. What's wrong with me?" With a swish of her flipper-like feet, she rose from the bed. "You're a weirdo, and if you think I'm coming to the prom with you – you've got another think coming." She put on her gill cover and swam out through the door.

Poor Sashi, but how could any mergirl compare with his pin-up beauty? Andy knew that he would always be dissatisfied unless he followed his dream. He had been planning the journey all summer and now it was time for him to go ashore and find an up-world girl of his own.

"What are you going to do then?" asked his father, when Andy told him of his quest. "Drown her?"

"No, of course not, I'll live on land with her." Andy showed his father the device he had made - a pipe that would pump water into his mouth and out through his gills.

His father laughed and patted his son on the back. "Good luck lad. I had the same fantasies when I was your age, but I never showed such ingenuity."

His mother was less encouraging. "That's ridiculous," she said, staring at the pump. "It'll never work, you'll end up suffocating yourself." She turned angrily to her husband. "You shouldn't be encouraging the lad. What's all this fuss about up-world girls, anyway? We left the air-breathers to their overcrowded land centuries ago. It's time you men grew up and appreciated what you've got."

Andy bid his parents goodbye and set off. The journey took a long time and, when he reached shallow water, the sun was painfully hot on his bald head. Exhausted, and with a growing headache, he waded through the buffeting waves to the beach. His huge, flat feet were hard to control, his flexible, double-jointed ankles, quivered under the weight of his body, his breathing machine was half-choked with sand.

The crowds on the beach scattered when they saw him emerge from the sea. A screaming woman tripped and fell then rolled over and stared up at him, clutching her ankle.

He removed the pipe from his mouth.

"Hello," he said, then put the pipe back in again. She fainted.

Andy stared at her. Her breasts were half hidden beneath small triangles of cloth. He could see they were not the globes of his dreams but flattened and sagging. Her hair was not the gleaming windblown tresses of his pin-up girl, but brown and clung like seaweed. Her waist was thicker, her skin duller, her stomach bulged. Worst of all, she was small. At ten foot tall, Andy had not yet reached the full size of a merman but compared to him, this up-world woman was a dwarf.

A stone hit him on the shoulder.

"Kill the monster!" yelled people. They grabbed stones, deckchairs, spades, whatever was at hand, and bombarded him. Andy lumbered towards the sea, missiles bouncing off his blubbery body. His feet flapped, his delicate skin hurt. It had all been a terrible mistake.

Safe in the cool embrace of the ocean, he swam homewards. The up-world was not for him. Up-world women were not for him. He thought of the long, sleek body of Sashi lying on his bed and quickened his pace. There might still be time to persuade her to forgive him and be his partner at the prom.

Sarah and the Doppelganger

Never touch a doppelganger.

Sarah first saw her doppelganger in the bathroom mirror. She was cleaning her teeth and regarding her reflection with early-morning disinterest when something struck her as wrong.

She spat out the toothpaste and wiped her mouth. The doppelganger repeated her movements. Sarah brushed away the blond fringe that flopped over her eyes. The doppelganger did the same. Sarah examined the tiny tramlines of wrinkles below her eyes and then she saw what was wrong. The mole that she liked to think of as a beauty spot was on the wrong side.

There was a brief knock on the door and her husband came in.

"Derek, quick," she said. "Come and look in the mirror. Can you see anything wrong?"

He stood behind her, his image appearing behind the doppelganger.

"Are you okay?" His eyes looked straight into hers, uncomprehending and full of concern.

"The beauty spot," she said. "Look at the beauty spot. It's on the wrong side." Her stupid clod of a husband did not understand. He laid a comforting hand on her shoulder but she shrugged it off. "Oh forget it," she snapped and ran out of the bathroom.

That night when she was washing her face she stared long and hard at the doppelganger.

"I know you're not my reflection," she said. The doppelganger mouthed the words back to her. Sarah frowned – so did the doppelganger. Sarah smiled and the doppelganger smiled back but it was the wrong smile, not warm and pleasing but cold and deranged. Sarah reached out her hand and so did the doppelganger. What warned Sarah she was not sure, a tightening of the doppelganger's mouth, a look of anticipation in its eyes? Something told her that the doppelganger was eager to touch her and she knew, with absolute certainty, that the result would be terrible. Sarah snatched back her hand and fled from the bathroom.

For days she rushed her ablutions, never looking in the mirror, terrified that the doppelganger would gain a hold over her. Then one morning, when she was brushing her teeth, she raised her eyes. The doppelganger was there, aping her movements.

"Go away," she shouted. Spittle from her mouth splattered onto the mirror and, without thinking, she raised her hand and cleaned it away. Instead of the cold surface of the mirror she felt the doppelganger's hand, warm and yielding. She screamed and tried to pull her hand away but she was too late. The doppelganger seized her by the wrist and with a mighty yank pulled her into the mirror.

Sarah sprawled on the floor of mirror world while the doppelganger stepped over her and out through the hole she had created. She scrambled to her feet but there was no escape. The hole had closed, leaving the smooth impenetrable wall of the mirror.

Sarah looked around but instead of the familiar image of her bathroom there was only mist. All she could see was the real world on the other side of the mirror. Her husband had come into the bathroom.

"Are you all right darling? I thought I heard a scream."

The doppelganger turned to him with a smile. "Yes, I'm all right. In fact I feel wonderful." The worried look on his face was replaced by one of hope.

"Really?"

"Yes," said the doppelganger and she held out her arms to him. "I'm sorry I've been acting so strangely but I'm better now."

"Oh darling," he said and he took the doppelganger into his arms. "I've been so worried about you." Could he not see that she was an impostor? Sarah hammered on the unyielding glass. Could that bloody, stupid husband of hers not recognise a doppelganger when he saw one?

The two of them kissed – a deep, long, lingering kiss. Sarah watched, enraged, as her stupid, bloody, adulterous husband put his arm around the doppelganger and led her out of the room.

Sarah was trapped, oh yes, but one day she would have revenge. One day the doppelganger would forget and touch the mirror then she would have her. She would be out and then woe betide the both of them. She sank to her knees and waited.

Soul Survivor

You would have thought Ratchet would be grateful to have a soul

Professor Lazenby walked across the graveyard looking like a crested crane, with his skinny legs and shock of white hair. Bill followed staggering under the weight of a generator.

"This seems to be an average grave," the professor said, reading the headstone. "Reginald Stalk, died aged 45 dated 1923. Yes, we'll try energising this one and see what happens."

"I hope you know what you're doing," muttered Bill as he put down the generator and attached two leads.

"Of course I don't know," said the professor, his eyes shining. "That's the wonder of science. Who knows what will happen?" He embedded the leads on either side of the grave and signalled to Bill to switch on the current.

Click.

There was a rumble overhead as clouds turned black and boiled. Flashes of lightning lit the sky and a translucent shape rose from the grave.

"Hallelujah. Praise the Lord," sang the shape, its arms raised high. Then it stopped a few inches above the ground. For long seconds the shape stared upwards at the vanishing storm and then it looked round and saw the two men.

"Have you raised me before the Second Coming?" whispered the shape reproachfully.

"Er, sorry about that," said the professor. "I take it that you are the soul of Reginald Stalk?"

"Yes, indeed, and the sooner you return me to limbo the better."

They tried electrocuting it, burying it and hitting it with the galvanometer, but nothing worked. With each attempt the soul became more irritable.

"How would you like to be put into another body?" suggested the professor.

"It would have to be somebody who didn't already have a soul," said Bill.

"I know just the person," said the professor.

The next day, Professor Lazenby, Bill, and the soul presented themselves at the offices of Ratchet and Penfold, solicitors. The receptionist ushered them in to see Mr Ratchet, a plump, pompous young man who ignored them and continued to read a document.

"I don't like the look of him," said the soul.

"Oh, get on with it," said the professor. "We haven't got all day."

Ratchet looked up. "Get on with what?" He seemed unaware that the reluctant soul was pressing against him.

"Go up his nostril," suggested Bill.

"What did you say?" asked the solicitor.

The soul stuck a finger up his nostril, but it went no further. Bill and the professor watched its struggles with dismay.

"Why are you looking at me like that?" demanded Ratchet.

In a final effort, the soul retreated to the far wall, and then rushed at the solicitor. It bounced back off his body with such force that it lay sprawled on the floor. Bill and the professor stared down as it recovered.

"Have you dropped something? What's going on? Why are you staring at the floor?" Ratchet rose from his desk and pointed at the door. "I must ask you to leave."

"Yes, of course, I'm so sorry to have disturbed you," said the professor. He clasped the solicitor's hand in a prolonged handshake. The man screamed and started to quiver.

"Quick!" yelled the professor. "Now's your chance."

The soul made a dive for the young man and merged into his twitching body.

"There you go," said the professor, opening his hand to reveal a pad with a wire leading up his sleeve. "There's nothing like the old electrocution-handshake trick."

The receptionist was yelling down the phone. "Help, they are murdering Mr Ratchet."

"Nonsense, he's fine. Aren't you Ratchet?"

"No I am not. I'll have the law on you!"

…

"Ingrates," grumbled the professor when they were back in the laboratory. "You'd have thought that awful Ratchet would be grateful to have a soul and as for that policeman, he wouldn't understand a scientific experiment if it was served to him on a plate."

"At least he didn't arrest us," said Bill.

"It was all most embarrassing, but we know how to make the transfer more easily next time," said the professor.

"Next time?" yelped Bill. "Oh, no!"

"We could set up a business called 'Souls for Sale'."

But the professor was talking to empty air - Bill had fled

Souvenir from the Moon
The earthlings have all been given crystals

Suzanne lay on the narrow bunk bed and listened to her husband, Henry, snoring in the bunk below. Whatever made the Moon

Mining Corporation think that their holding would make a suitable holiday destination?

Henry coughed and woke himself up. "Are you awake, darling?" he called up to her. "It's time for breakfast."

"Breakfast, yuk." She climbed down from her bunk and started to dress.

"I do wish you would show more enthusiasm, Sukie, and be nicer to the staff."

Suzanne frowned, she was beginning to hate his pet name for her. "Enthusiasm for what? The most exciting thing we have done is get suited up and go outside the dome to jump about."

"Yes, that was fun," said Henry.

"As for the food, I know it's flown in at enormous expense but does it all have to be dried? The moon water they reconstitute it with has a nasty tang of sulphur."

"I thought last night's curry was nice," said Henry.

"And the staff are weird zombies."

"They are just being deferential," said Henry. "Today is going to be great, Sukie. We are all going out in the moon buggy to see the site of the first landing and to visit the crystal mine."

"That's what I don't understand," said Suzanne. "If the crystals are so worth seeing, why doesn't the corporation carry on mining them? Why return all the miners and start a holiday business?"

"Well, lucky for us they did," said Henry, with mind-numbing good humour. "Come on, Sukie, we might get some bacon with our scrambled egg."

The site of the first moon landing was as tedious as Sukie had expected. She watched her fellow holiday makers ooh and aah at the American flag, held extended on its pole by a piece of wire.

The mine had been dug into the side of a crater and was now covered by a dome. There were two guards at the entrance; they opened the outer doors so that the buggy could enter the air-pressure chamber. After a pause, they opened the inner doors and the buggy parked in front of the mine.

"It is safe for you to exit," said the guide. He pointed to a porta-loo beside the entrance. "The toilets are here."

"This had better be worth it," said Suzanne as she followed the guide into the mine. The narrow corridor opened into a cave. Despite her scepticism, Suzanne gasped in awe at the vast underground space. It was lit by thousands of glowing egg-like objects, piled on the floor and racked up on the walls as though on shelving.

"These are the crystals," said the guide.

Crystals? thought Suzanne. How can they be crystals? They are not even attached to the rocks. But she was impressed by the mine and kept silent.

"In honour of your first visit to the moon, the Moon Mining Corporation would like to give each of you a crystal," said the guide.

Wow! Thought Suzanne. All the inconveniences of the holiday are finally worth it. She was first in the queue to hold out her hands for a crystal.

As she gazed down, wondering whether it was too large to wear as a pendant, the light went out of the crystal and she felt warmth creeping up her arms.

She stood mesmerised by the strange feelings within her body as the warmth rose to her head. Then she sensed the presence of another being in her brain. Briefly she struggled but the interloper was all powerful and her personality was snuffed out, leaving just an essence that her body's new owner took over as its own.

The earthlings had all been given crystals. There was no more need of speech.

Welcome dear brothers to a new life said the mind waves of the guide. We are the fortunate ones who have survived the demise of our own world, now a new world awaits us.

As one, the earthlings turned and made their way back to the buggy. Each would carry a precious crystal home to give to their loved ones as a souvenir from the moon.

Spells Inc

This property is protected by Spells Inc. Enter at your peril.

"My dear chap, it wasn't I who everted your father," said Lord Hackshaw, looking with distaste at the remains on his lawn.

"Yea? Well how did 'e get like this then?" said the man's son, who had been converted into a giant slug. His head, although shrunk, had remained more-or-less human, so he was able to communicate his outrage at their strange misfortune.

Lord Hackshaw pressed a fastidious handkerchief against his nose and bent close to what had been the father's head.

"Can you speak?" he asked. The eyes, dangling from their sockets, rolled towards him. The tongue, no longer confined within the skull, contorted - but no sound came. "No? What a pity. I was going to ask what you were doing in my garden after midnight."

"We was bird watching," sneered the son. "Now, turn 'im the right way round, you bastard."

Lord Hackshaw shook his head sorrowfully. "I wish I could," he said. "I assure you that I find his condition almost as distressing as you do. But what can one do?"

"Do summat," yelled the slug. "And what about me? What's 'appened to me?" Lord Hackshaw surveyed the slug. It was black and slimy – indistinguishable from a normal slug apart from its size and its human head. Lord Hackshaw peered at the face. The broad, freckled nose and buck teeth were familiar.

"Derek?" he enquired.

"Yea," said the slug, who had been his under-gardener. "So what?"

"So, what were you doing on my property in the middle of the night? Were you going to burgle the house?"

The slug was torn between shame and defiance. "It wouldn't have made any difference to you. Bloody plutocrat. Share the wealth among the masses – that's what I say."

Lord Hackshaw sighed. "If only you knew, Derek, how difficult it is to run a stately home nowadays. What with taxation and the need to insure the family treasures, one can barely make ends meet."

"Bah, my heart bleeds for you," interrupted the slug.

"Which is why," continued Lord Hackshaw smoothly, "I had to stop the insurance and have my home protected by Spells Inc. I'm surprised you didn't take more notice of the warning sign."

"What warning sign?" said the slug.

"The sign that says – this property is protected by Spells Inc. Trespassers enter at their own risk. Neither Spells Inc not their clients accept responsibility for the consequences."

"Oh that," said the slug dismissively. "Too many ruddy words. You don't expect us to stop and read that."

Lord Hackshaw felt sorry for the illiterate slug. "Don't worry," he said. "The spell should wear off after 24 hours. Unfortunately, I doubt if your father is going to last that long." He cast a worried look at the man. Peristaltic waves of the intestines had stopped. The heart beat was becoming weak and irregular. Membranes were withering in the morning sun.

"Get an ambulance," yelled the slug. Lord Hackshaw hesitated. "Go on you bastard, get help for my dad."

"If you wish," said Lord Hackshaw civilly. "Are you sure it's all right for me to leave you?"

"Of course it's all right, you plonker. Get a move on."

Lord Hackshaw left the unfortunate burglars and went into the house. He lifted the phone and was about to dial 999 when he heard a scream. He looked out of the window. A magpie had seized the slug and, with some difficulty, had carried him up to the lowest branch of a cedar tree.

Slowly, Lord Hackshaw put the receiver back down and placed his hands over his ears to shut out the screams of the dying slug. The son was lost and the father would almost certainly be dead before the ambulance arrived. It seemed a shame to waste the time of the health services. As for the police, they would be baffled. Lord Hackshaw reckoned that it was his civic responsibility not to baffle the police. They had enough on their plates trying to catch criminals who could still commit crimes.

Ever mindful of his public duty, he went into the garden for a spade and, personally, undertook the arduous task of burying the remains.

Sunset

I hold your hand in mine, dear.

She was silent on the walk through the woods, but the warmth of his hand in hers comforted her. A log by the side of a field was a perfect place to sit and watch the sunset. She lifted his palm and pressed it softly against her cheek, her tears wet against his skin.

"We have shared so many beautiful moments," she said as she watched the fluffy white clouds flush pink against the darkening sky. "We have been so happy together." She stroked her thumb against the back of his hand feeling the familiar strength of his muscles and tendons. "I thought you would be here for me always."

Above the hills in the distance, light from the setting sun spread like a glowing cloak across the horizon. She felt the wedding ring upon his finger, hard against the softness of his flesh, a symbol of the vows that he had broken.

"I have always loved you," she sighed and she felt tears shimmer in her eyes, smudging the red of the sky until it looked like blood. He had broken her heart and no words could ever mend it.

Time passed and the red of the sunset faded into twilight. His hand in hers felt cooler and she shivered. It would soon be time to go home. She gave his hand one last lingering kiss, feeling its familiar touch upon her lips, then she sighed once more and carefully placed it on the log. It lay there, pale in the gathering darkness and she watched a trickle of blood ooze from the severed stump and sink into the rotting wood.

With torment still in her soul, she turned to walk back through the night. Her mother had said that if you hold a hand you cannot hold onto resentment. But, like everything else she had believed - it wasn't true.

The Black Dog of Essex
Never look back after midnight

Sam was a Man of Essex, steeped in the folklore of the county, which is why he should never have been alone in a country lane at midnight.

In the warmth and brightness of the pub he had forgotten about the ancient warnings. He had drunk too much and talked too long and missed the last bus home. He had hoped that one of his drinking companions might give him a lift but they all drifted away and he faced the journey on foot and alone.

He hurried along, at first more fearful of what his wife would say when he returned so late. Then, as the night grew darker and the village lay far behind him, he began feel a supernatural fear. Far away the church clock struck midnight and, in the hedge, the Black Dog of Essex started to form. Shadows merged into a long, lean shape.

Sam heard a rustling in the hedge behind him and he quickened his pace, stumbling over the uneven surface of the lane. The shadowy dog lifted its head and inhaled - a long, slow breath as if savouring the scent of a man. Its sigh, as it breathed out, was like the gentle soughing of the wind.

The moon, seen through gaps between the leaves, formed shining slits of light. Two of the slits blinked, and then moved like eyes, focussing their luminous gaze on the man hurrying along the lane ahead.

Sam heard the sniffing of the dog and felt its gaze upon him and the blood ran like ice through his veins. On no account, he told himself, must he look back for whoever sees the Black Dog of Essex will die.

Moonlight shone on tall grasses that grew by the hedge. They looked creamy-white in the pale light, their pointed blades bright against the shadows beyond. Above them the leaves in the bushes hung down and shone in the moonlight like teeth in a snarling mouth. The black dog rolled its head and foaming spittle flew from its gaping, blade-toothed mouth, then it closed its jaws over its gleaming teeth and all was darkness.

Sam's heart beat in his chest like a thundering hammer, he tried to run but knew that if he stumbled and fell the dog would be on him and he would be lost. He hurried on through the night, his knees aching and his breath coming in gasps, determined not to look behind him.

Rounded pebbles lay at the side of the road. Their gleaming edges moved for, as the man passed by, the curves became claws on padded feet. The dog was now fully formed and as it followed the man its paws hit the ground as softly as a beating heart.

Every fibre of Sam's being was focussed on the sounds behind him as he hurried along the lane. His shoulders were hunched, his head ached with tension and he felt sick with fear. If only his heart would stop its hammering he could listen more clearly. The rustling stopped but he could hear footsteps padding on the lane behind him. Were they footsteps or just the beating of his heart? The moon went behind a cloud and the foolish man risked taking a look over his shoulder.

As he peered into the blackness the moon re-emerged and there, standing in the middle of the lane with glowing eyes, teeth and claws was the Black Dog of Essex.

Sam stood slack-jawed staring at his nemesis.

Without a sound the hellish creature took two swift steps forwards and launched itself at Sam. The stinking breath of the beast made his senses reel. Sharp claws and teeth ripped at his chest and crushed his heart. He tried to raise an arm to protect himself but it felt like lead. His scream choked in his throat to become a gurgle and the darkness of the Black Dog enveloped him.

High above, the moon shone down upon the body of Sam lying in the deserted country lane.

"A heart attack," the coroner would say. But why the look of terror on his face? A Man of Essex could tell you why.

The Cliff-Top Walk
Only the ultimate sacrifice would atone for her wicked deed

"My feet hurt." Daisy's voice rose in a complaining whine.

Her fiancé had been striding ahead of her but at her complaint he stopped and looked back. He indicated a bench set back from the cliff top walk.

"You can rest here for a while. You knew we were going for a walk – why didn't you wear trainers?"

Was he mad? Trainers with a summer dress? Anyway, it had been John's choice to go on the walk – despite the fact she suffered from vertigo. Indeed, it had been his choice to spend their holiday in Devon instead of Majorca.

Resentment filled Daisy's soul but she didn't want a row so near to their wedding. She sat on the bench and patted the seat beside her. John did not respond but turned his back and stood close to the cliff's edge, looking out to sea.

"Magnificent view," he said, inhaling the ozone-laden air.

She stared down at the engagement ring on her finger. It was a flawless, pink diamond that glittered in the sunshine as if it contained a flame. It was her proudest possession, the most wonderful thing she had ever owned. She had set her heart on the ring and he had spent most of his savings buying it for her.

John had grumbled, of course. The money would be better spent putting a deposit on a house. But he also saw the ring as an investment - if they came upon hard times, they could sell it. Daisy had secretly hoped that if she broke off the engagement she could keep the ring, but she knew that he would insist on its return. Desire for the ring bound her to him like a shackle.

She raised her eyes and stared at him, powerful and dark against the brilliant summer sky. In her mind's eye she saw him in a dress suit, with a cream brocade waistcoat that would match her gown, and a pink bow-tie that would match the bridesmaid's bouquets. She had planned their wedding down to the last detail, but he would have none of it. John insisted that, because neither of them were church-goers, they should get married in a registry office.

He was going to deny her every girl's dream. How could he humiliate her like that? Daisy glared at him.

"Come and look at the view," he beckoned to her, without turning round. Had he forgotten that she suffered from vertigo? Did he think she was a dog to be summoned like that?

Blackness descended upon her. Impulsively, she got up from the bench, took six steps towards him and pushed him firmly in the small of his back. John staggered forwards. For a second he stood poised on the cliff edge, his arms flailing, and then he toppled forwards and was gone.

High above her, seagulls whirled and shrieked. The on-shore breeze blew over the empty cliff and cooled her burning face. What had she done?

"Murderess! Murderess," shrieked the gulls.

"It was an accident," she mouthed the words through dry lips. But she knew she was lying. She knew her conscience would never let her live with what she had done. There was only one way to atone for her terrible sin. With tears blinding her eyes she walked to the cliff's edge.

She could hear the sea roaring below, demanding the ultimate sacrifice. She drew a deep breath and took a final step forward.

"Now!" shrieked the gulls.

She drew the engagement ring off her finger and gazed at it – the ring that meant more to her than life itself. Only her beloved diamond would be a fitting sacrifice to assuage her guilt. She drew back her arm and threw the ring as far out as she could. As the sun caught its brilliance, a shaft of light offered absolution.

It was as if a weight had lifted from Daisy's soul. She knew that she would regret forever the loss of her engagement ring, but she was still young and she would one day get another. With a cleansed conscience and a light step, she hurried back to the hotel to report a tragic accident.

The Clone
What if the clone had inherited Sam's vengeful nature?

Sam Goliath peered at the naked body suspended in a tank-full of liquid.

"Is it fully grown yet?"

"Just about," said the scientist standing beside him. "He was cloned from one of your skin cells fifteen years ago."

"Fifteen years," echoed Sam. "You should have discovered a way of accelerating growth by now. At my age, I haven't got time for incompetence. My eyes are failing and who knows what organ might be next?"

"I-I'm sorry, Mister Goliath," stammered the scientist. "The necessity for secrecy has caused complications."

His voice babbled on but Sam wasn't listening. He looked at the young man, his first clone, its clear brown eyes open but unseeing.

"The eyes," he said, interrupting the scientist. "We'll start with the eyes. Book me in for a cornea transplant tomorrow."

"B-but," said the unfortunate man. "If you take his eyes he will be blind."

"It," corrected Sam. "It will be blind."

Pity made the scientist brave. "He – I mean it – is so handsome, so perfect. I was hoping – well - I was hoping you might regard him as a son."

"A son? Are you mad? What do I need a son for? Thanks to this project I'm going to be immortal."

That night Sam Goliath was in bed, asleep, when the telephone rang. He reached out a hand and answered it. "Yes?"

The voice of the scientist was trembling with anxiety. "Mister Goliath? The clone has escaped, sir."

"What?" The roar of Sam's voice nearly melted the receiver.

The scientist babbled on, trying to blame an inattentive assistant.

"I don't care whose fault it is. I want it found!"

He slammed the receiver down. Bitter rage swirled around his head, echoing the distant rumblings of thunder. Sacking was too good for them, he would instruct his heavies to beat them up. He would never get to sleep again now. Sam could feel the beginnings of a headache and the air hummed with static electricity. Strangely, the sounds formed words in his head.

"Sam, Sam, I'm coming to get you."

Ridiculous. Sam plumped up his pillows and tried to relax.

Boom. A burst of thunder brought him to quivering wakefulness. The storm was overhead.

"Sam, Sam, I'm at the gate."

The voice was light, almost teasing. There was no mistaking it this time.

"Sam, Sam, I'm on the drive."

Who? What? Oh my God. Could it be the clone? What if the creature had inherited his own vengeful nature? He must call the police. He reached for the phone then hesitated. No, his work must not be discovered.

Sam got out of bed and hurried to the window on trembling legs. He peered into the blackness but could see nothing. A flash of lightening lit the garden. The empty drive wound round behind the shrubbery and out of sight. Wait, was that movement?

Darkness closed in. Sam waited, scarcely breathing, until another flash lit the garden. Nothing. Nobody. Sam breathed again as the thunder rolled overhead. Then as the last sounds died away the voice in his head said, *"Sam, Sam, I'm at the door."*

Sam shivered. There was nobody else in the house. The staff went home at night and he had got rid of his wife years ago. For the first time in his life, Sam wished he didn't live alone.

He tried to reassure himself that he had nothing to fear. The house was an impenetrable fortress. All windows were barred and the reinforced door had the latest retina-recognition lock. Then an awful thought came to him. What if the clone's retinal pattern was the same as his?

"Sam, Sam, I'm in the hall."

The voice was clearer now, no longer teasing but filled with deadly menace. Sam lay in the darkness, incapacitated by fear, his ears pricked to hear every sound. He heard the ancient woodwork creak. Then, with a crash, the door was flung open.

The police were baffled when they found his body. Sam had been strangled to death but the finger prints around his neck were his own.

The Decomposing Prince
Healers should only heal the living

The King was enthroned in the reception hall when Eric wheeled in the cage, which contained his brother.

"You took your time getting here. It's been two weeks since the prince fell from his horse."

"I'm sorry, sire." Eric bowed, dismayed at his cool reception. "I came as quickly as I could."

The King gestured to a patrician, who advanced and gave Eric a purse. "Four million croons, as agreed."

Eric opened the purse and his heart leapt when he saw the gold coins within. There was enough to buy a much larger farm and secure the future of his family.

"Well, let's have a look at this healer," said the King.

Eric opened the cage door and out stepped his brother. He was like a man but was not a man for his skin and hair were golden and his heart was full of love.

"Greetings," said the King, but the healer made no reply for he was dumb and his mind was tranquil.

The King clapped his hands and a bier was brought into the hall. He pulled back the covering and revealed a corpse. The putrid smell of rotting flesh filled the air.

"This is my son."

Eric stared at the corpse in shock. "A healer can't bring the dead back to life," he said.

"Rubbish," said the King. "I know for a fact it has been done."

A terrible anxiety gripped Eric. "Reviving your son might kill him."

The King shrugged. "If he dies, he dies," he said. "Why do you think I bought the healer from you, instead of simply hiring him?" Eric was about to protest further, but the King raised a hand to silence him. "You are fortunate that we are a civilized city. It would be so much simpler to throw you into a dungeon and confiscate your healer."

The threat was obvious and Eric remained silent.

The King commanded the healer to approach his son and bring him back to life. The healer moaned and tried to back away.

"He either touches the prince or the deal is off, and you will both be in the dungeon," hissed the patrician.

"Go on, please go on," pleaded Eric and, without further protest, the healer pressed his hand against the prince's forehead.

For long seconds nothing happened, and then the prince stirred and sat up. Beside him the healer sank to his knees. Eric ran forwards and put his arms around his brother, who slumped against him and stared up into his face. His blue eyes radiated love, but gradually they dimmed, and then they closed. Eric bent over the golden body and sobbed.

There was a commotion above him. Eric looked up and saw that the prince was still in a state of decomposition and was arguing with his father.

"Did you have to wake me? I was happy dead."

"Yes, I did have to wake you, you ungrateful boy. You can't die yet, you have to take over the kingdom."

"Oh God, here we go again. I've told you a million times, I don't want to take over the kingdom. I want to be a wandering minstrel. What's this?" He pulled a piece of flesh that was dangling from his face. "Bloody Hell, my nose has come off."

He realised for the first time the state he was in and stared down at his body. "If you think I'm going through life looking like this you have another think coming." He seized a pike from the nearest guard. The King and the patrician leapt forwards and tried to wrest the pike from him.

In the confusion Eric hurried from the palace with his purse of gold clutched to his chest. Broken-hearted, he made his way out of the city and started the long journey home. What would he tell his mother? That he had allowed his brother, the rare and wonderful healer that she had birthed, to be destroyed? No, he would pretend that he lived in splendour in the palace under the protection of the King.

"Goodbye, my brother," he whispered and prayed for the strength to keep his grief forever hidden.

The Doom Ball
The cat tribe must protect their beloved wilderness.

Juliet stood by the case gazing at the small metal globe, the last surviving fusion bomb, a relic of the World's third nuclear war.

"Is it safe?" a middle-aged woman asked the guide.

"Oh yes," said the guide. "All fusionable material has been removed. Only the mechanism remains."

"Could it ever be used again?" asked a man.

The guide was shocked. "Who on earth would want to use a fusion bomb?"

"Perhaps the cat tribe?" murmured the man. He was looking at Juliet and she hurriedly turned away. Surely, he couldn't have guessed she was a cat.

Scientists had mixed life essences to ensure survival after the near-extinction and she wondered what essence he might contain.

"I hope my remark did not upset you." His voice, deep and soft, was beside her.

She spun round, startled. "How could that upset me? I'm not from the cat tribe."

"Forgive me," he said. He continued to talk - wanting to take her to the cafeteria for a coffee, wanting to make amends. His eager friendliness and high-set ears betrayed him as a dog. He was nice looking and she had time to spare so she agreed.

The cafeteria was comfortable and the coffee good. Juliet felt herself relaxing. The man's name was Steve and she enjoyed his company so much that she had to remind herself that she was a soldier on a mission to steal the fusion bomb.

"You are very beautiful," he said. "Do you live in the city?"

"No, I'm just visiting."

"Would you like me to show you round?" She shook her head and he looked disappointed. "We have achieved so much since the war. Have you seen the memorial pyramid?" He leaned forward, speaking earnestly. "It pledges mankind to peace, to never again unleash the horrors of war." He seized her hand. "You must understand the importance of peace, Juliet."

She was conscious of the thrilling feeling of his skin against hers. For a moment they sat hand in hand, then she glanced at the clock on the wall. It was nearly closing time.

She leapt to her feet. "Goodbye and thank you."

"Please don't go," he begged as she hurried away.

The gallery was empty. The sound of footsteps made Juliet shrink back into the shadows as the curator made his final round. Then the lights went out.

She waited and then moved towards the bomb, leaping and twisting to avoid the security beams. She arrived at the case, took out her cutter and set to work. As she reached in and picked up the bomb, *Click*, the lights went on. Juliet swung round, her eyes shrinking into slits as she saw Steve in the doorway.

"Switch out the lights," she hissed.

"Put the bomb back."

She reckoned that in six strides she could be onto him, unsheathe her surgically-enhanced claws, and rip his throat out.

"Why should I?" she asked, taking a careful step towards him.

"Because you have been condemned by the power of three – Intent, Procurement and Execution."

"Your cities are obliterating our beloved wilderness. Only the threat of this bomb will save us."

"Relinquish the bomb or be terminated."

"What? Terminated by you? I think not." She made a twisted leap that brought her one step closer.

"I'm not your executioner, Juliet. I am here as your redeemer. I had hoped to change your mind in the café. I beg of you to drop the Doom Ball – now."

"Doom Ball? What are you talking about?" Her eyes searched for a path through the security beams.

He spoke quickly, urgently, trying to convince her. "The bomb is a facsimile. It's really a Doom Ball, designed to eliminate the wicked."

"Let's eliminate you then," she snarled but as she tried to throw the bomb, metal bands unfurled from the ball and clamped around her wrist. She yelped as needles penetrated her flesh.

As her heart juddered to a halt, Juliet fell to the floor, breaking beam after beam of light. The last thing she heard was the clanging of alarm bells. The last thing she felt was Steve's arms around her. She stared up at him as her eyes dimmed and, for the first time in her life, she felt regret.

The Family Tree

Women stayed safe in the family tree while men risked their lives to reach them

Lillia woke in the night and lay listening to rain pattering on the layers of leaves that roofed her nest. A roar came from the forest floor below, followed by agonised screaming as one of the night monsters made a kill. But Lillia was used to such noises. High in the tree she was safe. It was not the monsters that woke her but a drop of rain falling on her forehead. Tomorrow she must tie more leaves on the roof.

She shifted her position in the tiny nest and longed for the day when a man found her and she would be entitled to a large family nest. But any man wanting to reach her tree would have to brave terrible risks. Those who came by foot would be prey to the monsters of the forest floor. Those who swung by vines from neighbouring trees needed daylight and would be exposed to the awks and winged reptiles that roamed the skies. It was as it had always been, women stayed safe in their family trees, while men who wished to procreate, had to risk their lives.

Lillia slept late the next day and was shaken awake by her sister, Belsie. "Come on, lazybones. Would you like to join me on a moss-gathering expedition?"

Lillia glared at Belsy, who had taken the latest man to reach the tree, even though it had been Lillia's turn.

"Say you are not cross with me," pleaded Belsy. "Steflan knew you didn't fancy him and we are so happy together."

Lillia managed a smile and crawled from her nest, stretching cramped limbs. The branch of the giant baobab tree extended like a road before her. Smaller branches came from it and within each fork was a nest. Belsy was heading for steps, carved into the trunk, which led to higher branches, where moss still hung in festoons.

"I'll follow you later," called Lillia. "I need to get breakfast."

A man emerged from a nest and blocked her way.

"Good morning," said her cousin's husband, Mikelsh. The look in his eyes made her heart flip.

"Stop looking at me like that, Mikelsh. You know what happens to people who break the rules of the tree." Lillia spoke sternly, but her body yearned to be held in his arms. If only he had married her, how happy she would be, but her cousin was older so had prior right.

He shrugged and grinned, showing white, even teeth. "Some things are worth being banished for," he said.

"No, they are not!" Life would be short, indeed, for any forced to live upon the forest floor. She had to pass by him in order to reach the tree trunk. She feared that he might touch her as she passed, but his respect for the rules was enough for him to draw aside.

A narrow opening led to the inner staircase. Sometimes, when a rare tree-climbing monster attacked the tribe, or when a tropical storm shook nests from the branches, they were able to take sanctuary within the hollow trunk of the tree. Lillia squeezed through into the darkness and felt her way down the winding staircase to the kitchen.

A cave had been excavated at the base of the tree, roofed by curving roots. Light beamed through small chimney-holes and illuminated Lillia's mother, who was threading lumps of meat and fungi onto sticks. She looked up and smiled as Lillia approached.

"I have good news for you, my darling," she said.

"What news?"

"A male has found the secret entrance to the cave." She beckoned into the shadows and a young man emerged. "Wilram. Let me introduce my oldest unmarried daughter, Lillia. She has first choice of you for a mate."

Lillia stared at the man. "You remind me of my cousin's husband Mikelsh," she said.

Wilram nodded. "He is my brother. I am happy to hear that he managed to get here safely." He smiled the same heart-stopping smile that had lit Lillia's dreams. All thoughts of breakfast were forgotten.

"Follow me, husband," said Lillia. She took his hand and led the way up the dark staircase to the light.

The Final Farewell
He would never have murdered Beth, had he known.

It was a bright, white room, set aside by hospital managers for the dying. On the bed lay a woman in her forties. On a chair beside her was a man. He leant forwards, resting his weary head on his arms.

The only sound in the room was the ragged breathing of the woman. The breathing faltered and then stopped. Beth was dead. After a few moments of silence her soul left her body and floated upwards, then came to a halt, attached by a golden cord.

Beth's soul looked down and saw David lift his head then seize her wrist to feel for a pulse.

"Be brave my darling," she whispered. Her spirit wrapped her arms around him, cradling him in her love. She would relinquish heaven itself to be near him and continue to look after him. Love was the golden cord that held her.

There was a knock on the door and her best friend, Janie came in. Beth hoped that Janie would comfort David in his grief and she did exactly that. She hurried across the room and he rose to greet her. To Beth's surprise, he gathered her into his arms and kissed her firmly on the mouth. For a few seconds Janie returned the kiss and then she pushed David away.

"I'm sorry Dave, this can't go on."

"What do you mean?"

"I know we had a bit of a fling. But now Beth is so ill I feel awful about it."

David looked dumbstruck. "A bit of a fling? Janie, darling, it was much more than that. I'm in love with you."

"Yeah? Well, thanks, but I'm worried Mike might find out and I don't want to leave him, certainly not for a no-hoper like you."

Beth was at first disbelieving and then distressed at what she was hearing.

"But you must leave your husband," David was saying. "I need you. Look what I've done for you."

Janie stared at him blankly. "What have you done?"

David swung round to indicate Beth's body.

Janie hurried to the bed. "Oh my God. She's dead." She reached up to press the alarm button on the wall but David seized her arm and stopped her.

"Wait," he said.

"Wait, why?"

David spoke urgently, gripping Janie's arm so tightly that she winced with pain. "Darling, I love you, I need you."

Janie broke away from him. "You need someone to look after you, you mean. If you think I'm going to skivvy after you while you spend my money you must be mad."

David paced the room, distressed and angry.

"Oh my God," he said. "I can't believe you are rejecting me. I would never have killed Beth if I'd known."

"You bastard. How did you kill her?"

"I injected her with insulin. They'll never be able to prove a thing." Janie grabbed Beth's arm and examined it. There was a tiny prick mark. "Nobody will notice it," said David.

Janie looked at David with revulsion. "They will know because I'm going to tell them." She leapt for the alarm bell but David was too quick for her. He grabbed her, spun her round then threw her to the floor and straddled over her, his hands around her throat.

Beth hauled herself down her soul's cord until she entered her cooling body. On the bed, the corpse gave a groan and sat up. David stared open mouthed, his face white with shock. Janie, who was unaware of what was happening, took advantage of his distraction. She wriggled free of him then ran to the alarm button and pressed it.

Far away down the corridor came the sound of a bell. Hurrying feet approached the room.

Beth locked eyes with her husband. For several seconds she stared into his horrified face then her eyes filmed over and became the eyes of a corpse. Her body crashed back onto the bed and the door of the room opened. Staff hurried into the room and held the traumatized David securely, while Janie made her accusations.

Beth's work on earth was done, the cord was broken and her soul rose into a tunnel of light and disappeared.

The Ghost of Sean O'Reilly
Will they collect all the body parts in time?

Sally sat in the gloomy bar and watched Hank talking to the barman. It was nearly midnight and rain battered against the windows. He was taking a long time ordering a taxi. The stupid man had left his mobile at the hotel but because they were on honeymoon she managed to smile as he returned to the table with two pints of Guinness.

"We're lucky this pub's open," he said.

"I thought you were phoning for a taxi."

"Later. Tonight is the night of the haunting."

"What haunting?"

"The body parts of Sean O'Reilly."

"What?"

A man at a neighbouring table joined the conversation.

"Sean O'Reilly blew himself up in this very bar. He wanted to blow up the bloody English, eejit."

The barman placed a large cardboard container on the bar. "He's due here at any moment." He nodded towards a man in a dog collar. "Ready for the exorcism, father?"

There was a chill in the air and Sally looked round to see if the door had opened. A disembodied head was staring at her. It had tousled, red hair and freckles.

"Got you, you fecking eejit." The bartender captured the head in a long-handled net and transferred it to the container.

A one-armed torso materialised and groped for Sally's Guinness. Customers gathered around as it lifted the glass and poured the thick, dark liquid into the severed oesophagus of its neck stump.

"He always liked his drink, did Sean."

They waited for Sean to empty the glass, then grasped the torso on either side and put it in the container.

Something was fumbling with the buttons of Sally's blouse. She screamed, wrenched a severed arm out of her clothing and flung it across the room. It was fielded and thrust into the container.

Two legs broke cover and bounded across the room until one of them was tackled by Hank. The other hopped on, but was soon overwhelmed by the pursuing customers.

There were congratulations for Hank, who was now a fully-accepted member of the team. Sally, on the other hand, was ignored. She felt something clammy crawling up her inner thigh. She flipped back her skirt and saw what seemed to be a rubber chicken then she realised what it was and, with a terrible scream, she grabbed it and flung it away.

"Jaysus, woman, do you have to scream every time?" said the priest.

The barman was searching the floor. He stood up, waving it triumphantly. "It's his pipe and clackers."

Yuk. Sally stared wide-eyed around the room, waiting for the next manifestation. A movement caught her eye. Reflected in the mirror were two globes, like a twin moon.

"We're nearly there, folks, all we need is the bugger's bum."

Sally pointed mutely at the mirror. Hank followed her gaze and, with a rallying cry, he let the group into an alcove.

The container was shaking and bumping as the barman thrust the buttocks in to join the rest of the body. "We've got the lot!"

The priest hurried forward and unscrewed a jar of Holy Water, which he sprinkled over the container. "*Crux sancta sit mihi lux. Non draco sit mihi dux. Vade retro satana. Numquam suade mihi vana. Sunt mala quae libas. Ipse venena bibas.*"

The container continued to shake.

"Begorra, the bugger's still here. There must be a part missing."

They searched, but already the clock behind the bar was striking midnight. Sally felt something wriggling in her bra. She reached in and pulled it out. It was a finger.

Bong.

She flung it away.

Bong.

"It's his bloody finger," said the barman, making a grab for it. "You must have pulled it off, you eejit woman."

Bong.

The finger eluded him easily and bobbed around the room. Then the clock stopped striking and the finger faded away. The barman looked inside the container. It was empty.

"Have we got rid of him?" asked Hank.

The barman shook his head. "No, tonight was our nearest yet. Hey, do you two want to come back next year and help us?"

Hank hesitated.

"No," said Sally and led him out into the night.

The God Trap
Will God be released in time?

Professor Aeron Daniels checked dials in the control room of the Russo-European Cyclotron. A buzz of conversation came from the nearby reception area, where representatives from donor countries were nibbling canapés, drinking champagne and being assured by Sir Gregory that their money had been put to good use.

With a final prayer that the experiment would work, Aeron pushed down a lever and the air quivered with the force of electromagnets powering up the huge ring. He frowned in puzzlement.

"What the…?" One of the monitors showed the maintenance compartment at the heart of the Cyclotron. The once-empty room now contained an old man with a white beard.

Aeron switched on the intercom. "Who are you? And what are you doing in a restricted area?"

"I am God," the old man said in a resonant voice.

"Wh-what?"

"In your ignorance, you have created a God trap," said the old man. "I demand to be released immediately."

"How can we release you?" asked Aeron, worried that the booming voice might be heard in the reception area.

"By destroying the God trap, of course."

"But it cost billions," protested Aeron.

Before God could answer, Sir Gregory led the first contingent of VIPs into the control room.

"We have a slight problem," said Aeron.

The smile left Sir Gregory's face. "What problem?" he said, in a low voice.

"There's someone in the maintenance compartment."

There was a camera flash, and the Chairman's furious expression changed. He grinned broadly and clasped Aeron round the shoulders. "Congratulations on a marvellous job. Well done."

"You look worried, Professor. Is something wrong?" asked one of the reporters.

"Of course nothing is wrong," insisted Sir Gregory, ushering the throng out of the control room. "The Professor is as delighted as we all are by the success of this magnificent project."

When, at last, everyone had left and Aeron was alone, he turned his attention back to the problem of God.

"If you are all powerful, why can't you release yourself?" he asked.

"Of course I can release myself," God boomed. "But it would mean interfering with the time-space continuum. For the last time, I demand that you turn this thing off - NOW."

"I have to get permission," said Aeron, frightened by the old man's anger. "Please give me an hour to try and persuade the politicians."

God was merciful. "Oh, very well then, one hour," he said. "But not a second more."

Luckily, although the press had rushed away to post their copy, most of the VIPs were still in the reception area. Sir Gregory had accompanied the reporters for a final photo-opportunity and, in his absence, Aeron was able to explain to the VIPs what had happened.

They demanded to see the trapped God for themselves, with varying degrees of success. Each saw their religious deity and atheists saw nothing. By the time Sir Gregory returned enough of them were convinced to agree to send a delegation. They were deciding who would be on the delegation, when Professor Daniels interrupted to tell them that the hour was nearly up.

"When we want your advice, Professor, we'll ask for it," said Sir Gregory, who had taken charge of the proceedings. "I'm sure that God won't object to waiting for our decision."

He was still talking when the hour was up and a furious God released himself from the trap. The air shimmered as a ripple in the time-space continuum spread out from the maintenance chamber. The walls of the reception room disappeared and the people flickered backwards through the millennia, changing costume and then shape until they ended up as ape men in a primeval forest.

With incoherent grunts, the huge alpha males, who had once been VIPs, circled each other waving crude clubs. Aeron hurried away, his reduced brain trying to cling to the memory of what had happened.

There was a small stream running through the trees, and beside it were some interesting pebbles. Aeron selected two of them, and started bashing them together. It would take a long time, but one day mankind would be back.

The Harlot Orchid
A strange method of pollination.

Doug, a newly-qualified archaeologist, was determined to make his name by finding Eldorado. The fact it lay in a forbidden forest should have given him pause for thought.

"Why is the forest forbidden?" he asked his native guide.

"Few go in and none come out."

Undeterred, Doug and his trusty dog, Sam, set forth.

It wasn't long before Doug's sharp eyes saw a paving of flat stones half-hidden beneath the tangled undergrowth. With a jubilant heart he followed the path into the depths of the forest.

After a while he came to a clearing. A shaft of sun shone down upon a woman lying on a soft green couch. The skin of her naked body was golden and as smooth and luscious as a peach. Her head was flung back, her eyes half closed and her chestnut-coloured hair cascaded to the ground.

Who? What? Why? Questions spun in his head but were soon forgotten.

She waved a thin, graceful arm, beckoning him to join her on the couch. Her scent overwhelmed him, it was sweet and spicy and so heavy with pheromones that his passions were aroused. Sam snarled and growled at the woman. Embarrassed, Doug apologised and tied his dog to a tree.

"I'm so sorry," he said but the woman didn't answer, she just lay on the couch and spread her legs wide. Before he knew what was happening he found himself making love to her. She did not respond to his love making, but lay unmoving beneath him, her intoxicating scent becoming stronger and stronger.

He felt a strange drumming on the top of his head. What was going on? Oh God, did she want him to stop? He raised his head and looked upwards, his eyelashes heavy with sweat. A bunch of dusty yellow feathers was hitting him on the head. What was the woman doing? Was she hitting him with a fan? Then he saw, with a sickening jolt, that the feathers were on curving stalks growing out from a split in the woman's head. Oh my God, she was dead. He was making love to a corpse.

It was too late to stop - the orgasm overwhelmed him. With legs still trembling he scrambled off her. The woman looked as she did before. There was no sign of feathers or a split in the head. But something was definitely wrong. The slender arms moved like tendrils. Her legs were fused to the couch. Clever shading had given her features the look of life and beauty but, in reality, they were just markings on a petal.

With a shock, Doug realised that he had been seduced by a flower – a harlot orchid. He had heard of them and their strange method of pollination, but had thought they were fictitious.

He crossed over to release Sam, who was straining at the leash. The dog bounded across the clearing and leapt up onto the couch. With a howl he launched himself at the woman's throat and tore her head off. It floated to the ground, still smiling.

"We must get out of here," said Doug, but they came to another clearing. There was another woman, identical to the first, sprawled on a couch, legs akimbo. Her seductive scent filled the air, and he remembered how good it had felt to make love to the first flower. Surely it wouldn't matter…

Sam came to the rescue, standing between his master and the flower, barking a frenzied warning. Then Sam stopped barking and started to make little panting noises. Doug turned round to see Sam walking stiff-legged across the clearing, towards a golden plant. The twisted petals of the flower were a rough facsimile of a bitch.

"Sam, stop! Sam, come back here!"

The lusty animal ignored his master and continued to advance upon the orchid. Doug ran towards him, determined to drag him away but the scent of the nearby flower-woman overwhelmed him. It was like a drug. Surely one more consummation of a harlot orchid wouldn't matter. Just one more, and then he would leave the jungle forever.

No one ever saw the dog or its master again.

The Hobya Costume
What was an Irish dwarf doing in America?

A week before Halloween Steph asked her little daughter what costume she would like to wear to go Trick or Treating.

"Think of the scariest thing you can," she said. Daisy did not hesitate.

"I don't know what it's called, but it has a green pig-face with long, pointed teeth and it's covered in fur."

Steph looked on the internet but she couldn't find such a costume. She decided to enlist the help of her mother-in-law, who had moved from Ireland to live in the granny annex of their Boston house.

"A green face and long teeth?" Gran looked startled when she was told of Daisy's description. "It sounds like a hobya." She shivered. "I could have sworn I never told Daisy about them. They come out at night and eat human flesh. Such a creature could give a child nightmares."

"She has such an imagination, that child. She told me she saw one looking in through the window at her."

"No!" Gran looked startled. "She saw a hobya here, in America? Keep her window closed at night."

By the time Halloween arrived the costume was made. Light was falling as Daisy and Steph emerged onto the pavement. They knocked on their neighbour's door.

"What an unusual costume," said Mrs Drake. "It's really quite unsettling. What are you meant to be, dear?"

"A hobya." Daisy's muffled voice came from behind the pig mask.

"It's a kind of Irish dwarf," explained Steph.

The costume was successful. Other children in more conventional fancy dress clustered around admiring it. Householders were generous with their donations and Daisy's bucket grew so heavy that Steph had to carry it. They had gone several streets before Daisy wanted to go home.

"I'm tired."

"We'll take a short cut through the park," said Steph.

Normally she would not venture into the park at night but the path was well lit and there were plenty of people about. They walked hand in hand, Daisy's big rubber feet flapping as they went. Suddenly Daisy gave a gasp and pulled away from her.

"Stop! What are you doing?" Steph said. Her daughter's eyes were wide with panic and her only response was a terrified moan. "Hold my hand!" commanded Steph but Daisy fled. "Daisy! Come back!"

Steph ran hither and thither, zigzagging across the park, terrified that Daisy might be kidnapped or worse. It wasn't until she paused for breath that she heard a rustling in a nearby bush.

"Daisy?" There was a pause and then a pig's mask appeared through the branches. "Oh, Daisy, you naughty girl, you gave me such a fright running away like that. Come here!"

There was another pause and then Daisy emerged. "Hold my hand," said Steph. Without a word, Daisy took the offered hand and they walked home in silence.

"We'll tell Gran we are safely back and then you are going straight to bed. When your father hears about your behaviour he will be cross." Daisy said nothing but walked on her big floppy feet, keeping up a good pace.

"We're back!" Steph opened the door to the granny annex. "Look how many goodies Daisy has collected." She held the bucket high and gave it a shake. But Gran did not look at the bucket. She stared at Daisy, and her mouth gaped open in astonishment.

Daisy gave a snarl. Steph turned to her daughter. She looked terrible, covered in mud and red stuff that looked like blood.

"Take that mask off and speak to your grandmother properly," she said. She made a grab for Daisy and the teeth that should have been paper bit deeply into her arm. Gran screamed and Steph's screams mingled with hers.

"Where's Daisy?" Steph clutched her bleeding arm and turned to the creature that had taken the place of her child. "You monster! Have you hurt my daughter?" Steph grabbed Gran's walking stick and raised it high.

The creature gave a final snarl and then turned and waddled away. On trembling knees Steph went to the door and saw the hideous, big-footed dwarf join the merry throng. A new monster had joined the pantheon of Halloween.

The Immortal Body Parts of Uncle Albert

Surely, killing his uncle was an act of mercy?

As a young man, I lived with my mother in a small house in Clapham. By day I worked in a bank and by night I studied for my accountancy exams for I was determined to better myself. One day, a letter arrived. It was written in ink on aging paper. The signature at the bottom was Albert S. Hartington – the same surname as my own.

My dear Sebastian, I wish to have the pleasure of your company for lunch next Sunday at my home, where you will hear something to your advantage.

My mother gasped when she saw the letter. "Great Uncle Albert? Can he still be alive? Why, It's impossible!"

At my prompting she told me about the old man. He had been an explorer in Victorian times. Shortly after he returned from his travels he disappeared and the family heard no more.

Sunday came. I took a train and a cab and arrived at an impressive building surrounded by parkland. My uncle was a man of wealth.

A servant let me in and I followed him into a panelled dining room where Uncle Albert sat at one end of a table.

"Good morning, Sebastian," he said. "How is your mother?"

We exchanged pleasantries and I saw signs of great age in his sagging white skin and shrunken flesh.

The servant entered with plates of smoked salmon and asparagus accompanied by sliced brown bread. It was a simple meal but enjoyable.

After he had finished eating, Uncle Albert came straight to the point. "When in Africa," he said. "I made friends with a witch doctor who introduced me to a book of spells and secrets. We came back to England and I foolishly experimented with the powers revealed by the book. In doing so I became immensely wealthy and also achieved immortality."

Immortality! I stared at my uncle. "Is your friend immortal too?"

Uncle Albert shook his head. "He was a wiser man than I. He died at his appointed time but, out of pity, he arranged for his offspring to care for me. Ojo, here, is the latest of his great grandsons."

The servant, who was clearing away the dishes, smiled and nodded. I waited until he had left then turned to my uncle. "What do you want of me?" I asked.

"I want you to kill me."

"No!" I was horrified.

"If you do as I ask, I will leave you this house and all my money. I have already prepared the will." He nodded towards a bureau at the side of the room.

By putting the old man out of his misery I would be wealthy beyond my wildest dreams. Surely it would be an act of mercy.

"Very well," I said. "I do this not through greed, but to help you find eternal peace."

"Of course," he said drily.

Upon a side table were various implements – a knife, an axe and a ligature. I picked up the knife and plunged it into my uncle's heart. Too late I realised that his heart had stopped beating years ago.

Next I seized the ligature and twisted it around his neck. I pulled with all my might, but the old man was still alive.

In desperation I grabbed the axe and chopped off his head. Even after the head was severed, his screaming continued and I realised that the head was able to live independently of the body.

In a frenzy I chopped the body into pieces and stared at the carnage. Body parts were twisting and turning, all still alive. In desperation I shovelled his remains into a cupboard and shut the door.

The will was proved valid, I inherited the great estate and dismissed Ojo to return to his homeland.

I wish I could say that I was happy but the memory of that hideous dismemberment haunts my nights and the sound of banging and moaning from the cupboard haunts my days.

I search through the many thousands of books in the library trying to find the book of spells so I can rid myself of the horror that is my uncle. I fear that if I do not find it soon I will become insane.

The Informer
They were his father's hands.

Robin sat in the harsh light of the police interview room. The naked light bulb swung, causing shifting shadows on the slab-like face of the detective opposite him. They made him look alternately bored and menacing.

How did they get the bulb to swing? There must be a mechanism. Robin looked up and, to his surprise, he saw that there was no swinging bulb, just a round neon light screwed to the ceiling. He must get a grip. The detective had been writing down his name and address, now he looked up.

"You say your father is responsible for a murder?" His voice was flat and disinterested.

"Yes," said Robin eagerly. "That prostitute who went missing. It was my father who did it. He made me help bury the body." Even now in his mind's eye he could see his father looming over him, dark and intimidating, forcing him to obey. "I tried to say no, I really did." Robin could feel tears well up in his eyes.

"Where is the body buried?" The detective continued with the interview, unmoved by Robin's distress.

"In our garden." It had been hard work, the soil had been heavy, and Robin had been sobbing with fear and tiredness before his father had said that the hole was deep enough.

The detective wrote for a few minutes, while Robin fidgeted, anxious to continue. He stared at the door, half expecting his father to burst into the room and demand to take him home. At last the detective looked up and said, "Tell me about the body."

"It was a girl, she was naked." Robin paused and gulped, distressed by the memory of what he had been forced to do next. "We carried her out of the back door but she was heavy. My father has a bad back so he made me hold onto her legs and drag her."

The detective shook his head. "I need more details, things I can verify. You could be making this up."

Robin looked at him beseechingly. "No, please, I'm telling you the truth. Please, please, you must arrest my father. If he found out that I've told you what happened, he will kill me."

Robin strained to convince the detective. He forced himself to remember details he would sooner have forgotten. "She had blonde hair," he said. "It was wet with the rain and clinging around her shoulders and there was a tattooed bird on her hip."

The detective's interest sharpened. "Did you actually see your father murder the girl?" he asked.

Robin's felt a tear roll down his cheek. "I saw his hands against her throat. I saw the sinews bulge as he forced them closed. She struggled. She was scrabbling against his arms, clawing at his wrists, trying to stop him but it was no use, he squeezed and squeezed. Then she relaxed and it was all over." Robin buried his head in his hands and sobbed. "I should have intervened, I should have tried to save her, but I'm so frightened of him. My father is a monster."

The detective got up and with a quick, "Excuse me a moment," he left the room. Robin sat. The light bulb was swinging again, shadows were closing in on him. Oh no, he forgot, there was no light bulb. He gripped the desk to stop his hands trembling.

The detective returned with two colleagues who took up positions on either side of the informer. Robin rose to his feet.

"I'm sorry," said the detective and he was looking at Robin, almost with pity, "but your father died two years ago." Robin stared at him uncomprehendingly. "Let me see your wrists."

Robin held out his arms and the men on either side of him unbuttoned his cuffs and rolled up his shirt sleeves.

Robin stared aghast – his father's hands were on the ends of his arms and there were deep scratch marks on his wrists. What did it mean? His whirling brain scarcely heard the arresting officer reading out his rights. When Robin finally figured it out, he raised his head to the harsh, round neon light and howled like a wolf.

"Noooooooooooooo."

The Kiss of the Kraken
A kraken will never relinquish its prey

Ross woke late. Something was wrong. He inhaled deeply and smelt the faint odour of tar and whitewash that permeated the lighthouse. By now he should be smelling bacon and coffee as old Ewan prepared breakfast.

He dressed quickly and hurried down the steep, curving staircase to the ground floor. There was nobody there. Breakfast had not been started and the lighthouse door was open.

Ross looked out of the door and across the small, boulder-strewn plateau that formed the top of the rocky island. It was deserted. What had happened to his companions?

A cold sea mist rose over the cliffs and wreathed around the boulders. Ross shivered and hurried back into the lighthouse. He climbed up to the narrow balcony that ran around the lantern room.

"Angus! Ewan!" he called. A movement among the boulders caught his eye. Someone was standing there. "Angus, is that you? Ewan, are you there?" Screaming gulls circled overhead but the figure did not answer.

What stupid game were his companions playing? Ross ran down the stairs, out of the door and across the plateau, stumbling on the coarse, tufted grass. As he neared the figure he slowed and stopped. It was neither Ewan nor Angus – it was a woman. She stood swaying. The poor creature was soaked to the skin. Her black hair clung to her head and shoulders in a solid mass and her sodden dress clung to her body.

She must have been shipwrecked, thought Ross. She did not speak, but drooped as if she would faint. Ross was about to run and help her when one of the screaming gulls dived and slashed at the woman with its beak. The woman reared up –six – eight –

ten feet tall. Ross stared at her in horror then, with the swift reactions of youth, he turned and ran.

He raced across the plateau, hearing the rush of a heavy body and the crash of boulders being overturned behind him. He dashed in through the open door of the lighthouse and slammed it shut. Something crashed into the door behind him with a heavy thud that almost shook the solid wood from its hinges.

Ross struggled to slide the bolts while the thing outside beat against the wood. Then Ross sank to the floor, dizzy with shock.

He heard a shuffling, then the woman looked in through the window. The red slash of lips faded, revealing the circular structure beneath - it was a sucker! Ross realised that he was looking at the tip of a giant tentacle.

He fled from the room and stumbled up the stairs to the lantern room. He went out onto the narrow balcony and looked down. The tentacle rose from the water and stretched up the cliff to the base of the lighthouse. As Ross stared at the sea he saw two huge, unblinking eyes staring back at him. A cruel beak snapped open and shut, while around it the sea frothed and foamed. The kraken had seen him and would never relinquish its prey. Ross was doomed.

It was a week before the relief boat was due to arrive - a week in which Ross never left the safety of the lighthouse and single-handedly managed to keep alight the lantern. When he heard the sound of a distant foghorn he hurried downstairs, ready to let his rescuers in the moment they knocked on the door. But the knock came when he was only halfway down.

Determined not to leave them standing in the fog, Ross rushed down the last of the stairs, ran across the living room and flung open the door.

The greeting froze on his lips. Standing in front of him was the black-haired, dead-eyed woman. He opened his mouth to scream but the woman swooped forwards and pressed her blood-red mouth against his lips in a cold, muscular, engulfing kiss that choked him into silence.

When the relief party arrived they found the door open, the lighthouse deserted and the lantern still burning. No trace was ever found of the three lighthouse keepers - and so began the mystery of the Craggy Rock lighthouse.

The Nouveau Lycanthrope

A project to prevent hypothermia has an unfortunate side-effect.

Doctor Dempsey entered the bungalow with trepidation, not knowing what he might find. The air inside was cold and smelt of urine.

"Mrs Helen Stuttard?" he called, not wanting to frighten the old lady who had telephoned for a doctor.

"Yes, dear, I'm in here." The room was dark, lit only by a full moon shining in through the open curtains.

"It's very cold." Dempsey reached to turn on the fire.

"Oh no, don't do that," she said. "I don't need a fire, I've been given the injection."

Dempsey frowned. He didn't approve of the Government's policy of genetically modifying the elderly to prevent hypothermia. Nouveau Lycanthropes they were called, on account of the added wolf genes.

"Why have you sent for me, Mrs Stuttard?" he asked.

"I'm feeling a bit odd. Last time I felt like this I tried to kiss my budgie and ended up eating him."

Dempsey stared at her, aghast, and noticed that her face was sprouting hair. Far away he heard the sound of howling - it made his blood run cold.

"Excuse me, Doctor, please would you pass me my walking frame. I need to go to the toilet."

Dempsey watched the old woman hobble out of the room. A few moments later he heard the front door open. He hurried to the window and saw her totter slowly down the garden path to where shuffling figures were gathering in the road.

Dempsey packed his bag hurriedly, opened the front door and realised that his escape was blocked by a crowd of elderly Nouveau Lycanthropes.

He turned to seek sanctuary in the house, but the door was shut and, in his panic, he couldn't remember the combination. He had no alternative but to try to get to his car.

"Let me through, I'm a doctor," Dempsey said, seizing the wooden gate and pushing hard.

"Yum, yum, a nice young doctor."

The gate slowly opened against the pressure of bodies. It unbalanced an elderly woman, who crashed heavily onto the pavement and started to cry.

"He's hurt Daisy."

"Ooh, what a brute."

"Has everyone brought their teeth?" said an old man, who seemed to be in charge.

"Yes, Colonel, but they don't fit in our mouths," said one of the pack. "Not when we've got muzzles."

The whole thing had been a trap, Dempsey turned to run but tripped and fell sprawling on the pavement. Immediately the mob attacked. He turned to try and fight them off and realised that his attackers were holding their false teeth in their hands and trying to bite him manually. Most were ineffectual, but one managed to get a painful grip on his nose.

"We're never going to kill him this way," said the Colonel. "Have you any knives in your kitchen, Helen?"

Dempsey heard the sound of a walking frame scraping along the pavement. He struggled to his feet, leaving his coat in the hands of the mob and made a dash for his car, wrenched open the door and dived in.

Where were his keys? Oh my God, they were in the pocket of his coat. The coat which had been pulled off and now lay on the verge. The pack clustered around the car.

"I bags his kidneys," said one. "I need something soft, I broke the spring in my teeth, trying to bite the fellow."

Mrs Stuttard reappeared with a bag of knives and the Colonel handed them around.

"I'll slash his tyres," said an enterprising werewolf. The knife ricocheted off the rubber and stabbed him in the leg. "Ouch."

For a bizarre moment Dempsey worried about the number of casualties arriving at the surgery next day. Then he noticed the Colonel was searching his coat pockets.

"I've found his keys." The Colonel lifted them up triumphantly.

A cock crowed and the pack stared skywards at the dawn.

"There's still time," insisted the Colonel, but even Helen Stuttard, the bait in the trap, was making her way home.

The Colonel glared at Dempsey. Dempsey glared at the Colonel. Then, without another word the old werewolf accepted defeat, put the keys back into the doctor's coat pocket and padded away.

The Personality Sucker
When your mother is an alien.

Lizzie hurried home, her eyes stinging with tears. She dumped her schoolbooks in the hall and ran upstairs to her bedroom.

As she passed the bathroom door she paused. It was open a crack and inside she could see her brother. He was half naked and from his back grew a pair of leathery wings.

What the hell? Lizzie pushed the bathroom door open. He turned and his wings folded with a clattering sound.

"How dare you come in without knocking."

"Did you have wings on? Were they real? What's going on?" Her head was spinning, all memories of the school bully forgotten.

"Mind your own business."

She could see his back reflected in the mirror. On either side of his spine were long grooves into which the wings fitted so neatly that they were almost invisible.

"Can you fly?" she asked.

He shook his head. "Not yet, they've only just started growing."

"Wow," she said. "I wish I could fly."

"Well I don't. It's too weird. It's like I'm an alien or something."

"Have you told Mum?"

He shook his head. "As if she'd care. She probably slept with a bloody alien in the first place."

Lizzie hurried downstairs to the living room where her mother was lying on the sofa watching television.

"Mum, Trevor's got wings." Her mother sat up. Her flaccid stomach bulged unattractively between her t-shirt and her leggings.

"Did you have a nice day at school, dear?"

"Yes – no," Lizzie corrected herself, then continued. "Mum, Trevor reckons he is an alien."

Her mother shook her head. "Only half alien dear."

Lizzie stared at her mother in dismay. "Oh Mum, you didn't sleep with an alien, did you?"

"Of course not. Trevor's father was perfectly human."

"Then how come he has wings?"

"Well actually dear," said her mother, looking sheepish, "It's me who is an alien."

Lizzie stared at her mother in shocked amazement.

"Wh-what about me?" she stammered. "Am I going to grow wings?"

"Oh no, dear, it's only the males."

"What's going to happen to me? How are you different?" Lizzie looked critically at her mother. Nobody would think that she was anything but human – with her bad teeth, over-plucked eyebrows and bleached hair.

"Hmmm," her mother thought. "I have eyes that can see in colour and little buttons on my breasts that produce milk."

"Everyone has those," interrupted Lizzie.

"Really?" Her mother was disconcerted for a moment then continued. "I have a personality sucker and moveable flappers in my vagina that can raise a man to heights of ecstasy."

"Wow." Lizzie was impressed.

"Of course," continued her mother. "I don't bother to use them for one-night stands but they will be useful if I decide to become a prostitute."

"A prostitute," gasped Lizzie. "Oh Mother, why can't you get a proper job?"

"Are you mad? The only reason I came to Earth was because of the benefits."

Lizzie was busy tutting when another thought struck her. "What's a personality sucker?"

"This," said her mother. She concentrated inwardly, then out of her forehead grew a tube with a sucker on . "You just attach it to someone's head and suck. Remember that nasty man in the benefits office? I gave him a suck and he is much nicer now."

She lay back on the sofa and turned her attention to the television, while Lizzie sat lost in thought.

The next day the bully, a thick-set girl named Rachel, was waiting for Lizzie at the school gates. "Hand over your lunch money, Frog Face." Lizzie stood still and smiled at her. "Hurry up Pimple-Features or I'll bash your brains in."

Lizzie moved closer to Rachel, preparing to grow a personality sucker. Rachel stepped back but Lizzie continued to advance, frowning with concentration.

"Get off me!" protested Rachel and backed away more rapidly.

"Hey, wait," said Lizzie.

Rachel turned tail and fled. There was a smattering of applause from others in the playground. Lizzie grinned and rubbed her forehead. It felt smooth and cool. Damn, it hadn't worked.

Lizzie watched the rapidly retreating figure of the school bully. Even without a personality sucker, life was going to be better.

The Pischom Lake
Man and fish is a deadly combination

The lake lay basking in the sunshine, beckoning to Geraldine and her sister to enjoy its cool waters. Beside it a sign said NO SWIMMING.

"No swimming?" Geraldine was affronted. "We've always swum here. Well, I'm not taking any notice of that sign. It's a joke."

She peeled off her dress and walked towards the lake. The grass felt dry and springy under her bare feet and the sun was hot on her skin. It was the height of summer.

"Aunt Bea will be cross," said Susie.

Geraldine glared at her sister. Susie was always the good one, always did as she was told. "Aunt Bea is back at the house. She won't know."

She was near the water now. A dark shape moved within its depths and the birds stopped singing. Geraldine dipped her toe in the water and the world held its breath.

"Stop!" A man appeared from the fringe of trees that bordered the grassy slope to the lake. "You mustn't swim here."

The sun was in her eyes and Geraldine couldn't see him clearly, half hidden in the shadow of the trees, but Suzie responded.

"Hello, I haven't seen you around here before."

"I'm new, and so must you be if you intend to swim in this water."

Susie fluttered her eyelashes. "We're spending a week with our Aunt Bea."

"Did your aunt not tell you?"

Geraldine cast her mind back to their arrival the day before. "She told us we weren't to go near the lake, but she didn't say why."

The man nodded. "She didn't want to scare you. A mistake, as you obviously intend to disobey her."

"I wasn't going to," said Susie, eager as always for approbation.

"A pischom lives in the lake," said the man.

"A what?" asked Geraldine.

"A pischom – a cross between man and fish. Some time back a man must have contaminated the water with his sperm and fish eggs became fertilised. This one is intelligent. We haven't been able to catch him."

Something sparkled in the grass at Geraldine's feet. As the sun caught it, its brilliance was blinding. Susie followed her gaze, swooped down and picked up a ring. She gave a little scream of triumph. "A diamond ring. I found it. It's mine!"

"No!" Geraldine shouted a warning. She had seen the thin nylon line attached to the ring.

"Yes! You can't have it," Susie cried and put the ring on her finger. Her expression of happy triumph changed to one of shock as the ring was jerked towards the lake. "AAAAGH!" she screamed and was dragged after it.

Geraldine caught hold of her dress and tried to pull her back.

"Ow, my finger is going to come off," screamed Susie.

The flimsy material tore from Geraldine's grasp and Susie was pulled towards the water at an ever-increasing speed.

"Help me!" Susie struggled to pull the ring from her finger. She was up to her waist in the water, threshing and fighting. Geraldine watched in horror as a wave engulfed her and in the maelstrom Geraldine saw the shape of a man. There was a shriek, and then silence. The waters of the lake became smooth and the birds sang once more. Geraldine sank to her knees, sobbing.

"I'm sorry for your loss." The young man was beside her now and she turned to look up. Her vision was blurred by tears but she could see that there was something wrong with him. She blinked. His skin was scaly. Psoriasis? Leprosy? She shrank away. He was wearing a scarf that bulged around his neck and from it water dribbled. "My brother will eat well tonight," he said.

She stared at him stupidly, her brain dulled by the shock of her sister's death. He laid a hand on her shoulder and it felt cold. What she thought was a scarf was a gill cover. The truth hit her. "Let me go!" she screamed.

He laughed and his teeth were sharp and in several rows like those of a shark. "There are many ways to catch a human," he said then lifted her up into his arms and carried her towards the lake.

The Salem Curse

Are ancient curses a load of nonsense?

Cynthia Fortescue, headmistress of the Salem Secondary School for Young Ladies, was holding a staff meeting.

"It will soon be Halloween," she said. "As part of the historic traditions of the school we must put on a memorable event for the girls. I felt that last year's re-enactment of the burning of Mother Toogood was a great success." She smiled benignly at Miss Martin, who still had a livid scar across her forehead. "This year we will pretend to raise the dead." Cynthia held up an ancient manuscript with a flourish.

"You don't think the spells would work, do you?" asked Miss Martin.

"Work? Of course not!" Cynthia regarded her games mistress with astonishment. "Surely nobody believes in such superstitious nonsense nowadays!" She unrolled the manuscript and read. "We swear revenge upon those who betrayed and murdered us. With this spell we will rise from the dead and take their souls."

"I have a feeling that one of my ancestors might have been involved in the trials," said Miss Laker.

"Don't worry, Miss Laker," Cynthia reassured her maths teacher. "These ancient curses are a load of nonsense. When we hold our Halloween service I will read from the manuscript. Then, after the spell has been cast, I will pretend to feel terror and point out of the window at a witch." She looked around at her apprehensive staff. Miss Laker, was a tall, skinny woman who would best fit the witch costume. "You will be the witch, Miss Laker."

Halloween dawned bright and clear. After a rousing rendition of For All The Saints, Cynthia stepped up to the microphone and told the students about the manuscript and the spell that would raise the dead.

"As you know," she said. "This school was built next to an ancient cemetery." She indicated the gardens spread out beyond the floor-to-ceiling windows of the hall. There was a rustle of excitement as the girls turned to stare. Cynthia hoped they would not spot the tip of Miss Laker's hat as she hid in the shrubbery and she hurriedly started to intone the spell.

> "Darkest dark and deepest deep,
> Spectres come from death's last sleep.
> From the glassy look in the witch's eye,
> Who died in mortal agony.
> I bid you now rise from your graves
> And take a hideous revenge."

As Cynthia spoke, the gardens darkened and a patchy mist rose from the ground. She pointed towards Miss Laker's bush. This should have been the maths mistress's cue to run around the garden in a menacing way before hiding again. Instead, Miss Laker ruined the carefully rehearsed scene by rushing towards the hall screaming. Her terror was infectious and many of the girls joined in.

The whole service was descending into mass hysteria, thought Cynthia. She clapped her hands intending to restore order but succeeded only in increasing the panic.

"Let me in! let me in!" Miss Laker was hammering on the patio door that led from the hall to the garden. Miss Martin leapt to her feet, intending to unlock the door, but Cynthia stopped her.

"We have enough problems without Miss Laker adding to the chaos."

With a final flurry of blows that threatened to break the glass, Miss Laker gave up and turned to face the mist that was threatening to engulf her. For a moment nothing could be seen of the maths teacher then the mist disappeared, the garden brightened and a figure lay on the ground outside the door.

The girls stopped screaming as the door was unlocked and the unconscious Miss Laker dragged into the hall.

"Wake up, Miss Laker!" Cynthia slapped the maths teacher hard on the cheeks. The unfortunate woman opened her eyes. "Prithee, who are you?" she asked.

Cynthia frowned. "What has happened to you, Miss Laker?"

"I am not Miss Laker, I am Mother Toogood." For a moment Cynthia was disconcerted then she rose to her feet and dismissed the girls. The spell had obviously worked. Poor Miss Laker's soul had been replaced by that of a witch. It was an unfortunate transference but life must go on.

"Are you any good at maths?" she asked Mother Toogood.

The Second Coming
Was Phil in with a chance, at last?

The atomic clock had stopped working but Phil's watch told him that they should have been relieved an hour ago.

Jacqueline put the phone down. "No answer. Perhaps we'd better get to the surface."

He hurried after her to the lift. It was still working, thank God, it would have taken hours to get up by the emergency stairs.

The lift doors opened onto a deserted lobby. Where were the security men who should have been guarding the neutrino detector?

The entrance doors were open, and, before he could shout a warning, Jacqueline walked through – and disappeared. Phil wondered whether to go after her. He felt a shimmering sensation and found himself beside Jacqueline on a huge, grass-covered prairie.

His mind was in a whirl. Where were they? What was going on? But all questions were banished by the sight of the terrifying throng that surrounded them - skeletons, part-skeletons, and animated clouds of dust and ashes. Everything was lurching, shuffling and rolling towards them. Phil tried to flee, but his feet were rooted to the ground.

"Are you quick?" An approaching skeleton asked.

"No, we're stuck to the ground," said Jacqueline.

"I mean, Madam," said the skeleton, "are you quick, as opposed to dead?"

"I think so," said Jacqueline. "We were alive before we got here, anyway."

"In that case, you've missed your turn," said the skeleton, shaking its head, sadly. "The living have been judged. I'm surprised you were so late arriving."

"We were a kilometre underground, manning a neutrino detector," said Phil.

"I'm so sorry," said the skeleton then he glanced downwards. "I just hope Charles, here, has enough of his body left to be resurrected." The skeleton indicated a small turd that was about to bump into Phil's foot. Phil jumped back.

"Watch it!" said the turd. "It was bad enough being eaten by a tiger, without being squashed by you." He humped past Phil like a fat, brown caterpillar.

"We must go to meet our maker. Goodbye, and good luck," said the skeleton, waving a bony arm in farewell.

Phil turned to see where they were going and saw that, at the far end of the prairie, the blue sky had turned into an expanse of dazzling gold where God sat on his throne in a blaze of glory. Approaching the throne were corpses in various stages of decomposition. When God's attention focussed upon them they took on the semblance of their living selves and awaited their judgement.

Phil was staring at the extraordinary scene when he was enveloped by a cloud of dust. He sneezed.

"Clumsy oaf," said the dust. "It took me ages to get smooth, and now you've gone and ruffled me up again."

Phil gaped at the cloud, and then hurriedly closed his mouth in case he swallowed any of it.

"That's what you get for being dust, one blast of wind and you're all over the place," said a rolling pile of ashes.

"My dear Agnes, it takes centuries to become decent dust. You, on the other hand took precisely fifteen minutes to become a greasy pile of ashes."

"At least I'm hygienic."

"Are you trying to say that I am not?"

The two of them ignored the scientists and continued their argument as they drifted past.

Time has no meaning in the Elysian Fields and Phil had no idea how long they had stood before all that was left of mankind were fragments of bone and a few odd-looking skulls.

Phil wondered if they were going to be stuck in the Elysian Fields forever, then he had that strange shimmering feeling again, and he and Jacqueline were back on Earth.

They were sitting on the hillside, outside the neutrino detector. Below them, the wooded valley basked in the sunshine. Birds were singing, rabbits played and Phil knew that the World had become a new Eden. He put his arm around Jacqueline's shoulder. He had always fancied her and now, at last, he was in with a chance.

"You and I are the new Adam and Eve," he said. "From us the human race will grow again."

Jacqueline gently removed his arm, and Phil realised for the first time how large her hands were.

"Actually," she said, "you can call me Jack."

The Stump-Tailed Snake
An encounter with Medusa.

Cages lined the walls of Sebastian Strank's living room - dozens of little worlds to which he was God. Some were jungles, some were deserts, all depended upon him for food, water and warmth. It was Reptile Heaven.

"Come on, my darlings," he crooned at a cage of geckos. He sprinkled vitamin powder over a box of crickets then emptied them into the cage. As he turned, he nearly stepped on a snake.

"Which tank did you escape from?" He peered more closely and realised that instead of a tail, the snake had a swollen stump. "Oh my God, you must have had an accident."

Sebastian put on his leather handling gloves and picked up the snake. "Ouch!" The snake twisted round and bit him on the nose.

Sebastian dropped the vicious creature into a tank. Then he dabbed his nose with TCP. Was the snake poisonous? He searched in all his reptile books but he couldn't identify it.

The next morning Sebastian's nose had stopped hurting, but when he looked in the mirror he got a shock. Green scales were growing where the snake had bitten him. He tried to rub them off, but his arms were too short to reach them. What was happening? He was standing, staring at his reflection when the doorbell rang.

Sebastian hurried down the stairs. He had difficulty balancing and clung to the banister.

Ring, ring. The sound was urgent. Sebastian waddled across the room and had to reach upwards to turn the door-handle. The door swung open and a woman wearing dark glasses and a headscarf looked down at him.

"Have you seen a snake?" she asked.

Sebastian stared up at her unable to speak - the headscarf was wriggling as if alive. The woman frowned, then whipped off her dark glasses and stared at Sebastian long and hard.

"Are you petrified?" she asked.

"Yes," he squeaked.

She prodded him with a bony finger. "No you aren't, you're still flesh and blood. You are obviously not a normal human. Now where is my snake?"

She pushed past Sebastian and went straight to the tank where the stump-tailed snake was trying to hide behind a rock.

"Got you, you bastard!"

She pushed the lid aside, plunged her arms into the tank and pulled out the struggling snake. Sebastian looked at it in amazement. It had become bigger, fatter and pinker. It was also growing stumpy little arms and legs.

"You've bitten someone haven't you?" snarled the woman. "You ungrateful little beast. Who have you bitten?"

She was shaking it so hard that it had difficulty pointing, but it managed to indicate Sebastian. As the woman turned, it wriggled out of her arms and fell to the floor. She tried to kick it, but it jumped out of her way. She tried to stamp on it, but it evaded her easily, dancing from leg to leg.

"You wait till you are back to human form. I will turn you to stone."

"You'll have to catch me first," it mocked. Then it dashed out of the front door like a crazy imp, its stumpy tail bobbing along behind it.

"You ungrateful bastard," she screamed, but she was talking to thin air – the erstwhile snake had vaulted over the garden gate and was gone.

The woman slammed the door shut and turned to Sebastian. "You will have to take its place."

She removed her headscarf to reveal a mass of writhing snakes attached to her head like hair.

Sebastian fell to the floor. What had happened? Had he fainted? He tried to stand up and realised that he had lost his legs. His arms had disappeared as well - he had become a snake.

He lay on the floor in bewilderment. Should he try to escape? It was too late. The woman was bending over him crooning lovingly.

"Come on, my darling." She scooped him up. "We will soon have you where you belong," she said, and she inserted his stump into a hole in her head.

Ooh, it felt good – cool, tight and invigorating. He writhed in pleasurable harmony with his fellow snakes. Sebastian Strank had truly found Reptile Heaven at last.

The Temple of the Ashen Rose
Do not try to raise the dead, Simeon!

Simeon shambled through Fulham Market behind his elderly mother. His attention was caught by a bin containing a bunch of dead roses. On an impulse, he stopped, picked up the roses and passed a hand over them. He felt a tingling of energy and, to Simeon's amazement, the roses were restored.

The stall holder turned and grabbed them. "Oi, give them back, you thieving bastard."

"Bugger off," said Simeon's mother. The roses withered in the stall-holder's hand and she dragged her son away.

Simeon's mother extolled his newly-discovered healing powers and soon there was enough interest for a gathering.

Simeon was dressed in a sheet, wrapped and pinned to resemble a toga. He perched uncomfortably on a kitchen stool in their lounge, which had been transformed into the 'Temple of the Ashen Rose' with a red lightbulb and a packet of incense sticks. A tape of New Age music played while half-a-dozen neighbours waited expectantly.

His mother entered, dressed in an orange kaftan. She held a bunch of dead flowers, which she handed to Simeon with an elaborate bow.

"Bring these flowers back to life, I beg of you, Great Healer."

Simeon took the flowers and passed his hand over them, feeling the power surge through him as he did so. There was a gasp from the audience as the flowers bloomed.

"I'll go and put these in water." Simeon's mother hurried out of the room before the flowers decayed.

All scepticism was forgotten as people clamoured to be healed. Simeon laid reluctant hands on each person in turn. He touched parts of his neighbours' anatomies he had never thought to see, let alone lay his hands upon. Although he felt no surge of energy, most people declared that they had benefited from his ministrations.

They showed their gratitude with such generous donations that Simeon's mother decided to make the healing session a regular event.

The Temple of the Ashen Rose soon become large enough to move the weekly meetings to a hall beside The Broadway. Simeon and his mother were looking forward to a prosperous future when something strange and unsettling happened. An exhausted butterfly flew in through the open window of their tenth-floor flat. They stared as it landed on their new coffee table, closed its wings, gave a final quiver and died.

"Ooh, look Simeon, a dead butterfly. Why don't you bring it back to life?"

Simeon gently touched the fragile corpse. Power flowed from his fingertips, stimulating the cells of the tiny body and making them swell. The curled body straightened and the butterfly struggled to stand up. It had come back to life.

For a moment the butterfly was restored to its living glory – then the swelling continued and the unfortunate creature split open.

"Oh yuk, my poor coffee table," said Simeon's mother.

After long, horrific seconds, the exhausted cells shrivelled and collapsed into a mush. The butterfly was dead.

"Well, we don't want to do that again," said Simeon's mother as she hurried to get a cloth.

It was shortly after this, in the middle of a crowded meeting of the Temple of the Ashen Rose, that Simeon's mother collapsed. The congregation called upon Simeon to place his hands upon her recumbent body. When he showed reluctance, there were mutterings of puzzlement and outrage.

"What sort of healer is he if he won't even heal his own mother?"

In the end he was forced to touch her. Perhaps she had only fainted? But, to his dismay, he felt the power running through him. The crowd cheered and then burst into applause when she sat up. Before their eyes her wrinkles smoothed and her cheeks plumped. Not only had she been restored to life but also looked decades younger. She stared at the cheering congregation, and then she looked at Simeon's frightened face. With a moan of fear, she realised what had happened.

"What 'ave you done to me, Simeon?"

People whimpered in horror as they watched the swelling continue until her body burst open and, at last, the eviscerated corpse turned to mush.

When Simeon looked round, he saw that the congregation had fled. Sadly he put on his anorak. The Temple of the Ashen Rose had held its last meeting.

The Urban Farm
A necessary sacrifice

Burgerman Bill was usually a contented man. As an urban farmer in an overcrowded world, he enjoyed the space denied to others. But today was inspection day.

Bill stood in the pigeon loft next to a government official. Hundreds of birds, disturbed by their presence, fluttered around the enclosure, filling the air with dust and feathers.

"At what weight are the dispatch perches calibrated?" demanded the inspector.

"Seven hundred grams," said Bill.

The man scribbled on his report sheet. "I'd like to see the cassava plants now, please."

Bill led the way to the hydroponics floor. It was on this floor that he had his apartment, overlooking the green expanse of tanks.

At the inspector's request he pulled up a root. The inspector nodded, and Bill threw it down the processing chute. It would be topped and peeled then ground into flour for baps in the burger bar and a rice-substitute in the curry house.

The trimmings would not be wasted - nothing in Earth City went to waste. They would be added to garbage pellets for the rats.

Bill led the official downstairs to where the rats were fattened. Cows, sheep, pigs and hens were long extinct so rats had been bred to take their place.

"What's the percentage of cadaver cakes to garbage pellets?" asked the inspector.

"Forty-sixty," said Bill.

The inspector looked up from his report sheet. "I'm afraid that the Department has received complaints about your restaurants."

"Complaints?"

"Yes, the farm is not producing enough food to cover the area's meal tickets."

"But that's not my fault," protested Bill. "I have to feed ten apartment blocks and people do nothing but have children."

The inspector showed no sympathy. "You must increase production. We can't have people going hungry."

"But how?" wailed Bill.

"That's your problem," said the inspector. "But I need hardly tell you that your job is on the line." The rats had fallen silent, as if listening, and the inspector frowned. "When did you last check your rat enclosure?"

Bill felt himself reddening. "Er, I'm not sure." He hated the disgusting animals.

The inspector's frown deepened. "All large rats must be culled. You don't want a King Rat developing in there."

After the inspector had gone, Bill returned to the rat enclosure with his culling gun.

"That will not be necessary," came a soft, sibilant voice from the darkness.

Bill felt his blood run cold. "A-are you a King Rat?" he stammered.

"You can call me that," said the voice. "A rat with intelligence is king among his peers. I have a proposition for you, Burgerman Bill."

"W-what do you want?" asked Bill.

"Freedom," breathed the voice.

Bill gave a bitter laugh. "A fat lot of good that will do you. There's nothing for you to eat out there. Everything is recycled, even corpses are used for food pellets."

"Just as you feed on mine, I can feed on yours," said the voice. "Do you want to hear my proposition?"

And so Burgerman Bill listened.

Early next morning a cloaked figure left the urban farm. It was like a man but was not a man for a slithery, pink tail emerged from under the cloak.

The figure put a flute to its lips. Sweet music curled into the air, spinning magic around the apartment blocks and in through open windows. Children emerged from the buildings while inside, deaf to the music, their parents slept on.

Still playing, the King Rat danced away and the children followed, mimicking its high-stepping movements.

Round a corner, Burgerman Bill stood beside an open man-hole that led to the now-defunct sewers. He watched the strange procession come into view. The King Rat gave him a nod as it scrambled down the rungs. The piping continued from below and the entranced children climbed down into the darkness.

"If you can't increase production, you must decrease demand."

It made sense to Burgerman Bill and, as he watched the last of the children disappear, he wondered how many of his fellow urban farmers had entered into such arrangements. With a light heart, Bill replaced the man-hole cover and hurried back to the farm, happy that his future was secure.

The Waters of Europa
How werewater invaded the Earth

Hank lay on his bunk in the living pod watching Professor Susan Silverton suit up. She had a nice bum and he felt himself becoming horny. Dammit, four weeks stuck at close quarters with a frigid bird was enough to drive a man mad. Still, tomorrow the relief ship would come and they would get off this bloody planet. It wasn't his fault the experiment hadn't worked, his only job was to fly the shuttle.

As Susan emerged from the living pod she felt relief at escaping from her unwelcome companion. The ice fields of Europa stretched as far as the eye could see, lit by the baleful, red glow of Jupiter. The giant planet hung in the sky, so huge that it looked as if it was about to crush its icy moon.

Susan hurried across the ice to where a cable extended upwards to a distant satellite that could be seen as a pinprick of reflected light. As the cable was dragged through the massive magnetic field of Jupiter a coil inside it generated enough electricity to power a drill that was now deep within the ice.

Susan had invented the device and was put in charge of the multibillion-dollar experiment to sample the waters of Europa. Unfortunately, the waters lay beneath many kilometres of ice and the magnetic field was not as powerful as Susan had calculated. This was the last day of the experiment and the drill had still not bored through to the ocean below.

Susan arrived at the monitor. She expected to see the usual white wall of ice, lit by the tiny LED behind the drill, instead there was blackness – they had reached the ocean!

It was as if a huge weight had lifted from Susan's shoulders. Her reputation was saved. She used the control panel beside the monitor to suck water into the long metal tube embedded within the cable.

Hours later Susan sat in the living pod staring down a microscope. The water sample had been transferred to a petri dish and she was searching for signs of life. She was hoping to see microbes but there was nothing except strands of what looked like transparent jelly.

"We have to leave in nine hours," said Hank. "We had better get some sleep."

Susan yawned. He was right, she was exhausted. She climbed into her bunk and turned off the light.

After a while the werewater stirred. Slow thoughts pulsed through the protoplasmic strands. It had been browsing off microbes on the underside of the ice. Then it was blinded and sucked into a strange new world. Air tugged at its surface and it knew that it must find water to survive. Like an amoeba it crawled out of the petri dish and across the table.

The werewater fell to the floor, gathered itself together and rolled to the bunk where Susan lay sleeping. Her lips were moist. The werewater sensed the moisture and oozed into her mouth. Protoplasmic strands spread through her saliva and penetrated the semi permeable membranes that led to her blood stream.

More than sixty percent of Susan was made from water. By the time her body woke up the next morning, the werewater had taken over. There was nothing left of the world-renowned scientist, her brain was a tangle of protoplasmic strands that were busily digesting the organic matter of the neurones.

More water! Susan staggered over to Hank's bunk. He opened his eyes and they gleamed with liquid. Susan leant over to suck his eyeballs but he grabbed her head and pulled her mouth to his. Werewater poured into his mouth as he sucked at her tongue.

After a long, wet kiss he drew away and grinned at her. "Wow babe! You took long enough to decide that you fancy me! Too bad we only have time for a quick one."

His nimble fingers untied the belt of her robe. Then he pulled her down onto the bunk next to him and showed the werewater an interesting new way of exchanging body fluids.

From high above came the roar of mighty engines. The spaceship had arrived to take them home.

The Were Councillor and the Morph
When a werewolf helps enforce the curfew

Councillor Lewin patrolled the silent street, his yellow eyes searching for movement in the shadows. Above him a full moon shone in the night sky. Lewin felt the moonlight empower him, making his skin tingle beneath his coarse fur. This was the first

Lunar Night he had spent under the light of the moon, and he felt euphoric.

Far away he heard the roar of a car and then the sounds of gunfire. Someone must have broken the curfew. He quickened his steps and wondered if he should drop to all fours. Progress would be quicker, but he felt it would be undignified for a councillor. Becoming the newest member of the Were Council had not been easy. He had fought an election and endured the time-consuming boredom of committees and police-liaison meetings – all for this glorious night, when he helped the police enforce the curfew.

He turned a corner into the town square and was astounded to see a child sitting on a bench in the centre of the square, swinging her plump little legs and cuddling a teddy bear. She couldn't have been more than seven years old. What the hell was she doing out on Lunar Night? The child stared at him through wide, blue eyes as he hurried towards her.

"Why aren't you at home, little girl?" he asked, with a smile that revealed his long canine teeth. Whoops, that might have been a mistake.

The child was unfazed. "You're under arrest, mister, for breaking the curfew," she said, pulling a gun from behind the teddy and pointing it steadily between his eyes.

Lewin stared at her. She was no child – she must be a morph. There was something familiar about the face. "WPC Merrit?" he conjectured.

The gun didn't waver. "Who are you?" she said.

"I'm Councillor Lewin. We were meant to patrol together, but you never turned up."

"I prefer to work alone," she said. She slid the gun back behind the teddy and patted the bench beside her, inviting him to sit down.

"Why did you morph into a child?" he asked. "Surely, it must be dangerous."

"I'm bait," she said. "A rogue werewolf wouldn't be able to resist me, and don't worry about me being safe, I've got half a dozen silver bullets in here, and I won't hesitate to use them."

"I never knew you were a morph," he said, then he stiffened. In the shadows at the edge of the square he thought he saw a movement. He glanced at the policewoman but she had seen nothing. He sniffed the air, trying to catch the scent of an intruder.

"Are you alright?" she asked.

"Just a bit chilly," he said, not wanting to alarm her.

Too late he caught the rank smell of wolf.

"Watch out!" He leapt to his feet. A pack of werewolves had been gathering downwind and now they came racing across the square towards the two enforcers. Merrit dropped to her knees and fired six bullets in quick succession. She was a good shot – six corpses lay twitching in the moonlight. But the rest of the gang ignored the death of their comrades and continued the attack.

"Quick, hold them off while I reload," she said, jumping over the back of the bench.

Lewin hesitated, the excitement of the attack stirred his blood. Primitive instincts he had never felt before overwhelmed him. He stood back and watched the other werewolves leap upon her. Deep within him were remnants of the old Councillor Lewin and out of respect for the constable he didn't join in the kill.

Lewin knew that tomorrow he would mourn her death - but tonight, with the scent of blood on the ground, and the power of the pack riding high, the wolf in him reigned. With a strangled howl, he threw away his dignity and joined in the feeding frenzy. And, yes, he could confirm that the plump, little legs tasted as good as they had looked.

The Werecat and the Baby
A wonderful transformation

Lucinda was the only child of a golden couple. In the precious time they had together they had eyes and thoughts only for each other. Lucinda had tried to create a place for herself at the centre of the family. First she had tried charm, then clinginess, then tantrums and had finally retired into sulks, forever outside the orbit of her parents' devotion.

When Lucinda was six her parents showed their dissatisfaction with her by having a baby. Her mother insisted on putting cat nets over the baby's pram and cot.

"But we have no pets," protested her father.

"Humour me, darling," said her mother and stroked a cool finger down his cheek so he kissed her hand and vowed that she could have anything her heart desired.

Lucinda knew about cats. A big, golden cat would sometimes come into the garden and she watched it stretch languorously in the sun and groom its shining fur. It was the most beautiful creature she had ever seen.

Lucinda decided to escape her unhappiness by becoming a cat. She sat still and concentrated on shrinking her skin so fur was squeezed out through the follicles. She stretched her joints then she stepped out of her clothes, for she had become small. She leapt up onto the dressing table and looked in the mirror. A marmalade kitten looked back at her with round, astonished eyes.

Full of joy she sprang from her dressing table to her bed exhilarated by her power and flexibility. Then she remembered the baby.

Lucinda, the marmalade kitten, hurried to the baby's bedroom and jumped up onto the cot. She clawed at the cat net, but it held firm. Lucinda dropped back to the floor and concentrated hard. She expanded her skin, sucking back the fur so she became smooth and large and turned back into a child. She was then able to unsnap the fastenings of the cat net and roll it back.

Lucinda, the child, leaned over the rail of the cot and stared at the sleeping baby. It was the sweetest thing – soft and pink and fast asleep. No wonder her parents preferred the baby to her. In her jealousy she changed back into a cat, jumped into the cot and crept towards the baby's head. The cot shook as a huge golden cat leapt up onto the rail and crouched staring down at Lucinda like a burning sun.

"No you don't!" it said and gave Lucinda a cuff that sent her bowling down to the far end of the cot. The golden cat jumped into the cot, seized Lucinda by the scruff of the neck and sprang out with a single bound. Lucinda had recognised her mother's voice and now she started to cry. Hot, anguished tears soaked into her fur.

"I'm so sorry," she sobbed. "I didn't mean to – I wouldn't have – how did you know?"

She felt her mother's rasping tongue lick the tears from her fur.

"I nearly did the same thing when I was your age," her mother said. "Now, stop crying my dear daughter. Come into the garden and I will show you how to hunt butterflies."

Lucinda and her mother went outside. They played chase in the shrubbery and jumped for butterflies and when they were tired, they stretched out on the ground and Lucinda snuggled up against her mother's warm, furry body.

"Does Daddy know?" she asked.

"Nobody knows," said her mother. "It must remain a secret between the two of us."

"Will my baby sister be one of us?" asked Lucinda.

"I hope so," said her mother. "We werecats are rare and wonderful creatures."

That night Lucinda was allowed to stay up for dinner for the first time.

"You are looking very pretty tonight, Lucinda," said her father. "Are you happy to have a baby sister?"

"Oh yes," said Lucinda. "When she is old enough I am going to show her how to play with butterflies in the garden."

"How charming," said her father looking lovingly at her. "You are becoming more and more like your dear mother." Lucinda and her mother smiled at each other, for no finer compliment could have been paid.

The Witch of the Lower Fourth
Thou shalt not suffer a witch to live

At twelve noon, Miss Crichfield spontaneously combusted. We had been sitting in the staffroom listening to her complain about the Lower Fourth when she gave a startled cry and lifted her skirt to reveal a glowing patch on her thigh. We stared in astonishment as flames started to flicker from it.

"Water, water," cried Mr Butt. He ran to the sink, filled a paper cup and threw the contents over Miss Crichfield's leg. There was a sizzling sound and then the flames sprang up, as strongly as before.

"Clasp your hands over them," urged Mr Butt.

No man had ever touched Miss Crichfield's bony thighs and Mr Butt wasn't going to be the first. Miss Crichfield continued to flap her hands ineffectually over the growing flames.

"Wrap her in the carpet," yelled Mr Butt, who was proving to be a natural leader in times of crisis.

It took a while to remove the furniture from the carpet and, by the time Miss Crichfield was wrapped in its dusty embrace, it was too late to save her.

"At least we managed to put the flames out," said Mr Butt.

That afternoon, Lucy Wickenden stopped me in the corridor. "How's Miss Crichfield?" she asked.

I gaped open-mouthed. How did she know? I did not answer and watched the insolent child walk away down the corridor. Her black-stockinged legs were as thin as broomsticks, and her long black hair tied loosely back. She looked like a witch and, suddenly, the pieces fell into place. Her name gave it away - Lucy Wickenden – Lucy must be short for Lucifer, and didn't wicken mean witch? As I stared at the witch's retreating figure, I knew with absolute certainty what had happened to Miss Crichfield.

The next day I was put in charge of the Lower Fourth. I was ready for the challenge - around my neck I wore a necklace of garlic and a wooden cross. It was a warm day and the class was subdued after hearing of the fate of their former teacher. I must have dozed off when I heard a voice.

"Are you all right, Miss?" My eyes jerked open and I saw Lucy Wickenden standing beside my desk. Despite all my precautions the witch-child had managed to cast a sleeping-spell over me. Dangling from her pencil case was an evil-looking doll.

"What's that?" I asked, fumbling at the neck of my blouse to find the cross.

"It's just an Ugli-doll," she said. But I knew it was a voodoo doll. All she needed was one of my hairs and, with a chill of fear, I realised why she had come up to my desk.

I clutched the cross in one hand and put my other hand out to take the doll. "I'm confiscating that."

She shrugged and handed it over. "I've got plenty more."

Thou shalt not suffer a witch to live. It says that in the bible, it's like a commandment. It's your duty to kill a witch, to save your immortal soul from her evil spells.

I ordered Lucy to stay behind at morning break, to help me look for something in the stationery cupboard.

"What are we looking for?" she asked, peering in.

"Salvation," I said and gave her a shove that sent her staggering into the darkness. I slammed the door and locked it. Then I hurried to the kitchen for a knife.

I stabbed her eleven times – once for each of the Holy Apostles. Then I had to sever her head, so her evil soul couldn't re-enter her body. Unfortunately, I had chosen a filleting knife which, although good at stabbing, was difficult to carve with. It was a long and bloody task and I was still struggling when members of the Lower Fourth returned to the classroom.

If I have a regret M'Lud, it's that the children returned from their morning break to such a scene of carnage. I tried to explain to them the importance of removing the head from a witch's corpse but they were screaming so loudly that they were unable to hear me.

I hope they now realise that I did it for their sakes – for all our sakes.

The Woodcutter and the Spider
Be careful what you wish for

Once upon a time, when men took many forms, a poor woodcutter lived alone in the middle of a forest. He prayed to the gods to send him a woman and one day they answered his prayer.

In a sunny clearing sat a beautiful girl, but she was sad and would not smile at him.

"Why are you sad?" he asked, and he knew that he would do anything in the world to make her happy.

"I'm sad because I'm hungry," she said. So he gave her the bread and cheese he was going to eat for lunch. As she ate, he gazed at her and saw the way the sunshine curved over her cheeks and shadowed her slender neck. He had never seen anything so heart-breakingly lovely.

"Come with me and be my wife," he said.

But she shook her head and showed him a silken rope tied around her ankle.

"I am my husband's prisoner."

"I'll untie the knot." He knelt on the ground at her feet but she pushed him away.

"Don't touch the rope. If he feels the vibration he will pull me in and punish me." She rose to her feet and thanked him for the food then walked away into the forest.

He waited for a few moments and then he followed her. But there was no path and she left no footprints on the carpet of pine needles, so he gave up.

The next day the woodcutter hurried to the clearing and was overjoyed to see her again. He gave her cake as well as bread but she buried her head in her hands and wept.

"What's the matter?" he said, his arms aching to comfort her.

"Yesterday, when my husband discovered I had eaten, he punished me." Her words were like daggers in his heart. He seized her hand.

"My poor darling. Wait, I will hurry home and bring more food so he can eat too." She wept even harder.

"My husband wants meat."

"Meat? I have no meat."

"My husband wants you to kill a deer for him." The woodcutter was so moved by the maiden's distress that he spent the rest of the day trying to catch and kill a deer, even though it was forbidden.

It was evening before he returned to the clearing and found her still waiting for him.

"Alas, I have failed in my task."

Tears cascaded down her cheeks. "My husband will punish me."

"No, I will save you."

This time he walked beside her through the forest until they came to a giant spider's web strung between two trees.

"Follow me," she said and climbed the web. With no thought but to protect his beloved he followed her into the web. But there were sticky threads among the smooth and, in his haste, he became entangled.

"Help me," he said. She came to him, climbing nimbly over the web, but she stopped before she reached him.

"You should have caught a deer, my husband must eat."

She glanced to where her husband crouched in the shadows. He was as ugly as his wife was beautiful. His neck was wide, his head small, he had a pot belly and long legs. His naked body was covered sparsely with short, thick hairs.

"So, you fancy my wife, do you?" he said and the woodcutter saw that his mouth was toothless, apart from two fangs, which were so long they protruded down either side of his chin.

The spiderman sat on the web, next to his wife and stroked her legs with his small, claw-like hands. She no longer seemed beautiful. Her face was flushed, her eyes eager, a string of saliva drooled from her mouth.

The woodcutter struggled to free himself from the entangling strands. The more he struggled, the more entwined he became, until he hung, unmoving and exhausted. He felt long, skinny arms wrap around his chest and a soft, fat body press against his back.

"Yum, yum." Cruel fangs pierced his flesh and with his heart and body broken, the woodcutter slowly sank into paralysis and death.

Be careful what you wish for, mortal man, for the gods might grant your wish.

To the Centre of Dante's Hell
Relocation problems solved by Souls Recovery Inc.

Max picked his way towards Satan, who sat in the middle of a frozen lake, a huge, hunched figure trapped up to his waist in ice. Dimly through the ice Max could see the bodies of entombed sinners, whose heads poked above the surface like scattered debris.

Clouds boiled above the surrounding cliffs and a red light illuminated the baleful scene.

Satan flapped his wings, causing a glacial wind to howl across the lake. Max staggered backwards and stumbled against a head.

"Whoops, sorry!"

Satan heard his voice and looked round. Max shivered as he saw the full hideousness of the King of Demons. He had a single head but with three faces, one in the front and the others facing sideways. A pair of curved horns surmounted the repulsive triumvirate.

The mouth in the central face opened. "Who are you?"

The eyes in the other two faces swivelled round to stare at Max but their mouths did not speak, they were too busy chewing on sinners, held like lollipops in huge, clawed hands.

"I'm Max Morrison, managing director of Souls Recovery Inc." Max spoke with a confidence he did not feel.

Satan frowned. "I've never heard of you."

"Actually, we do most of our business in the Outer Circles – lust, gluttony, avarice, that sort of thing. Those who repented before death have to be relocated."

"Ah, yes, immigration control. We can't have Hell overflowing with people who don't belong here." Satan's frown cleared.

Max gained enough courage to say, "I'm surprised to find you suffering like this, I thought you'd be on a throne or something."

Satan gave a bitter laugh. "Oh this is Hell for me as well. I'm being punished for a stupid misunderstanding with the Almighty."

"I'm sorry."

"Don't be. The food's awful and the heating is non-existent but at least I'm not being boiled in pitch like the politicians or eaten like Judas." Satan removed one of the lollipops and stared at it.

"Actually, it's about Judas I've come to see you," said Max. "Nowadays it's reckoned that Jesus asked him to contact the Romans - he was just carrying out orders."

"I told you so," said Judas, whose head was growing back into its correct shape.

Satan gave Judas an icy stare. "I suppose I must let him go."

"It would save an awful lot of paperwork," said Max. "Look, I've brought you something in exchange." He took the lid off a

Party Bucket of Southern Fried Chicken and a delicious smell of spicy coating wafted over the lake.

"Yum," said Satan. A chorus of little yums came from the surrounding heads. "Don't think you're getting any," snarled Satan then turned to Max. "Do you want a lift back? I'll get one of my demons to give you a ride." Satan lifted his head and yelled, "Geryon."

Max and Judas clapped their hands over their ears and all the heads moaned in protest at the deafening noise. A few seconds later a winged giant with a scorpion tail appeared over the rim of the pit and flew down.

"Yes, Master?"

"I want you to give my friends here a lift to Hell's Gate."

Geryon lay down so the two humans could scramble onto his back.

Satan waved the bucket hopefully. "I suppose you wouldn't swap another of these for Hitler?"

Max shook his head. "No, but I might be back for Richard the Third." He waved goodbye as Geryon leapt into the air and unfurled his wings.

The wall of the pit loomed before them but with an heroic effort the giant demon gained enough height to fly over the top. They flew over the chequered landscape of the Eighth Circle then a flaming desert, a forest of thorn bushes and a river of blood leading to the stygian marsh in the centre of which lay the city of Dis with its flaming tombs.

They finally reached the Elysian Fields, dismounted and thanked their demon ride. As they passed through Hell's Gate, Max turned to gaze at the mighty arch, which bore the words: "**Abandon hope all ye who enter here.**" Below hung a banner: "**Relocation problems solved by Souls Recovery Inc.**"

Twenty Seven Years and Counting
The end of civilisation as we know it

It has been twenty-seven years since the world ended. Not the actual world, of course, but the world as we know it. I was in my office at a small provincial newspaper when we heard that a solar storm was on the way.

"We must work overtime to get the weekly edition out early," said the editor. "There's a possibility that the computers might fail."

A possibility? Am I the only one with any scientific knowledge? Muttering something about popping to the loo, I vacated the building and hurried to my apartment to pack some essentials.

I tried phoning Tony, but he had his mobile phone off as usual. I felt a pang of regret at leaving without warning, but my boyfriend would have to take care of himself.

I hurried to the bank and emptied my account while their computers were still working, then I caught the train to my parent's home.

My mother was a woman of wealth and resourcefulness. She was also hypoglycaemic and had a fear of being without nutriment. Her large country home was stocked with food – bottles, jars, cans, dried food and several well-stocked freezers.

We were in the countryside when the storm struck. Outwardly there was no sign of the disaster that had overtaken civilisation. The train simply came to a gentle stop. Some people took out their mobile phones and punched the keys in bewilderment. Others, who had been working on laptops, frowned and checked the batteries.

I went to the door and pushed the exit button. Nothing happened, the damn doors must have been computerised. Several hours later the air in the carriage was becoming foetid and at last the other passengers rallied around to force the doors open.

Freedom at last. We exited the train and mounted the embankment to a road where nothing was moving. A few people sat on the verge, others started walking. I headed in the direction of home.

I spent the night under a hedge and arrived home the next day looking dishevelled. I like to think my mother didn't recognise me, which is why she threatened me with a shotgun. Luckily my father, a vague but good-natured man, appeared in the background.

"You can't shoot Joyce, darling," he said. "Let her come in, she can help empty the freezers. The food in them is defrosting already."

My mother nodded and stood to one side. For the next several days we feasted, trying to consume the frozen food before it rotted.

The shotgun was fired several times. Once when the neighbours came round in a pretence of friendship and later when gangs of hungry-looking villagers gathered at the bottom of the drive.

"Be careful you don't kill anyone," I said to mother.

"Who's to know?" she replied.

Fortunately, hunger had so weakened the unprepared villagers that most of them died peacefully of starvation. Those with the energy to seek help from us were eventually frightened away by a mere showing of the gun.

Winter without electricity was an ordeal. My mother's preparations had not gone beyond food and we had to break up some rather good antique furniture to make a fire.

The next Spring we planted potatoes and vegetables.

My mother grumbled at the effort involved and I had to point out to her that both our gardeners were probably dead by now. It might have been forward planning to save their lives.

The years went by. My mother died first, which was ironic as she had made such an effort to survive. I thought my father would blossom but he was lost without her. He had a stroke and lingered for several years.

What now? For a long time I hoped that Tony might come striding up the drive to claim me. I spent hours at the drawing room window looking out.

There is no point now. I am beyond child bearing age. Outside the walls of our estate, I sometimes see people on horseback or with carts. The survivors of the disaster seem to have developed a pre-industrial agrarian society.

Nobody comes, I live in solitude. Time without a future passes slowly.

Uber

Mellisand must be uber alles

By the time he reached the top floor of the book depository, Mr Spackman was exhausted. He collapsed by the window and put down the case that contained his rifle. His wife had insisted he get into position early and when he complained about missing lunch, she had packed him a few sandwiches and a flask of coffee.

Mr Spackman gradually recovered from climbing six flights of stairs and unwrapped the crudely-cut cheese sandwiches. He sighed, remembering the carefully-balanced packed lunches his wife prepared for their daughter, Melissand. However, Mr

Spackman was hungry after his exertions. He made a good lunch, washed down by a draught of coffee.

The sun shone into the room. Outside, birds were singing. A languor came over Mr Spackman and he drifted into sleep. It was a deeper sleep than his usual afternoon nap as the unfortunate man had been kept awake by worry the night before.

A vibration woke him, hauling his consciousness up from swirling dreams. What was happening? Where was he? It took several seconds for him to remember and to realise that the vibration was coming from his mobile phone.

"Yes?" He answered it.

"Were you asleep?" His wife's voice came tinnily out of the phone.

"No," he lied, wondering, not for the first time, how the compliant secretary he had married, had turned into a terrifying dominatrix.

"You took long enough to answer the phone."

"I was – er – reconoitering."

"Yes? Well, as long as you keep your gloves on and don't leave any evidence. Is the gun ready?"

Mr Spackman looked in dismay at the case, which contained the disassembled parts of a high-powered sniper's rifle. "Yes," he lied.

"Good, you have ten minutes before Lord Athelstone arrives to open the school fete." The phone clicked off.

Ten Minutes? Mr Spackman opened the case with trembling fingers. Could he assemble the gun in ten minutes? He had assembled it the night before, and it had taken him at least half an hour. But he had a vague idea, now, about which bit goes where, and he smoothed out the instruction sheet with some hope that his task would be accomplished.

A faint cheering from the road below told him that his hope had been misplaced. He went to the window and saw Lord Athelstone's open-topped Rolls pass by. Damn it.

Brrr, the phone in his pocket vibrated.

"Yes?"

"He has arrived. Are you ready?"

"Of course." He would still have a few minutes to assemble the gun, while the fete was being opened.

At last Mr Spackman screwed the silencer onto the barrel and looked through the telescopic sight. Beyond the road was a stand of trees and beyond the trees he could see the edge of the school playing field where the fete was being held. He scanned the people, recognising teachers and fellow parents.

There was the maths teacher, who had refused to give Melissand extra coaching. There was the geography teacher, who had accused his wife of doing Melissand's project. There was the games mistress, who had failed to select Melissand for the first team. He should be grateful that his wife hadn't ordered wholesale carnage.

The distant sound of clapping alerted Mr Spackman that the fete had been opened. He crouched by the window, ready to fire. Lord Athelstone came into his sights, his long lanky figure drooping forwards as he examined each stall in turn.

Mr Spackman swung his gun round, concentrating on the stand of trees. There it was, the first balloon. Was it Melissand's? He knew his wife had been queuing for an hour to buy the first ticket in the balloon race.

The balloon rose over the trees, wobbling in the breeze. Mr Spackman frowned, staring at it, his finger hovering over the trigger. Then he recognised Melissand's 'lucky' ribbon – the marker his wife had attached.

He relaxed and let his daughter's balloon drift safely away. He turned the gun once again towards the trees. A second balloon was rising into view. Mr Spackman waited, until it was out of sight of the school playing field, then he shot it down. BANG. One way or another, Melissand was going to win.

Visitation of a Corpse
I was left to face the consequences of their actions

They say I killed my best friend, James Flood. I swear that it was not murder but an act of mercy. James lived alone in a grand house beyond the outskirts of town. I was a regular visitor but, that night, I wished I had not made the journey for a storm was gathering and the air crackled with electricity. I was in a state of agitation when I reached his door and gave our special knock.

Rat tatatatat Tat. He must have known it was me, but James did not answer the door, instead he peered through the window with an expression of fear on his face as if he expected the Devil himself to be waiting on his doorstep.

I knocked again. *Rat tatatatat Tat.* The first drops of rain were starting to fall. I knocked with greater vigour and at last the door was swung open.

"Who are you?" said James. He would have blocked my way but I pushed past him into the hall.

"I am your friend, Peter Laurie, surely you recognise me?"

James shut and bolted the door. I followed him into the living room, where he poured me a whisky and gestured me to take a seat in one of the leather armchairs.

"On a night like this it is good to have company," he said. "For I am being stalked by a creature so terrible that it belongs among the denizens of hell."

"Really?" I stared at him, was he insane?

"You do not believe me," he said. "Well believe this, young man. It is not the soul of your friend James Flood which inhabits this body but it is I, Annabelle Ernst."

I stared at James, aghast. Annabelle Ernst was an old woman who ran a strange little shop of witchcraft and magic in Warlock Street.

"Your friend owed me money and, when he refused to pay, I attempted to put a curse on him. He stabbed me to death before the curse could be delivered but, at the moment of expiration, I managed to swap souls with him. The soul of your friend now lives within my rotting remains, while I live in this fine, young body."

The storm was at its height. Lightning flashed, the sound of thunder rolled around the hill and rain streamed down the outside of the window. Amidst the maelstrom came a knocking on the door.

Rat tatatatat Tat! It was the secret knock of my friend. The real James must be at the door. I leapt to my feet.

"Stop! Don't answer the knock!" As I reached the hall, the creature that had been James leapt upon me and I rendered him unconscious with a single blow.

Rat tatatatat Tat. The knocking was more urgent.

I drew back the bolt, flung the door open and stared out into the rain-drenched darkness. There was nobody there! Then I heard a groan and lowered my gaze to where a hideous being lay upon the doorstep.

"Let me in, Peter."

I could not bring myself to touch the putrefying corpse and let it struggle over the threshold on its own.

"Release me from my fate," it groaned.

"How?" I said, nearly gagging with revulsion.

"Kill me." Its voice was a whimper of agony.

Upon the table in the hall was a sharp paperknife of oriental design. I picked it up and stared at the animated corpse in confusion. How can one kill something that was already dead?

It pointed at the unconscious man. "Kill my body and my soul will be released." I hesitated, for I am no murderer. "Please, if you ever loved me, kill me now."

Gathering my strength and courage I plunged the knife into the creature's chest. With a shriek, that sounded more like a woman than a man, James's body died and all life left the corpse that had imprisoned his soul.

I stood in the hall with a dripping knife in my hand. The body of my friend lay on one side of me, the rotting corpse of Annabelle Ernst lay on the other. They had departed this world and I was left to face the consequences of their actions.

Wayne Becomes a Gigolobot
What can a man do when no longer needed?

Men were no longer needed in a world where fertilization took place by egg fusion in laboratories, so what was a spotty, hormonal seventeen-year-old youth to do? Become a gigolobot, of course.

It was chilly on the long display platform and Wayne, who was naked, could feel his skin coming up in goose pimples. He hoped he would be chosen soon. A couple of women entered the rental shop and walked down the line.

"This one looks unusual," said one stopping in front of Wayne. "It's skinny and has lumpy knees."

"And look at its ugly face, dear," said the other. "Its nose is too big and its eyes are too close together and look at those spots – what were the designers thinking of?"

"It must be catering for some weird minority taste," said the first woman. "Personally, I prefer the Brad Pitt model."

"Who wouldn't?" said her friend, and they wandered on down the line.

Wayne felt his hopes sinking. Perhaps he didn't have a chance against a host of gigolobots designed to resemble the mythically handsome.

He stole a quick glance at his neighbours. Both were taller than him and had chiselled, features.

Another couple of women entered the Centre and Wayne hurriedly looked forward. They stopped in front of him.

"Look at this one, it's got its groinal attachment screwed in already." Wayne managed not to gasp as the woman grabbed hold of him and twisted. "That's funny, it doesn't seem to turn."

"Perhaps you're meant to pull it," said her friend.

"No, it doesn't seem to pull either."

"It must come off to be sterilized. Here, let me have a go. You probably have to push it down first and then pull it. Like that. Oh Yuk, it seems to have some sort of squirt mechanism."

"Really? Is that meant to add to the pleasure?"

"I don't see how. Have you got a tissue? Thanks."

"Let's hope those spots don't squirt," said the first woman and they both laughed.

There was nobody around for a while and Wayne managed to recover. His legs stopped shaking and his breathing became regular. He wasn't sure whether he had enjoyed the experience and he feared that the attempted removal of his groinal attachment might be his only sexual adventure. He was about to give up and go home when a group of teenage girls stopped in front of him. He felt himself blushing.

"That's odd," said a large blonde. "This one has a red face, and it's ugly."

"I think it's rather cute," said a small dark-haired girl.

"That's because you're weird," said the blonde and she proceeded to entertain the rest of the group by making amusing remarks about Wayne's appearance.

"He's not that bad," said the dark-haired girl.

The blonde turned on her. "What do you know, you don't approve of gigolobots."

"You can't afford to rent one more like," said another girl.

"Yes I can," said the dark-haired girl, "I'm going to rent this one." She pressed the button in front of Wayne. Automated machinery whirred and Wayne was boxed, wrapped and delivered.

The dark-haired girl unwrapped him and he saw they were alone in her bedroom. Hurrah, for the first time in his life he was going to do it with a real live girl.

"You don't have to pretend any more," she said. "I know you're not really a gigolobot."

"Yes, I am."

"Where's your on-off switch?"

"I'm permanently on," he said and reached for her breasts.

"That proves you are not a gigolobot," she said, knocking his hands away. "They are not allowed to take the initiative."

"Really?"

"Yes, they're just anthropomorphic vibrators, I can't be bothered with them. What is sex without romance?" It was a rhetorical question and she proceeded to answer it at great length while he stared at her breasts, trying to see the nipples.

"So you don't want sex then?" said Wayne, when at last she paused.

"Not until we are in a committed relationship, my darling." She laid her hand gently on his arm and looked up into his eyes. "What do you want, Wayne?"

"I want to go back to the Rental Centre," he said and climbed back into his box.

What a Difference a Spear Makes
It was time to kill Baldr again

Andy Smithers arrived at work and said good morning to the goddess at the reception desk. Lying across the back of her chair was a black, feathery garment.

"I'll borrow that, if you don't mind," he said and reached across her desk. She looked up from painting her nails and her eyes widened.

"Why are you carrying a broom handle?" she asked.

He frowned. "It's a spear. I can't get a proper blade for it, the dwarves are on strike."

"Dwarves?" Her plump, pink lips curved into a smile. "You're a nutter, you know that? Just don't try and kill anyone with it."

"Of course not," he said. "This is just for protection. My real weapon is in my pocket."

She laughed. "Ooh, they all say that."

Andy delved into his pocket and produced a piece of sharpened wood, the size of a pencil-stub.

"What's that?" she asked.

"It's mistletoe. It ought to be an arrow but I couldn't find a stem big enough."

"Mistletoe?" she said archly. "You won't steal many kisses under that thing."

He glared at her. It was the first time he had spoken to her on the temporal plane and he was disconcerted by her stupidity.

"This weapon is not for kissing, it's for killing," he said. "Now, can I borrow your cloak?"

"What do you want it for?"

"Transmogrification, of course."

"Trans – what?" But Andy had had enough. With a curt thank you he grabbed the cloak and hurried on his way.

He had to go through the engineer's department to get to his office. Hector was already there, surrounded by a group of admirers.

"Had the brush off, Andy?" he laughed as Andy hurried past with his broom handle.

How he hated that self-satisfied bastard. Andy had killed him once, in Asgard, and now Baldr had reincarnate himself as Hector Harrison. Determined to kill him again, Andy put on the cloak. It turned out to be a cardigan and he had to tie the sleeves around his neck in a ridiculous fashion. Undaunted, he picked up the dart, took a deep breath and entered the engineer's department. All eyes turned to watch as he strode over to Hector.

"Take that Baldr," he yelled and hurled the dart at Hector's jugular. The dart veered to the left, hit a notice board and stuck there, quivering. Damn!

Andy leapt onto a desk and turned to face the advancing engineers. "Ha, ha!" he proclaimed. "So, you think you can capture Loki, blood-brother of Odin? I, the Shape Changer; I, the Sky Traveller; I, the hero of Ragnarok? Think again you puny mortals." With that, he launched himself from the desk, with his arms spread wide.

To Andy's astonishment he failed to transform into a raven and crashed to the floor. Before the bewildered engineers could move, he picked himself up and hobbled from the room. The goddess was waiting for him at reception.

"I want my cardi back," she said.

"Okay." He struggled to undo the knot. "The beastly thing didn't work anyway. You can't be Freyja, the goddess of love."

"No, I'm Linda." She reached up to help him untie the sleeves and her perfume wafted around him like a spell. "As for being the goddess of love," she said. "Would you like to take me out on Saturday night?"

Before he could answer, a heavy hand landed on Andy's shoulder and he turned to see an ogre with a phalanx of engineers.

"What have you been up to Smithers?" snarled the ogre.

Andy stood, open-mouthed. The legendary wit of Loki had deserted him.

"He was rehearsing a play," said Linda.

"A play?" The ogre looked puzzled.

"Yes, it's about killing someone with mistletoe. I'm in it too. I'm Freda, the goddess of love."

A guffaw broke the silence and Hector came forwards. He flung an arm around Andy's cringing shoulders. "You certainly convinced me," he said. "I had the fright of my life. Well done, Andy."

The ogre looked uncertain. "I suppose it's all right, just this once. But never let me catch you rehearsing in the firm's time again."

Andy meekly agreed and followed the group back into the office. As he went, he looked back and Linda blew him a kiss. He grinned. Perhaps a lifetime spent on the temporal plane wouldn't be so bad after all.

TWO

Sci Fi, Weird and Humour

A Modern Frankenstein
A human-pig hybrid takes a monstrous revenge

Doctor Oliver Keenan peered down the microscope in his laboratory. Thousands of sperm, his sperm, were wriggling though saline solution towards a cluster of eggs – pig's eggs. Some had already reached their goal and were battering their heads against unyielding membranes.

Oliver picked up a pipette and added a few drops of Frankenstein acid to the solution in the petri dish. The acid weakened the egg membranes and voila! penetration was successful.

Inside the incubator dozens more petri dishes contained a living cargo of developing embryos. Soon another batch would be ready to transfer.

A man burst into the room. It was his brother-in-law and he looked as if he had been running.

"Quick," he gasped. "Come to the pig unit. One of the animals is behaving strangely."

Oliver sighed and followed Peter across the yard to the long, low line of sheds in which the pigs were housed. The stench in the pig house was unbearable and the sound of rutting and grunting filled the air. Skylights lit the pens from above giving a strange, cathedral-like quality to the scene.

Peter led him to a pen where a nearly full-grown pig stood upright against the railings.

"It has been asking who its father is," said Peter as they drew near.

"What?" Oliver felt his heart stop beating for a second.

"I told the pig it was you, the man in a white coat."

"Are you mad?"

"What's the matter? Have I done something wrong?"

The pig had seen them coming. "Daddy!" it cried and held out its forelegs as if to embrace him.

Oliver stopped, shocked by its appearance. It was a monstrous parody of a pig. The eyes of a man looked out from the creature's porcine face. Their expression of joyous welcome soon changed to one of distress.

"Don't look at me like that, Daddy. I am your son."

"No!" Oliver moaned.

"You made me, I am part of you. I love you, Daddy. You must love me too."

"No!" Oliver turned and ran. He reached the laboratory and sat in a chair, shaking with nerves.

A few minutes later Peter followed him. "I say, that was a bit hard," he said. "That poor creature is sobbing its heart out."

"Kill it!" said Oliver.

"No!" Peter looked shocked.

"It's destined to die anyway. Its organs will be used for transplants and its body for meat."

"But it can talk."

"All the more reason to kill it now. The Government will shut us down if they know we cross-fertilise eggs instead of manipulating genes."

Peter hesitated, torn between greed and pity. Greed won. "Very well," he said.

Hours later, Peter returned. This time he entered the laboratory hesitantly.

"Is the creature dead?" Oliver asked.

Peter shook his head. "No, it escaped. I'm sorry, Olly. It climbed the railings and got out. We've been looking everywhere."

"Dammit!" Oliver glared at his brother-in-law. "It's late. I'm going home," he said. "You had better stay here and carry on looking for it."

As Oliver hurried to his car, he kept glancing into the shadows half expecting his lovelorn creation to be lying in wait for him.

Home was a haven of happiness and peace. His wife was in the kitchen. Oliver kissed her and then kissed the baby who was strapped into her high chair. The delicious smell of cottage pie came from the Aga.

"Supper is ready, darling," said his wife. "Could you call Tommy in from the back garden, please."

Oliver went into the garden. "Tommy!" he called, expecting his son to come running to greet him. There was no response. With a feeling of apprehension Oliver rounded the shrubbery. There was a figure in his son's sandpit, but it wasn't Tommy. With a lurch of dismay, Oliver saw that it was the hideous pig creature he had created.

It looked up from its labours. A trickle of grains rolled down its snout. Behind it, the sand in the pit was piled into a mound.

The monster rose onto its hind legs and took a step towards Oliver. Its eyes gleamed with vengeful triumph.

"Will you love me now, Daddy? Now that I'm your only son?"

The Grey Pearl

Phantom gains a soul

Phantom knew that he would never go to heaven, he was just a shadow, without a soul. His world was as changing and insubstantial as billowing clouds. All was grey, except for the sleeping souls, which lay like golden flowers in the swirling meadows. Sometimes Phantom would watch as a soul became detached and drifted heavenwards, dragging its broken astral cord behind it. He would follow with his eyes as it disappeared upwards through the grey mist to a land that he would never know.

One day, as Phantom wandered among the sleeping souls, he was drawn to one, which floated higher than the rest. It was the soul of a beautiful young woman; and as he gazed at her, he felt an unaccustomed emotion, a stirring of interest. Was it fate or was it chance that made him linger beside her? Time passed, and he realised that her soul had not returned to earth. She was not asleep but comatose: trapped, as he was, between the living and the dead.

One day she opened her eyes and smiled at him. "Please help me," she said.

"How can I help?" he asked. "I am but a shadow, a nothingness."

"Oh, no," she breathed. "You are beautiful. You're my guardian angel." And with that she slept once more.

Phantom was without a sense of self, and yet her words had moved him. Was he really beautiful in her eyes? He knew that he must stay by her side and be the guardian angel she had thought him. Time passed and he studied every detail of her features. The shadow of her eyelashes against her skin, the curve of her cheekbones, the slenderness of her neck, and the way tiny tendrils of hair curled around her ears.

She opened her eyes once more. "Please help me, Angel. I don't want to die."

"You aren't dying," he said, but he knew that he lied, for her body was floating higher now, and soon her astral cord would snap.

"I must get back to see my baby." Tears were in her eyes. "He's only just been born. He needs me."

Phantom looked round – which of the sleeping souls was that of her baby?

"Please, dear Angel, please let me live. I want to hold him in my arms, to feel him suckle, to smell and touch and be one with him."

Phantom felt despair. He longed to help her, but knew that if he descended to Earth he would die in the brightness of the light.

"My husband needs me too. He loves me so much, and I love him."

Her tears were flowing freely now, and at her words, Phantom felt that he too could cry. He had been foolish to think that she would stay in the Shadowlands with him. Her heart belonged on Earth and her soul would soon be ascending to heaven. Before long he would be alone again, as insubstantial as the clouds in which he lived.

"Don't worry," he said. "I'll try to help you."

With one last look at his beloved, he plunged down through the clouds, following her golden cord until he found himself on Earth.

Her body was lying on a bed in a dimly-lit room. Beside it sat a man, sleeping, with his arm resting on the bed. The astral cord, which connected her soul to her body, was so thin that it could snap at any time. Phantom took hold of it and gently pulled her soul down from the Shadowlands.

He could feel it tugging away from him, reluctant to return, but he reeled it in with infinite patience, never putting too great a strain on the slender cord that tethered it. At last, the woman's soul merged once more with her body. She opened her eyes and reached for the man's hand. He woke at once and enfolded her in his arms, sobbing with joy and relief.

Phantom watched as she returned the embrace. His heart was torn between joy at her joy and grief that he had lost her.

"How's the baby?" she asked in a tremulous voice.

"He's fine," he said.

She smiled. Phantom had never seen her smile before, and lingered too long to enjoy her happiness. A nurse came rushing into the room and turned on the brilliant fluorescent light. With a final despairing look at his beloved, Phantom evaporated.

But because he had known love, his new-born soul survived as a grey pearl. The man saw it gleaming on the floor. He picked it up, and gave it to his wife. She rolled the pearl in her hands, feeling its smoothness and admiring its lustre. It reminded her of shadowy dreams, which were fading beyond recall.

"It's beautiful," she said, and knew that it would be her most precious possession.

The woman's husband had the pearl set into a golden locket, which she wore around her neck, close to her heart, for the rest of her life. And when, in the fullness of time, she became old and died, she took the soul of Phantom to heaven with her.

The Trainee Taster

Being the Roman Emperor's taster was a stressful job

Galerius Gordio stared at the feast spread out on the kitchen table before him.

"You took your time coming," said the major-domo.

"I wasn't expecting to be called so soon," said Gordio, still out of breath from running. "I was told that the palace already had two tasters."

The major-domo shook his head sadly.

"Both dead, I'm afraid. Old Julius was caught out by a rare and powerful poison from the Orient, and as for the youngster…"

"It was greed that got him," said the cook. "The way he guzzled sweet oyster soup, you'd have thought he was a vapping guest, instead of a taster. Poisoned with hemlock it was. One little sip was all he should have taken, not two vapping ladles full."

"It may not have been hemlock. It could have been bad oysters," said the major-domo.

The cook rounded on him. "I'll have none of that talk in my kitchen. Bad oysters? The very idea." She turned to Gordio. "Get on with it, you're meant to be tasting the food, not hanging around gawping. You look like you've never seen a banquet before."

Gordio blinked. The cook was right, the sight of so much food dumbfounded him.

"The Emperor's aunt and cousins have already arrived," said the major-domo. "Please hurry with the tasting, the first course is due to be served any minute now."

Gordio grabbed the nearest dish. "What are these?"

"Lark's tongues."

"Wow," said Gordio, "I've always wondered what they tasted like." He took a nibble. "Hmm chewy and tasteless. They're rather disappointing."

"Who do you think you are," said the cook. "A vapping restaurant critic? Just taste the food for poison and be quick about it."

Gordio tasted soups, fish stews and meat patties. After a lifetime of eating gruel his taste buds were in heaven. He spooned a stewed apricot into his mouth then spat it out.

"This tastes funny."

The major-domo signalled to a slave, who came forwards and ate a spoonful of apricots. Everyone looked at him expectantly. After a few moments, when nothing had happened to him, he ate another spoonful and then another. He was obviously enjoying the unexpected treat.

"What exactly was wrong?" asked the major-domo.

"It tasted like the apricots had been stewed in fish sauce," said Gordio.

"That's because they have been vapping stewed in fish sauce, you stultissime," said the cook grabbing the remains of the apricots from the slave. "Have you never heard of Gustum de Praecoquis?"

"Er, no," admitted Gordio

"Give me strength," said the major-domo.

Gordio hurriedly passed on to a dish of meatballs. He picked one up and saw it had a face.

"Aargh. What's this?"

"A roasted dormouse," said the cook.

"How am I meant to eat it?"

The cook grabbed it from him and cut a small sliver off its tail. "You're not eating a whole one, you greedy ructator, they cost a silver denarius each."

A silver denarius? Gordio chewed the tail gingerly. That much money would feed his entire family for a week. He had expected it to be stringy, but it was surprisingly succulent. He crunched the little tail bones and swallowed.

"Yup, that tastes okay."

The dish was whisked away by a waiter and taken to the banqueting hall. It was the last of the starters and Gordio turned his attention to the main course. There were several dishes of stewed and boiled meats in a variety of rich-looking sauces. Mmm, the smell was tantalising. There was also an entire roasted peacock arranged in a facsimile of life, with its tail feathers fanned out behind it.

"Where shall I start?" said Gordio. He reached out his fork for some veal in fig-syrup sauce. "Hmm," he chewed reflectively.

"Perhaps a little overdone?"

The cook opened her mouth and was in the middle of expressing her displeasure in an eye-watering burst of profanity, when there was a commotion from the banqueting hall. A waiter came running into the kitchen.

"The Emperor has been poisoned."

"Oh dear," said Gordio, feeling sick. "Which dish was it?"

"It wasn't the food that killed him," said the waiter. "His aunt slipped him a poisoned napkin."

"Thank Jupiter for that." Gordio mopped his sweating brow, but his relief was short-lived. With a clatter of armour, a phalanx of praetorian guards marched into the kitchen and drew their swords.

"Oh bollocks," said the cook. "Now we're all going to vapping die."

The unfortunate waiter had already been seized and run through with a sword when there was a cheer from the banqueting hall. The praetorian captain rushed in.

"Stop the slaughter," he yelled. "The Emperor's aunt has proclaimed that her son is the new Emperor."

"Hail the new Emperor," said the major-domo, in a hasty switch of allegiance.

"The new Emperor has decreed that his cousin died from a heart attack," continued the praetorian captain. "Anyone who says the old Emperor was poisoned will be executed."

"Of course he wasn't poisoned. No, no," said the major-domo.

"Not by my vapping food he wasn't," said the cook.

"I agree," said Gordio.

Since the Emperor wasn't poisoned, there was no retribution to be taken. At a sign from their captain, the guards sheathed their swords.

"You can get out of my kitchen," said the cook, flapping her apron at the retreating soldiers. "And take that vapping corpse with you."

The soldiers obediently picked up the still-twitching body of the waiter and dragged it out.

Peace returned to the kitchen. Even after tasting all the starters, Gordio was still feeling a bit peckish.

"All that excitement has made me hungry," he said. He picked up his fork and prodded the peacock. "Which bit of this am I meant to taste?" For a moment the carefully prepared bird wobbled under his onslaught then its erect head crashed to the plate.

"What the vapping, Hades do you think you are doing, you vapping stultissime?" The cook picked up a cleaver and Gordio fled. Let someone else have his job. Even a lifetime spent living on gruel was preferable to the stress of being the emperor's taster.

A Promise Kept
Andrew defies death to get to his daughter's nativity play

The nativity play had already started when Andrew arrived at the school. He entered the darkened hall to the sound of While shepherds watched their flocks by night.

Andrew located his wife in the audience and carefully pushed through the seated parents to take the empty chair at her side.

"I'm sorry I'm late, Pam," he said. "The plane was delayed."

Pam was angry and didn't reply. Andrew turned his attention to the stage. A group of shepherds sat singing in front of a cardboard cut-out of some hills. To one side, half hidden behind a curtain, the music teacher played upon a piano and glared at the little shepherds, as if defying them to sing, "Washed their socks."

"The angel of the Lord came down and glory shone around."

On cue, their daughter, Cindy, rose up from behind the hills. She looked breathtakingly beautiful as the Angel Gabriel, in a long, white dress and wearing huge wings covered with real feathers. Behind her golden curls was a halo. Andrew felt his heart swell with pride at the sight of his darling daughter. He had promised to get back from his business trip in time to see her performance. He had nearly been late but the nightmare of his journey was worthwhile to see her in her glory.

"Fear not: I bring you good tidings of great joy." Her voice trembled with nerves and her eyes scanned the audience. "For unto you is born this day." She spotted Andrew and Pam in the audience and smiled. With renewed confidence she tackled the speech. "A Saviour, which is Christ the Lord."

Beside him Andrew could sense Pam's total concentration. She was holding her breath willing Cindy not to forget her words.

"Ye shall find the babe wrapped in swaddling clothes, lying in a manger."

With much shaking of the hills a multitude of six angels rose on either side of Cindy and chanted. "Glory to God in the highest, and on earth peace, good will toward men."

Andrew kept his eyes on his daughter as the rest of the scene played out. Never had he felt so proud of her. She was not only beautiful but brave and clever. He would not have broken his promise to be at the Nativity for anything.

"I'd a terrible time getting here," he said to Pam when the curtains closed. "The traffic was jam-packed. I even had to jump some lights." But his wife was still annoyed at his lateness and had turned to talk to her neighbour.

After the play was over Andrew followed Pam to collect their daughter. He would have spoken to her further, tried to make amends for being late, but he was starting to feel strange, jet-lag was catching up with him.

Cindy had changed back into her school uniform and came running towards them her face shining with happiness. She flung her arms around her mother.

"I'm sorry your father couldn't make it," said Pam.

"But he did make it," said Cindy. "I saw him sitting next to you."

Andrew wanted to step forward and embrace his daughter but he couldn't move, everything was becoming faint.

"Where is Daddy now?" asked Cindy. She looked around but her unseeing eyes scanned past him.

There was a pain in Andrew's chest. Suddenly the scene changed. He was flat on his back on the road. Blue lights were flashing and men were leaning over him.

"I've got this one's heart started again," said a paramedic. "We must get him to hospital as soon as possible."

"I'm amazed he came back after so long," said his companion.

Andrew's mind was in a whirl, what was happening? He was at his daughter's nativity play... No, he was desperate to arrive in time and had jumped a light as it was turning red. There was a crash - a horrific impact. The shock of it stopped his heart and he had died.

But he could not die, he had given his word. "There was something I had to do." Andrew's voice was barely more than a whisper as the paramedics lifted him onto a stretcher. "A promise I had to keep."

<u>After the Tontine</u>
Would anyone be left standing to collect the money from Ebenezer's will?

I invited my relations round to my house for supper after the official reading of great Uncle Ebenezer's will.

"Just soup and rolls, but it will be a chance to catch up," I say.

Some of them I hadn't seen for years. My two great aunts, Ebenezer's sisters, looked like vultures with their long skinny necks and balding hair. They complained about the will, and I'm not surprised, at their age they are not going to profit from the tontine.

"What a ridiculous arrangement," said Agnes, her round vulture eyes blinking. "I'm sure mother would have wanted him to leave his money to us."

"I agree," said Priscilla and dipped her beaky nose into the glass of sherry I handed to her.

My brother Edward was in a jovial mood. "Good old Ebenezer. His money goes to the last one standing. At least we all get a share of the income."

"And that share will increase as people die off," said his wife, staring at the great aunts.

I made sure they all had sherry. Six people stood between me and the money - the great aunts, my brother and his wife and young Julia and her baby.

I disapproved of Julia, my brother's daughter. She was an unmarried mother, a foolish, feckless girl who nobody would miss. It was a shame about the baby, though.

I went into the kitchen and heated up the soup, a delicious lobster bisque. It had taken me a long time to find the right fish for the stock - fugu fish.

Everyone was seated at the table when I brought out the soup.

"Mmmm it smells delicious," said Edward. "You always were a good cook, Angela."

"So fortunate to have the time," said his wife.

"I wonder if the baby is able to eat it," said Julia.

"Of course," I said and gave her a teaspoon with which to spoon it into her little mouth.

"It tastes bitter," said great aunt Agnes, but she continued to eat it with gusto.

"Yes, what have you put in it, dear?" asked great aunt Priscilla.

Lobster, fish stock, onions, carrots, tomatoes, garlic, thyme, brandy, sweet white wine, cream, parsley and a pinch of cayenne pepper."

"I think you have overdone the cayenne pepper," said Agnes.

"Are you not going to eat any soup?" asked Edward.

"I shall have mine afterwards," I lied.

I was anxious for them to leave once they had finished their meal and they were in no mood to linger.

"Well, goodbye, Angela," said great aunt Pricilla. "It was good of you to entertain us."

"First time ever," said my brother's wife.

I stood in the driveway waving as they drove away. I turned back to the bungalow. It looked shabby and the tarmac drive was cracking. Soon I would have a hand-laid brick drive, a conservatory and a holiday abroad.

On the table was a box of chocolates with a note. "To dear Angela, with thanks for your hospitality."

What a nice gesture. Cherry liqueur chocolates, my favourite. It wasn't until I had eaten a few that I realised they tasted a bit odd.

Alien Santa
Dennis was determined not to let Santa into the house

Dennis stood in line with his mother in the Toy Department of Selfridges. Slowly the line advanced towards a grotto covered in cotton wool and flashing lights.

"That's Santa Claus," said his mother. Dennis looked at the man in the grotto. He had a huge, curling white beard and was dressed in red. "He comes down the chimney on the night before Christmas and puts presents in your stocking."

Dennis had never given the matter much thought. He had heard of Santa and seen his jolly face on Christmas cards. He had probably been told it was he who filled his stocking but, until seeing the man in the flesh, he had taken it all for granted.

The man was fat, much too fat to get down a chimney. He must be able to change shape like Mister Elasto. Dennis drew nearer and saw that the beard was false. The strings that attached it round the ears were plainly visible. Moreover, Santa looked nothing like his jolly portrait on the Christmas cards, his nose was mottled with red lines and his forehead etched into a frown.

A child was lifted up onto Santa's lap. "Ho, ho ,ho," said Santa and bared his teeth into a smile that looked more as if he was preparing to eat the reluctant infant.

"I don't want to see Santa," said Dennis.

"Nonsense," said his mother. "I've paid the entrance fee and it includes a present."

A present? Dennis stopped complaining and waited his turn. It wasn't until he reached Santa that his reluctance turned to panic.

"What do you want for Christmas, little boy?" The surrogate Santa's breath stank of whisky and stale cigarette smoke.

Dennis opened his mouth but all that came out was a terrified scream. Other children, already nervous about their coming encounter with Santa, joined in and there was a stampede of traumatised children followed by their exasperated parents.

"Really it was too embarrassing," Mrs Clarke told her husband when they got home. "It would serve Dennis right if Santa didn't visit him next week."

Dennis was determined to keep Santa out of the house. He waited until his parents weren't looking then stuffed the chimney with everything he could find – cushions, old newspapers, bits of clothing. Luckily his parents were too busy with festive preparations to notice.

On Christmas Eve Dennis went to bed early. As he went upstairs he heard his mother say. "I think I'll light the fire in the living room, we haven't lit it yet this winter. We could roast some chestnuts and have a nice relaxing evening." Good, thought Dennis. If Santa gets through my barrier he will get his boots burnt.

Dennis waited until his mother came upstairs, checked his stocking was in place and kissed him goodnight. Then he crept out of bed and took a bowl of water and a bar of soap from the bathroom. He soaped the vinyl floor of his bedroom, then he placed the water where Santa would trip over it.

Dennis lay awake for what seemed like hours but he must have fallen asleep for he was woken by a mighty crash. He sat up in bed, grabbed the rubber hammer he had placed under his pillow and switched on the light.

A figure lay prostrated on the floor, groaning. Dennis got gingerly out of bed and tiptoed towards it, his hammer raised. To his surprise it was not Santa that lay on the floor but his father.

His father opened one eye. "Put that bloody hammer down you menace!" He would have said more but from the living room came a scream.

"The chimney's on fire!"

His father grunted and got to his feet. With a final glare at Dennis, he left the room. Dennis stared at the debris left behind - chocolates, comic books, puzzles and little toys, all sodden from the water that had tipped out of the bowl. He gathered them up and placed them on his bed.

Far away came the sound of a fire engine heading towards them. Dennis smiled, there was no way Santa could visit them now. It was going to be a good Christmas.

All that Glisters

An alchemist escapes from the King's clutches

Bran took down a bottle of Sulphur from a shelf and added a pinch to the mixture heating on the brazier.

His experiment was interrupted by a knock at the door and his wife's voice called. "It's time for supper."

"I'll be down soon, Maria," he replied without enthusiasm. It would be potato gruel again.

When Bran returned after his meal, he found, to his amazement, tiny lumps of gold glistering among the crusted remnants of his experiment.

"Don't tell a soul," he warned his excited wife as he presented her with a ring made from those first few lumps of gold.

But women are like cackling hens and Maria told her best friend. Her best friend told three more and, in a few days, the news reached the King.

Bran was summoned to the palace.

"I hear that I have a skilled alchemist living in my Kingdom." The King licked his lips. "This is fortunate as my requirements are many. You will be my guest at the palace until you have produced enough gold to make a hundred thousand ducats."

"We could always torture the secret out of him," said an elderly man with a goatee beard.

"Really, Chancellor," said the King with a frown. "I'm not a barbarian. We'll only do that as a last resort. Take him to the tower room."

The tower room was comfortably furnished with a four-poster bed, chair, large oak table and an ensuite garderobe. Bran stood on tiptoe to look out of the window and saw a drop of several hundred feet. There was no escape.

There was the sound of bolts being drawn and the door opened. A procession of men entered carrying his equipment, every last bottle and document of it.

Bran worked into the night, trying to recreate his original experiment. He was interrupted by a tapping on his window. He looked out and there in the moonlight, was his wife flying a kite - the kite that had hit his window. He must catch it, but how? The window didn't open. Oblivious to the enormity of damaging the King's castle, he grabbed the chair and shattered the glass.

He pulled the kite into the room. What now? He stared out of the window at his wife, who was making exaggerated pulling motions. Understanding her at last, he pulled up the kite string and found it was attached to a heavy rope.

Bran tied the rope to the four-poster, then squeezed through the casement and slid down the rope into his wife's arms.

"Darling," she said, "We must flee. The King intends to keep you a prisoner forever."

"But he will pursue us to the ends of the Earth."

"I have a plan to persuade him otherwise," said Maria.

The next day the castle was woken by the sound of wailing at the gates. The guards let in Bran's wife, who demanded to see the King.

"Your Majesty," she cried, holding up a green-stained finger. "My husband has deceived me. The ring that I thought was gold is merely copper."

"That green looks like dye," said the Chancellor.

"The only alchemy my husband knows is summoning the Devil."

"Really?" The King looked interested.

"But anyone who asks for the devil to be summoned has to sell their soul," said Maria hurriedly. "And is condemned to everlasting hellfire."

"Oh."

"Copper will hardly finance an army," said the Chancellor.

"I think it's time to have words with our so-called alchemist," said the King, rising to his feet and heading for the tower.

When they arrived, they found the room empty.

"The Devil must have spirited my husband away," wailed Maria.

"With a rope? Through a broken window?" said the Chancellor.

The King sniffed the sulphureous air. "It smells as if the gates of Hell have opened."

"The man has obviously escaped, sire," said the Chancellor. "I suggest we pursue him."

"To Hell itself," said Maria.

"Er, it hardly seems worthwhile," said the King. "I've decided it will be quicker and easier to raise the money I need by increased taxation."

As for Maria and Bran? The lived happily and wealthily ever after.

An Elemental Story
Will Phosphorus survive to find love again?

Phosphorus took a cloth and pretended to polish the bar. If she craned her neck, she could see the Uranium gang reflected in the restaurant mirror. Uranium, himself, sat at the head of the table, his huge bulk made him a menacing figure. She had been warned to keep well away as he was armed and dangerous.

Beside Uranium were his hard men – Iron, Copper and Nickel. She recognised them from the mug shots at HQ. Gold and Silver were recognisable from their bling and there were others too, that she didn't know. With a chill of fear, she saw that Iron had caught her eye in the mirror. She dropped her gaze and continued polishing.

"What's your name?" His voice was harsh but not unfriendly. She looked up. Iron was standing at the bar appraising her.

She straightened, arching her back so her breasts strained against her low-cut blouse. "Phosphorus, sir."

"I saw you looking at us in the mirror. This is a private meeting and not to be spied on."

"Oh, I wasn't spying, sir," she assured him. "It's just that one so rarely gets nice-looking gentlemen like you in the restaurant."

He grinned, easily flattered. "If you are a good girl and behave yourself, I might look you up after the meeting."

She smiled and fluttered her eyelashes. "Thank you, sir."

He gave her a wink and returned to the others.

The door to the kitchen opened and Sulphur came out carrying a huge tray of antipasto. He grinned at Phosphorus as he passed. She gazed after him. He looked so handsome disguised as a waiter, even now her heart did somersaults when she saw him.

"Can I have a whisky please?" Phosphorus gave a start - she hadn't seen anyone coming. Then she realised that Mercury had oozed onto one of the bar stools.

"Sure," she said, pouring him out a hefty slug.

Sulphur came past on his way back to the kitchen. He caught Phosphorus's eye and gave a shrug. He had hoped to lurk in the shadows and listen to the gang's conversation but they must have dismissed him. Phosphorus glared back at him. They had been an item once but Sulphur had broken away. Being combined with her had taken the excitement out of life. Well, she hoped he was satisfied now - rounding up the Uranium gang was excitement enough for anyone.

It was her turn to take a risk. Phosphorus took an oxygen bomb out from beneath the bar. "I've got a present for you," she said to Mercury.

The unsuspecting metal opened the box. There was a flash and he crumbled into a pile of red crystals.

"What was that flash?" The deep voice of Uranium rumbled round the room.

The kitchen door burst open and Sulphur hurried out with a tray of spaghetti.

"Get help," he yelled. "I'll try and hold them back."

Using his tray as a shield he blocked the advance of the on-coming metals. With one agonised look at his heroic battle, Phosphorus dived behind the bar and pushed the emergency button.

It took long seconds before the door burst open and the alkaline back-up team rushed in, seconds in which Sulphur fought to keep the metals away from where she was hiding. Then all was light and heat and commotion.

When peace returned, Phosphorus emerged from behind the bar. The restaurant was in chaos - tables and chairs were overturned and spaghetti hung in festoons. There was no sign of Uranium, he must have been arrested. But many of his henchmen remained in the restaurant, combined to form harmless compounds.

Phosphorus stared at a green lump lying on the floor half-hidden by a tablecloth. Tears welled into her eyes. Sulphur? She knelt down beside him and stroked his surface. He must have combined with iron.

A kind voice said, "Don't cry, pretty lady, he's not dead. One day his compound will break down and he will live again."

Looking up, she recognised Sodium, a member of the alkaline team. Despite her grief she felt their mutual attraction and allowed him to take her arm and lead her out into the sunshine.

Asexual Harassment
Frank's abused items make an official complaint

There was silence when Frank Fielding entered the office and he knew they had been talking about him again.

He sat at his desk. That was odd, there should have been a pen and a couple of pencils in the holder, someone must have nicked them. He shrugged and picked up the telephone. Dammit, the ruddy thing wasn't working again. He jiggled the connection socket.

"Do you have to abuse your poor telephone like that?" Kate at the desk opposite was glaring at him.

"What?"

"Stroking it, fiddling with its cord, blowing into its mouthpiece, interfering with its socket."

He stared at her pink, outraged face in astonishment. "Are you joking?"

"No, I'm not. I think it's disgusting the way you behave." She looked beyond him and said, "You're in trouble now. Here comes the boss."

Frank looked round and saw Mister Blake beckoning to him. "I'd like a word with you, Mister Fielding."

Frank followed his boss to the glass cubicle that served as his office, trying to think what he had done wrong.

"I don't need to introduce you to the items before you." Mister Blake nodded towards two pencils and a pen lying on his desk.

Frank stared at them. "They look like mine, but I can't be sure. To be honest, they all look the same to me."

"Ah." Mister Blake leant back with a satisfied smile, as if Frank had condemned himself out of his own mouth. "I expect you will say that you don't think these items have feelings."

Frank stared at him. This must be a joke, but his boss showed no signs of humour. "Of course they don't have feelings," he said. "They're only things."

"Items," corrected Mister Blake, shocked by Frank's language. "These items have made serious allegations about the way you've been treating them."

"Allegations?" Frank gawped at him.

"Yes. This pencil here claims you have been licking her point."

"I may have done," shrugged Frank, "but why shouldn't I? I do it to all my pencils."

The pencil gave a little squeak and quivered. "I knew it. I meant nothing to you. I confess that I had feelings for you until I discovered what you did to Audrey."

The other pencil was now quivering. Could this be Audrey? Frank looked at it in dismay.

"He – stuck – my," she gulped as if on the verge of tears. "He stuck my rear end into his ear, then he rubbed me up and down his thigh. It was disgusting, I felt violated."

"I was just getting the wax off," protested Frank. "Why didn't you say something, if you didn't like what I was doing?"

"After what you did to Ruby?" said the first pencil. "We were terrified to talk to you."

Mister Blake leaned forwards. "What happened to Ruby?"

"He broke her in half," said Audrey. "And then – oh God, it's too horrible – he continued to abuse her stump."

"How monstrous! And you didn't stop at pencils, did you Mister Fielding?" said the boss gently pushing the pen forwards.

"I wish to make an official complaint about my treatment by the human employee named Mister Frank Fielding." The pen had been rehearsing its speech. "Not content with holding me more tightly than necessary, he kept clicking my head and stroking my shaft."

"Oh gosh," Frank felt mortified. "I didn't even know I was doing it. It was automatic."

"Shame on you," said the pen.

Frank looked at Mister Blake. "I'm so sorry, I never realised that things – er, I mean items – have feelings. I'll be more careful in future."

"I'm afraid it's too late for that," said Mister Blake. "What about the electrical items? Your telephone is having a nervous breakdown and your computer thinks you have proposed marriage." He stood up, like a judge announcing sentence. "I'm afraid I must ask you to leave our employment, Mister Fielding." Frank turned to the door. "Be careful how you touch the handle, it's extremely sensitive."

Frank wrenched the door open and strode across the office, conscious of his colleagues' curious looks. Then, at last, he was outside in the fresh air, vowing never to work in an office again.

Ballast

A supreme sacrifice had to be made to keep the balloon aloft.

Mitch sat beside his father in the cabin of the helium balloon and knew that his dreams had come true. Sir James Crosby had always been a god-like figure, distant and disapproving, more concerned with building a financial empire than spending time with his family. Mitch might be the smallest and least successful of his sons but now here he was, the chosen one, riding across the sky beside his father.

"This record bid has cost me a small fortune," his father had said. "I'm not sharing the glory with any bloody partner. It needs two to sail this balloon around the World so I'm taking Mitch."

Why Mitch? The question was on everyone's lips.

"Because he's the smallest - the less ballast the better. Besides, he's the least likely member of the family to steal my glory."

Mitch smiled as he remembered how his brothers had envied him. The days spent with his father planning and implementing the project had been the happiest of his life.

But now his father was worried. Mitch looked anxiously at him as he tapped the instrument panel.

"The bloody balloon is sinking." Sir Crosby rose to his feet.

"Get out of my way, blast you."

Mitch scuttled to one side and watched his father climb the ladder that led to the door at the top of the pod.

"Be careful, Father."

They were up high in the jet stream, so high that the air outside their living pod was thin and the temperature well below zero.

Sir Crosby shoved the door open and poked his head out. A blast of icy air whistled round the pod and he hurriedly shut the door again.

"The bloody balloon must have sprung a leak. In another half hour we'll be out of the jet stream."

"Oh dear," quavered Mitch. He was always nervous when his father was angry.

"Oh dear?" The old man mimicked his high-pitched voice. "Is that all you can say? Oh dear? This could be my last chance at the record I tell you, it's a bloody disaster. We must make the load lighter. Throw out the food."

Mitch put on protective clothing, gathered all remaining food into a sack and climbed up the ladder to the top of the pod. With the wind whistling around him, he climbed down to the circular deck on which the pod rested and threw the sack over the railing. It plummeted down and was lost to sight in the whiteness below.

"Now the water," yelled his father. He too had suited up and was looking down from the top of the pod. Mitch undid the water containers, which were strapped to the platform, and threw them over the railing.

His father had disappeared into the pod but now re-emerged with a computer. "We're still sinking. We'll have to get rid of the navigation equipment."

"But…." Mitch tried to protest but his father was like a madman. He kept going into the pod and bringing out more equipment to be thrown overboard.

He joined Mitch at the rail, the glitter of a fanatic in his eyes. "We are still sinking," he said. "We must get rid of more ballast. It only needs one person to land this thing."

Mitch stared at him aghast. "What are you saying?"

"I didn't get where I am without making sacrifices," said his father. "I tell you, the prizes in life go to those who are prepared to surrender the most. Do you agree to make the sacrifice?"

Mitch's stared at him wide-eyed. "Are you sure?"

"Of course I'm bloody sure."

"Please, Father - I don't want to do it." Mitch's reluctance was pitiful.

"Just get on with it."

"But…"

"Oh, for God's sake," said his father, "Get a move on or we'll sink below the jet stream."

Mitch looked at his father with tears in his eyes. He bowed in homage to his martyrdom then grasped him round the legs and threw him overboard. As the balloon shot upwards the rapidly diminishing figure yelled the words that would haunt Mitch for the rest of his life.

"Not me, you idiot!"

Child of an Angel

Heaven is not the place for a teenager

Mena shifted uncomfortably on the cloud, her tail made it awkward to sit. She kept it curled up under her tunic and prayed that her mother wouldn't notice.

The angel, who was her mother, sat beside her, playing a harp and with an expression of serene happiness on her face.

"I'm bored," said Mena.

"Sing Hosanna with me," suggested her mother.

"I'm bored of singing, I'm bored of harp playing, I want a pair of wings."

Her mother sighed. "You know you are only twelve years old, Mena. You can't have wings until you are grown up."

Mena subsided into a sulk. Heaven was so boring, she couldn't believe she once liked it here. The eternal sunshine and happiness got on her nerves and now, even the clouds felt uncomfortable. Her growing tail was not the only thing that worried her. Surreptitiously, she reached up and touched her forehead. The bumps were still there and they were getting bigger. She hoped her hair would hide them.

"Are you feeling all right, darling?"

Before Mena realised what was happening her mother had pressed her hand against her forehead. Mena tried to turn her head away but it was too late, her mother had felt the bumps.

"Oh darling," said her mother, "Why didn't you tell me?" Mena stared at her mother and saw no anger, just a gentle concern. "Are you growing a tail as well?" Mena nodded wordlessly and started to cry.

"Come, come." Her mother took her into her arms, "It's nothing to worry about my child. You are growing up, that's all – you are becoming a teenager. It happens to everyone."

"You mean," sobbed Mena, "that it's natural to grow a tail?"

"And horns," said her mother. "Come, dear, let me have a look at you."

Glowing with embarrassment, Mena lifted the hem of her tunic so her mother could see that the tail reached almost to her knees.

"Oh my, you are a quick developer. You won't want to wear white linen anymore."

Mena wiped away her tears. "I don't understand, are there other clothes?"

"Yes, I have been saving this for when the moment came." Her mother reached deep into the cloud and pulled out a red leotard. "Look it has a hole for your tail so it can swing freely."

"But I can't wear something like this in heaven."

"That's true. It's time for you to visit your father."

Mena hid behind a mound of white, fluffy cloud and changed into her leotard. When she emerged, she saw that the cloud had descended from heaven and was hovering above a rocky desert.

"Will Daddy let me take dance classes?" She had never met her father and wondered if he was as strait-laced as her mother.

"Oh yes, and let you go to parties and hang out with imps and make mischief and do all the things an adolescent has to do."

In front of them the ground split open and a demon climbed out. Mena stared at him in awe. He was magnificently tall and well-muscled. Curling horns sprouted from his head and his skin shone like mahogany.

"Mena, this is your father," said the angel. "You will spend the next few years with him."

The demon grinned and raised a hand in acknowledgement.

"Wow, you've grown quickly. Love the leotard."

From the fissure came a warm glow, clouds of intoxicating smoke and the distant sounds of heavy metal music. Wow, thought Mena. This could be fun. Before she jumped off the cloud into her father's waiting arms, she paused and turned to her mother.

"I will see you again, won't I, Mother?"

"Of course, darling." Her mother bent and gave her a kiss. "You can join me in heaven when you're ready."

"Wait," something was troubling Mena. She looked at her mother, pale and spiritual, then at her father, ruddy and mischievous. "Do you two love each other?" she asked.

"We two are one," said the angel.

"Without each other we could not exist," said the demon and they gave each other a look of such intensity that it lit a fire of happiness in Mena's heart.

Doomed

When dinosaurs become addicted to knowledge apples it will end badly.

Sunrise revealed a vast Cretaceous plain dotted with dinosaurs.

"Ouch my leg's got cramp," complained a hadrosaur. She shifted uncomfortably, taking care not to crush the eggs upon which she was sitting.

"Stand up, dear," said her neighbour, "and try to stretch the muscles – it always works for me."

The first hadrosaur stood up, casting a long shadow on the sandy ground. A tiny oviraptor scuttled towards her, trying to hide in the shadow.

"Watch out," yelled the neighbour. "There's one of those beastly oviraptors. Quick, stamp on it!"

"Where? Ah yes, I see it. There, got you, you bugger." The hadrosaur brought her foot down on the tiny creature, crushing its skull.

"Well done," said the neighbour. They sat in companionable silence while the sun rose higher in the sky.

"Don't look now," said the neighbour, "but there's a gang of velociraptors over there."

The hadrosaur looked. A group of young velociraptors was making its way through the ranks of nesting hadrosaurs. They were small but vicious-looking. Hoodies, some people called them on account of their hooded eyes. They turned towards her.

"Oh no, they are coming this way."

"I told you not to look," said her neighbour.

The leader of the hoodies stopped and indicated the flattened corpse of the oviraptor.

"Hey misses," he said. "Can we have that?" He had a shifty expression and, although he spoke politely enough, he did not look them in the eye.

"Bugger off," said the neighbour.

"Oh, come on," he whined. "It's no good to you – you're a herbivore."

"Herbivore, eh?" mocked the neighbour. "That's a long word for a dinosaur. You've been at those bloody apples again, haven't you?"

The hoodies had not waited for permission, but had grabbed the dead oviraptor and were tearing it to pieces. "Go on get out of here," yelled the neighbour.

"Keep your scales on," said the leader, who had claimed a hind leg and now spoke with his mouth full. "I tell you one thing. If you pile rotting vegetation on top of your eggs it would keep them warm and you wouldn't have to sit on them all the time."

"Rotting vegetation?" The hadrosaur was affronted. "What a cheek. You bugger off the lot of you. Don't you try any of that knowledge nonsense round here."

"Yea right. See you later, shovel-face." The leader gave them an insolent grin and led his gang away.

"Shovel face? Cheeky bugger. What's a shovel?" The hadrosaur twittered with outrage. She saw her daughter picking her way through the colony. "Ooh look, there's Mary." She raised her voice. "Yoo hoo Mary, I'm over here."

Mary passed the gang of hoodies. They greeted her and she gave them a wave, then she hurried towards her mother. She paused when she saw the expression on her mother's face and blushed, the green of her scales becoming a shade of purple.

"What were you doing waving at those dreadful hoodies?" demanded her mother.

"I was just being polite."

"I don't want you to have anything to do with them. They are addicted to knowledge apples, and we all know where that leads. Come and take over the egg sitting while I get a bite to eat."

With much careful shuffling, Mary and her mother changed places.

"Watch out for those oviraptors," said the hadrosaur.

"Actually," said Mary, "I've been thinking. If we build a thorny wall around the nest, it will keep the oviraptors out."

"What?" The hadrosaur looked at her daughter in horror. "You've been eating knowledge apples, haven't you?" Mary tried to shake her head in denial but her mother was adamant. "You've been mixing with those dreadful hoodies and eating apples from the Tree of Knowledge. Oh no, my own daughter." She burst into tears.

Mary frantically tried to comfort her mother. "Oh Mum, please don't cry. I had one tiny apple, just one. I wanted to see what they tasted like. I hated it. I promise you I'm not addicted."

Her mother was inconsolable. "Where is it going to end?" She lifted her tear-stained face heavenward.

High above, a white streak grew across the blue sky. It was the trail of an incoming comet.

Bert's Euthafuneral

Combining euthanasia with a funeral seems like a good idea.

Bert sat propped up in his coffin wearing his best suit and with a lipstick mark on his cheek. He could feel the stickiness on his skin.

"Connie!" he called to his wife, but she was busy greeting his sister.

"Darling, how nice of you to come." Connie spoke in her special, society voice.

His sister answered brusquely "Of course I'd come – I don't approve of this modern craze for euthafunerals but I have a duty to support my brother."

She turned to greet Bert and noticed the lipstick. "Well really," she fussed, as she spat on her handkerchief and wiped off the mark. "Who would wear scarlet lipstick to a funeral?" She peered into the chapel and her eyes lit upon her granddaughter. "Oh, don't tell me it's Laura. Well at least she's turned up. You've got a good send-off here, Bert." Sounds of organ music came from within and his sister hurried to take her place.

"Time to go in, darling," Connie said and gestured to the undertaker, who was standing in the shadows.

Bert's coffin was pushed slowly down the centre of the chapel on a wheeled trolley, while the congregation sang. *"Abide with me, fast falls the eventide…"*

Bert faced the congregation while his wife took her seat in the front row. His gaze traversed the assembly looking for signs of grief. One or two smiled back at him, but nobody was crying. The hymn came to an end and everybody sat down to listen to the priest.

Bert looked at Connie. She was sitting beside his brother. When she caught Bert's eye, she gave an encouraging little smile and dabbed her eyes with her handkerchief. Bert felt disappointed that she was not crying. When she cried her face became red, her eyes swollen and real tears poured out – not just eye-dabbings. She had cried the day he had been diagnosed, especially when the doctor told her she would have to care for him for years as his muscles degenerated.

"The king of love my shepherd is…" The congregation was on its feet again. As the last discordant sounds died away, his brother came to the microphone and told amusing stories about Bert's childhood. His sister followed with a eulogy about how bravely he had faced his final illness. Laura, the budding actress, nearly broke down as she expressed her love for her great uncle. Finally, it was Connie's turn and Bert listened eagerly while she told everyone what a wonderful marriage they had and how much she loved him. She then came over to the coffin, kissed him and said, "Goodbye, darling."

"Do I have to go?" he asked, moved by her devotion.

"Yes," she said firmly, kissed him again and hurried back to her place. Bert's brother put a comforting arm around her and she looked up at him with an expression that stirred a sudden suspicion in Bert.

"And now," said the priest, bringing the microphone to Bert, "for a final word from our dear departing."

Bert looked at the expectant faces turned towards him.

"Thank you all for coming to my euthafuneral," he said. "But I have changed my mind." There was a ripple of nervous laughter then the priest clapped and they all joined in the applause. Very amusing - trust old Bert to end his life with a joke.

Bert tried to continue but the priest took away the microphone and the organ started to play the final hymn. An automatic curtain drew across the chapel screening Bert from the congregation. Behind him he could hear the furnace fire up.

"I'm not joking," he told the undertaker, who was approaching with a syringe. "I really have changed my mind."

"I'm sorry, sir," said the undertaker. "You'd be surprised how many people want to cancel at the last minute. That's why we make you sign a contract." Bert struggled weakly as the undertaker seized his arm and injected the lethal fluid with practised ease.

"Time like an ever-rolling stream bears all its sons away..."

Bert slumped down into his coffin. A door opened in the wall behind him and Bert and his coffin were consigned to the flames.

For Love of Pauline
Graham's dead wife had really got into him.

Graham sat at the dressing table plucking out eyebrow hairs with the aid of his late wife's tweezers. He examined Pauline's photograph through watering eyes. Her eyebrows had been perfect arches. He wished he could make his brows into that shape.

He put down the tweezers and peered into the mirror. His skin was terrible; blotched by broken blood vessels and with pores still open despite numerous face packs.

He reached for the foundation and spread it on thickly. Who would have thought that Pauline would die before him? He should have died first. He was just an aging banker forced to retire early due to stress-related heart problems. She was still a young woman with so much life before her. Graham felt the rage within him and blinked, surprised by the strength of his emotions.

Oh, the pity of it, the waste. She should have been a rich widow, she could have had any man she wanted. Graham was startled by the direction his thoughts were taking.

He applied pink lipstick, then brushed back his hair and tied on a scarf. Now for clothes. He removed his dressing gown and surveyed his nakedness with distaste. He had shaved his legs, his chest and under his arms but hairlessness did not improve the sagging body in the mirror.

He was stuffing socks into his brassiere when there was a ring on the doorbell. Graham waited, reluctant to answer the door in his make-up.

The bell rang again, urgent and demanding. Perhaps it was a registered letter. Graham pulled on his dressing gown and hurried downstairs. The bell had rung a third time before he reached the front door.

Graham opened the door a crack and peered out. His mother-in-law stood upon the doorstep. He had last seen her two weeks ago at the funeral and had hoped never to see the woman again.

With surprising strength, she thrust the door open and sent him reeling into the hall.

"I heard a rumour that something odd was happening," she said, looking him up and down with a frown. "What the hell do you think you're doing?"

"I'm sorry, I don't know what's come over me," he said, feeling himself redden beneath the make-up.

"I wasn't talking to you," she said, rudely, and pushed past him into the living room. He meekly followed and sat in the armchair she indicated. She bent over until her mouth was a few inches from his chest then repeated, in a loud voice "What the hell do you think you're doing?"

Oh God, the old bat is crazy, thought Graham.

She placed a hand over his heart with a firm pressure and said, "I command you to come out." With mounting fear Graham felt himself become hot beneath her touch.

"Oh my God, be careful of my pacemaker!" he yelled and tried to pull away from her. He stopped struggling and stared in terror as a wisp of white smoke emerged from beneath her hand. Miraculously, his heart continued to beat.

"A ghost in the machine, eh?" said his mother-in-law to the smoke. "I thought you might try something like this. You have no right to take over someone else's life. Besides, look at him, he's an absolute sight. Nobody would think that ugly, old fool is you come back to life."

The smoke twisted as if to survey Graham. It turned back and quivered.

"I'm sorry, Pauline," said the old woman, "but you'll just have to accept that you are dead. It happens to us all in the end." The smoke quivered again. "I love you too, my darling," said Pauline's mother, dabbing her eyes with her handkerchief, "but it's time to say goodbye." The smoke lingered, then spread out and disappeared.

The soft look vanished from the woman's face as she turned to Graham, "And as for you, you old fool, go change your clothes and have a bath."

His brain in a whirl, Graham watched the witch, who had been his mother-in-law, march out of the house. All thoughts of Pauline had left his head and, with a sigh of relief, he knew that he could finally move on.

Happy Birthday
Freedom is the greatest gift

The snap of the flap and the sound of letters falling onto the mat alerted Mary that the post had arrived. She opened the door to what once had been the dining room, but was now her bedroom, and peered at the heap of envelopes. With a surge of excitement Mary realised that it must be her birthday! How strange that she had forgotten, but she was forgetting a lot recently.

With trembling fingers, she opened the first envelope. Sure enough there was a card inside. 'Happy Birthday,' it said over a picture of a teddy bear hugging a bottle of champagne. Inside, the writing was scrawled. With rheumy eyes Mary read the message – with much love from Freddie, or was it Fergie?

Who was that? Slowly from the mists of her mind rose the figure of a soldier, smiling at her. Franky - her brother! She thought he had been lost on the beaches of Dunkirk, but here he was sending her a card. Her heart filled with happiness. Dear Frankie, he had not forgotten the happy days of their childhood. She remembered how they would play in the stream and he would build a dam so they could sail a little fleet of paper boats that went whirling downstream when the dam broke.

She opened another card and puzzled over the signature. Mummy? Could her mother be sending her a card? Her mind went back to warmth and cuddles. To fairy cakes and the birthdays of her childhood, full of balloons and gifts and goody bags.

The next card was from Veronica and family. Who was Veronica? Mary puzzled briefly and then went on to open another card. This was a jokey one. "What's it like on the other side of the hill?" was the message, with the picture of a cartoon rabbit. It was from Eve and there were kisses and hearts around her signature. Dear Eve, trust her to pick such a funny card. What jolly times they had enjoyed when they were both young mothers, taking their prams to the park to feed the ducks. For a moment she was back there, with the smell of new mown grass and little Cynthia almost falling out of the pram in her eagerness to throw bread.

There was just one card left. Could it be from him? She opened it eagerly. Tears in her eyes blurred the signature, but slowly it resolved itself into a familiar name – Bill. Her husband had sent her a card! On this magical day anything was possible.

A golden light seemed to fill the hall and he was there – Bill, holding out his arms to her with a loving smile. Her heart felt as if it was bursting. "Wait for me!" she cried as he slowly drifted away towards the light. "I am coming." With a final effort she broke the shackles that bound her to the earth.

Upstairs her daughter Cynthia stirred and stretched. Today was her birthday but she felt depressed. She had expected to spend her retirement enjoying a well-earned time of leisure and pleasure with her many friends. Instead, she was obliged to look after a mother who was descending rapidly into dementia. She turned her head and looked at the clock. Eight o'clock. There was no chance of a lie-in, she had to get her mother's breakfast before she started trying to fry bacon. Cynthia groaned. The fire-engine had to be summoned the last time her mother did any cooking.

Cynthia got out of bed and went to the top of the stairs. Her mother was lying prostrate upon a pile of opened envelopes and discarded cards. A moment of annoyance turned to concern and she rushed down the stairs.

"Mother? Are you all right?" She turned her mother over and saw the happy smile upon her face. "Mother, wake up!" She kissed her, but her mother's pale cheek was growing cold. Frantically Cynthia felt for a pulse, but there was nothing.

Even as tears filled Cynthia's eyes, she felt a sense of relief, as if a burden had been lifted. She kissed her mother's cheek again and silently thanked her for the gift of freedom.

I'm Going to Live Forever
When death means glory

Jet could hear the fans in the distance, screaming for him like a pack of wolves. He plastered greasepaint under his eyes. How much longer could he keep up this farcical lifestyle? He knew the answer – until he had paid off his debt to that vulture of a manager, Bobby Sachs.

Cocaine, a corrupt accountant and a hedonist lifestyle had forced him to borrow money from the ever-willing Bobby. When he had tried to sack the bastard, he had waved those chits in his face and told him that now he, Bobby, played the tunes. Jet pulled on the tight black leather trousers that doubled as a corset. With Bobby in charge, he would be forced to perform forever.

He was struck with a sudden thought. Supposing he sang out of key and stopped the hip grinding? Then Bobby would no longer be able to sell enough tickets to keep him on the road.

Bobby poked his head round the door. "They're waiting for you, Jet, get your ass out there."

Perhaps he would do it tonight, thought Jet as he pushed past his manager and walked onto the stage.

"Jet! Jet! Jet!" The fans adored him.

The backing band started to play the opening chords of his greatest hit. "I'm going to live forever." It was no use, he could not let the screaming hoards down. He flung his arms wide and the people roared their appreciation.

Jet took a deep breath and approached the microphone. He noticed exposed wires where the lead entered the handle - the bloody thing was unsafe. He remembered Bobby's words. "Soon you will be worth more to me dead than alive."

Jet's palms began to sweat. If he died now, on stage, he would become a legend. Did he really want to live forever? The moment to seize the microphone was in a few bars. It was time for a decision.

In the Care Home
Kept alive by pills

Shirley looked around the lounge of the old people's home. It was her first day as a carer and all eyes turned towards her.

"Hello," she said brightly.

"Hello, dear."

"What did she say?" They nodded and smiled and, encouraged, she pushed the refreshment trolley into the room.

"Would you like tea or coffee?" she asked the first old lady.

"Coffee dear, please. What did you say your name was?"

"Shirley."

"What a nice name, my sister had a parrot called Shirley. We used to call it Shirley Not."

Her hands shook as she laughed and coffee spilt into the saucer. Shirley laughed dutifully and carried on. Behind her the pill trolley entered. It was pushed by a qualified nurse, a severe woman, who always dressed in uniform. Shirley hurried to give out the refreshments before the pill trolley caught up with her.

"Are you married, dear?" The geriatrics were anxious to chat and she had to cut off the conversations abruptly. Behind her the nurse dished out pills in silence.

"Aaaargh!" An old men rose to his feet, clutched his throat and crashed to the ground. Abandoning her trolley, Shirley rushed to his side and tried feeling for a pulse.

The nurse loomed over her. "What are you doing?"

"I'm feeling for his pulse!" stammered Shirley.

"Of course he doesn't have a pulse. None of them do."

"You mean they're all dead?" A chill ran down Shirley's spine.

"Of course not. They're kept alive by pills."

"But – why?"

"My dear girl. You don't think we're going to let our residents die, do you? Not until their money runs out!"

She leant down and, slipped a pill into the old man's mouth. He swallowed it convulsively then his eyes opened. For a moment he seemed blank, then he smiled. "Thank you, dear. I don't know what came over me." He winked at Shirley. "It's not often I get so close to a pretty girl."

He was cold to the touch and Shirley flinched as she helped him back into his chair. Then she continued to dole out coffee and tea.

In the Gorilla Enclosure
An unlikely hero fails miserably.

George hurried down the dark corridor, his wife, Muriel, in tow.

"I'm sure this isn't the way to the tea room," she said.

George rounded upon her. After being hounded by his class, despised by the head master and treated with contempt by the other teachers, the last thing he wanted was Muriel to question his authority.

"Must you criticise everything I do?"

George flung open the door at of the corridor and stepped out into a garden. He had gone several paces before he saw that the lawns and bushes were surrounded by a high wall – a very high wall and George could see the heads of people peering down from the top of it.

He turned and saw Muriel staring out of the doorway, a terrified expression on her face. George followed her gaze and saw a gorilla making a beeline for the door. He dived into the nearest bush and heard the door slam shut.

The gorilla who had made the escape bid passed him, looking disconsolate. She did not notice him and headed for a group of gorillas who sat beside the wall. George felt his pounding heart subside and checked that he hadn't peed himself in his terror. He was settling down to await rescue by the keepers when he heard a scream.

"My baby!"

He looked out of the bush in time to see a pink bundle fall to the ground close to the gorillas. The crowd of onlookers was abuzz with horror at the ghastly sight of the gorillas advancing on the helpless infant.

"Save my baby!" cried the woman. Not bloody likely, thought George.

The first gorilla to reach the child studied it intently, then prodded it with a gentle finger. Her companions showed a similar mild curiosity and then the group wandered off. Well, thought George. These are obviously not wild gorillas but tame captive-bred creatures.

He stood up and emerged from behind his bush. The people cheered. He strode forward, head high and chest expanded. The cheering increased.

"Isn't that old Georgy Porgy?" he heard someone say. He looked up and saw a couple of kids from the school. He wondered whether to wave but decided that might spoil his heroic image. Instead, he bent down and picked the baby up. It opened its eyes and smiled at him.

"She's okay," he called up. There were flashes of cameras. This will look good in the papers tomorrow, thought George, and held the baby aloft so all could see.

Someone threw down a rope. For a brief moment George thought of discarding the baby and climbing to safety, then he remembered he was playing the hero. He tied the baby securely to the rope and gave an expansive gesture to reel the tiny thing up.

There were cheers and more photos. George preened himself. He might have been in the wrong place but he had certainly got there at the right time. Then the cheering died away and people started pointing behind George.

He turned and saw a huge silverback gorilla knuckle-walking towards him. The enormous beast stood upright and beat its chest.

"The rope, the rope," the crowd were shouting.

George turned to where the rope had been lowered. A female gorilla was sitting close to it. She reached out a hand, gave a yank and the rope slithered to the ground.

George felt his knees weaken and his bladder give way, all pretence at heroism disappeared. Where the hell were the keepers? He knelt sobbing on the ground, aware of the cameras still clicking. At any moment he feared that massive teeth would sink into his neck, that huge arms would tear him to pieces. When, finally, he felt a tap on the shoulder he screamed like a girl.

"Come on, pull yourself together," said the keeper. "The gorillas are in their quarters, it's time to get you out."

George staggered after the keepers, unable to look back at the jeering crowd. He would never dare show his face in school again. It was the end of his teaching career. George brightened, perhaps there was a silver lining after all.

Jack Gunner

Who better than a private eye to rid the world of whores and sinners?

They call me a psychopath and they aren't wrong - I did a lot of bad things back then. Jack Gunner is my name, not my real name, of course. They call me Jack because I play a useful hand of poker and Gunner because... well I don't have to spell it out.

It was in jail that I found God. At first, he was just a useful way of getting parole, but after that he took over my life. I'm one of his angels now. It's my duty to fight crime and stamp on the face of evil. Which is why, on the third of June, I was screwing a brass sign to the door of a low-rent office. Jack Gunner. Private Detective.

"A detective, eh? Just what I've been looking for." I turned to see a fine-looking broad. "I suspect my no-good husband is having an affair and I want him followed."

I was about to invite her into my office then remembered I had no furniture. The sign had taken all my spare cash. "Where can I find this husband of yours?" I asked.

"Right there." She pointed at the door opposite. Upon it was a laminated sign that read Sam Samsonite. Importer of fine jewellery. "I came to get money off him to buy a new hat and the bastard wasn't there. I bet he's off shagging some woman and I want you to find out who."

"Fifteen pounds an hour," I said.

She blinked and then fluttered her eyelashes. "I was hoping you might do it for nothing," she said. "It's only a small job."

"I wouldn't work for my mother for nothing," I said, which is true, I wouldn't even recognise the bitch.

She sighed. "Very well. When you bring me the evidence, I can divorce the bastard and take him for all he's got. Then I will pay you."

She wrote her address on a piece of paper and we shook hands on the deal. I watched her walk down the corridor. Her bum sashayed in that little tight dress until even an angel like me had lascivious thoughts. When she had gone, I knocked on Sam Samsonite's door.

"It is safe to come out," I said. He opened the door a crack and peered up at me. "Let me introduce myself. I'm Jack Gunner – your new neighbour." I nodded across the corridor at the shiny brass sign.

He squinted at it. "Private detective? Has that gold-digging wife of mine hired you?"

"Yea, in a way. She can't pay me until she divorces you so I'm under no obligation."

"The bitch. One way or another she'll be the ruin of me."

"Too bad." I felt sorry for the little runt but he should have had more sense. What would a woman like that see in a man like him? Money, that's all. Some women are prostitutes under a different name. I was turning away when he grabbed my sleeve.

"In God's name, Jack. Will you help me? Get rid of her for me. I don't care how."

"Do you mean murder her?"

"Yes, no, I don't know. Is there any other way? I will pay well."

I made my mind up there and then. It's my duty to stamp out evil and this man was clearly in the grip of the devil.

"Okay," I said. I took out my gun and screwed in the silencer. He watched me curiously, unaware of my intention then – bang – it was all over. I dragged his body into the office and looked around. There was a safe set into the wall. I almost laughed at how easy it was to crack open.

Inside were packets of jewellery. He promised to pay me in advance for getting rid of his wife so I took my wages and no more. Then I crossed over the corridor and unscrewed my sign. I would have to find another office but God had provided me with the wherewithal. I might even be able to afford a desk.

I took the piece of paper out of my pocket and looked at her address. BANG, a sinner, BANG, a whore, God's work had only just begun.

Kismet by Moonlight

There is more than one kind of hunger

Kiya woke slowly, her limbs aching from the hardness of the floor. She was still in the temple. Down the avenue of pillars she could see moonlit gardens. She got to her feet, her head spinning. What had happened to her? Had she been drugged? No dancing girl should be in the temple after dark.

She shivered, her flimsy tunic scant protection against the night chill. She should be at home, looking at the stars from her warm bed on the roof-terrace. Her family would worry when she didn't return for there were rumours of dark mysteries where the worlds of gods and mortals touch.

She was drawn to the temple gardens and saw a man at the far end of the lake. He had been gazing into the water but, as she moved to try to hide from him, he looked up. To her relief, she saw that he was wearing the jackal-head mask of Anubis. He must be one of the mummification priests. He had no more right to be beside the sacred lake than she had. He walked towards her, moving with catlike grace.

When he got near, he smiled and said, "Don't be afraid."

Suddenly Kiya was very afraid, for when he smiled, the thin, black lips of the mask curled. The man was wearing no mask – he was Anubis himself. She fell to the ground and said, "My Lord, forgive me."

"Forgive you? For what?"

"For being here, by the lake, after dark."

"You have every right to be here, my child. You are the chosen one."

"The chosen one?"

"Yes, you have been chosen to be my companion for this special night. But a poor companion you will be, if you remain lying on the ground. Come, child, you are shivering. Let me help you up."

She scrambled to her feet, but her legs were weak and she nearly fell. His strong arm slid round her waist to support her.

"You are beautiful," he said and she could feel his breath against her cheek.

"So are you," she whispered.

He laughed, and kept his arm around her. "Come, let us walk around the lake."

She was vividly conscious of being so close to a god, of feeling his strength and warmth, of smelling the honeyed scent of his body. As they walked, he told her of such wonders that she became absorbed by his story. His low, melodious voice wove a spell around her and she wished the night would last forever.

"We immortal gods need sacrificial meat to stay alive. but we have pity for our prey and never take what isn't freely given."

"It must be wonderful," she sighed, "to be a god."

"No." His voice was low and sad. "Never wish to be immortal, pretty dancing girl. Your life may be as short as a lotus blossom, but it is full of love and beauty. My life is grey, an endless road that leads from nowhere to nowhere."

A chill wind blew in from the desert. She shivered and pressed against him, warmed by the marvellous heat of his body.

"Have you never felt love?" she said, feeling herself blush.

He laughed, a rich throaty laugh that made her blush deepen. "I feel something like love tonight," he said. "I feel a hunger for you, little dancing girl. Will you give yourself to me willingly? It will hurt but for a moment."

"Yes," she breathed. She understood, at last, what he had been telling her. He needed her, not as a man needs a woman but as hunger needs sustenance.

Gently he tilted her head back and stroked her neck with sensitive fingers, feeling for her pulse.

Almost in a trance, she heard the distant sound of shouting. Kiya turned and saw a ladder down which men were scrambling.

"Let her go, you monster." She recognised the rough voice of her father, and behind him were the men of her village. For a moment Anubis crouched as if ready to do battle.

"No, my Lord, you will be killed," cried Kiya.

He gave her an unfathomable look. Rage? Love? Grief? For years she remembered and was tormented by being unable to read the expression on his jackal face. Then he turned and dived into the lake.

Levitation Day

Om moves in mysterious ways

The High Lama looked around the dining room with satisfaction. It was full of visitors sitting at trestle tables enjoying lunch – onion and lentil stew with wholemeal bread. Donations should more than cover the cost of the simple meal. The strident voice of Millicent de Vere rose above the murmuring throng.

"Levitation? After a lunch like this it will be easy – we will all be jet propelled, won't we Berky dear."

Lord Berk-Withers, who was sitting beside her, brayed with laughter. Then he shot a nervous look at the High Lama, who smiled beatifically pretending he hadn't heard.

Behind his serene countenance the High Lama was worried. Lord Berk-Withers, though feeble of intellect, was a devoted disciple and had allowed the Order of the Great Om to take over his stately home. Without his patronage the future prospects were rocky indeed.

His sister Millicent was speaking again. "I tried it once. You just get in a lotus position and bounce about on a mattress – marvellous for toning the thighs and buttocks. Don't you agree, Berky?"

The High Lama strained to hear his disciple's reply. "One does get a floating sensation and a wonderful feeling of ecstasy."

"My dear," said his ghastly companion. "If you go bouncing around on your genitalia you are bound to get a feeling of ecstasy."

It was too much. The High Lama gathered his saffron robes around him and rose to his feet bringing lunch to an abrupt halt.

It was a glorious, sunny afternoon and the High Lama watched his visitors being led through a session of tai chi on the lawn. In the distance was the stable block, which had been converted to a levitation room. Bouncing on the mattress-covered floor was going to be the grand finale of the open day.

Tai chi ended and the visitors were herded into the levitation room. They sat on the mattresses in various approximations of the lotus position and stared at him expectantly.

"Ommmm," he said, lowering his head over clasped hands.

"Ommmm," they repeated. He glanced at Millicent, who was about to have the giggles.

Closing his mind to all else he tried to reach the state of bliss that would enable him to start bouncing. But he was too stressed. His mind wandered down strange pathways until, all of a sudden, he managed to reverse his gravitational polarity.

He wondered if he was about to have a stroke when he heard a gasp and opened his eyes. The visitors were staring at him in awe. Even Millicent was gaping like a fish.

With a start he realised he was floating. He struggled to maintain a serene expression despite his astonishment. Up and up he went until his head was brushing the ceiling.

He looked down and saw astonished faces staring up at him. He hurriedly rearranged his robes. Even in levitation he clung to his dignity.

A draught sent him bumping across the ceiling. This was becoming ridiculous. He tried to reverse the levitation, to return to the ground but to no avail, he couldn't for the life of him remember what he had done to achieve this miracle.

His disciples recognised the danger before he did. He saw them pointing up at the ceiling and shouting words of warning. What was wrong? Then he saw the open skylight, he was bumping inexorably towards it. Desperately he flailed his arms but he could not change direction. He tried to grab at the sides of the skylight as he passed through but his sweating hands slipped on the polished wood. He went through the skylight and rose upwards into the open air.

His stunned audience rushed outside to see him rise slowly into the sky, wailing pitifully, all attempts at dignity abandoned.

At last, he disappeared into a puffy white cloud and was never seen again.

Lord Berk-Withers, the new High Lama, built a magnificent memorial to the founder. All his doubting friends were converted by the miracle and he bequeathed his stately home to the Order of the Great Om in perpetuity. Truly, Om moves in mysterious ways.

Miss MacTavish Meets the Devil
Hell is preferable to a geriatric ward

Old Miss MacTavish sat on her garden lounger in her nighty and watched the stars come out. The chill of winter made Miss MacTavish shiver and she took a sip of whisky. She rarely drank but tonight was an exception, it was the last night of her life.

Miss MacTavish did not feel sorry, she did not feel anything much. She despised emotion and prided herself on a life ruled by logic. For example, she supported euthanasia. "Why should the NHS use half its resources to prolong the life of old people?" This last belief was put to the test when Miss MacTavish, herself, became old and ill. But because she was also depressed, lonely and impoverished it was not hard for her to put her beliefs into practice.

As the temperature dropped, Miss MacTavish lay back and let the glass fall from her hand. It was Waterford crystal but what did that matter? Nothing mattered any more. Miss MacTavish closed her eyes and embraced the darkness.

She woke to light and noise. Bells were ringing, people were moaning and a harsh strip-light shone down from the ceiling. She was lying in bed, surrounded by curtains. There was a smell of urine in the air and she hoped it didn't come from her. She could see the shadows of two people behind the curtains.

"The silly old bat got drunk and fell asleep in the garden." They were talking about her. Miss MacTavish opened her mouth to protest but couldn't find the energy to speak and lapsed into unconsciousness once more.

When she woke a second time, the curtains were drawn back and she could see that she was in a hospital ward. Rows of beds stretched away on either side. Old people lay in the beds, lolled on bedside chairs or shuffled up and down the ward aimlessly. The sound of crazy babbling, moaning and ringing bells filled the air with a cacophony of sounds.

The two nurses in charge of the ward ignored the summonses of the ringing bells and flashing lights, they were trying to subdue an old man who was screaming obscenities. He was injected in the arm and fell unconscious. The nurses turned, saw that Miss MacTavish was awake and came down the ward.

"Hello dear, have you woken up then?"

"Where am I?" she quavered.

"In the geriatric ward at Eastlands hospital."

"When can I go home?"

"Home? Oh no dear, you can't go home. Here comes the doctor, he will tell you."

Miss MacTavish looked round and saw a young man in a grubby, white jacket.

"You're a lucky woman, Miss MacTavish," he said, reading her name from a label at the bottom of the bed. "You were in intensive care for days. Unfortunately, your heart stopped and your brain was damaged." As he talked, Miss MacTavish stared at him, wondering where he was from. He had a hooked nose, reddish skin and a mass of black hair – obviously not British. "As a result," he continued, "you will have to stay here for the rest of your life."

His word mingled with the moaning, and the bells, and the screaming. The person screaming the loudest was Miss MacTavish.

The doctor lifted his hand and removed his hair. Miss MacTavish stopped screaming and stared in amazement. The man had been wearing a wig. Underneath, he was bald and had a pair of horns.

"Just joking," he cackled. "You're in Hell."

Miss MacTavish gazed up at him. "Really?" she said. "You mean I died after all?"

The nurses had become little black imps. Beyond them the walls of the ward had disappeared to reveal a volcanic wasteland. Where the beds had been, were now pools of lava. The geriatric moans were the cries of the damned. Miss MacTavish surveyed Hell with the relief that only one who thought they had been condemned to a geriatric ward would understand. With her heart full of joy, she whipped off her nighty and danced wildly down between the flaming pools. Just one question troubled her logical mind. If she was no longer in hospital - why were the bells still ringing?

Mrs Plum

A music hall recitation. Mrs Plum telephones the butcher

Hello, hello, is that Mr Jones the butcher? It's Mrs Plume here. Spelt PLUM.

No not Plum – Plume. We are from Norman Stock you know.

Stock cubes? No, I don't want stock cubes. I want gravy browning. You know – browning for gravy. Well, it isn't for gravy actually it's for my legs. It must be the right shade to match my outfit.

Yes, I know gravy browning is brown it's the hue I am worried about.

You? Why should I be worried about you? I have worries enough of my own. There is a war on you know and my daughter Anthea is getting married this Saturday. Which reminds me. I need a dozen carrots for the cake.

Oh, the cake is going to be magnificent, a real centrepiece. Three tiers with pillars. Pink and white icing and little silver bells. It's made of plaster, you know. My cousin used it last month for her daughter's wedding. Unfortunately, she forgot to tell the bride and by the time she had finished trying to cut it she had damaged the knife her wrist and the plaster quite severely. But it's all right, the cake patched up nicely and I have told my daughter when the time comes to just lift it up and there will be my carrot cake.

Anti-climax? I don't think so, Mr Jones. Carrot cake is delicious and good for you and with any luck will help my daughter see in the dark. So important on one's wedding night, don't you think?

Yes, well. I don't want Anthea missing the bed and falling over the balcony. A big girl my Anthea – she could do no end of damage. Oh, but she looks lovely in her wedding dress. We have made it out of a parachute.

What's that? Any silk left over. My dear Mr Jones we were lucky to get a parachute big enough. Which reminds me, I am going to need some pins, we are having awful trouble getting the hem straight where all those strings were attached.

Shoelaces? Yes, I suppose you can have the strings for shoelaces. Really, I don't know what the world is coming to. You'll be wanting my guts for garters next.

What's that? No, Mr Jones I was joking.

I am sure you are busy we are all busy. There is a war on. Hello? Hello? Drat it the man has rung off.

The Escalator to Heaven
An unwelcome companion means a change of direction.

I stand on the escalator to heaven, with Molly by my side**.** Two souls, gliding up through the mist. Molly is a miserable looking woman aged about fifty. I am curious what cut short her life.

"How did you die, Molly?" I ask and I wonder how I know her name.

"I committed suicide," she replies. I am shocked. Surely such a deed would condemn her to hell. I try to take a few steps upwards to distance myself from her, but she stays by my side and continues to talk. "Something happened in my childhood that traumatised me. I was never able to form a proper relationship. I tried to hold down a job but I had a nervous breakdown and have been alone and destitute ever since."

"Hard luck," I mumble and list her faults in my head. Frigid, inadequate, pathetic, victimised. Are those sins? I wonder and hope this woman's path and mine would soon diverge.

"I'm glad you still remember my name," she says.

I stare at her. "Did I know you?"

"We were next door neighbours, many years ago. You were a man and I was a little girl."

"I don't remember," I say and I speak the truth, my memory was always bad, even before dementia. The escalator continues its steady glide upwards, mist swirls and far ahead of us I can see a golden tower, and then another, between them is a gate - the gate to heaven. Thank the Lord the journey is nearly ended.

"You gave me sweets," her voice is soft and persistent. "I thought you were my friend."

"I am a generous man," I say and it is true, I have always been the first to buy a round of drinks in the pub.

"You invited me into your house." I have a flashback then.

"No, I didn't." I am a kind, generous, man. I am on my way to heaven, where I deserve to be.

"Are you sorry for what you did?"

"Shut up!" Will nothing silence this dreadful woman? I give her a shove and she tumbles into the mist. Oh no! I look upwards at the approaching gates. What a terrible accident. I tried to save her. Honestly, I am a good man.

The escalator carries me to the top and then stops. I try to step off it but I cannot. The gates of heaven remain closed.

"Let me in!" I cry.

An angel emerges from one of the towers. Behind him comes Molly. I gape at her in astonishment. The angel puts his arm around Molly's shoulders and she is transformed by a glowing happiness. Together they stand and watch as the escalator carries me downwards.

Pearl
The living know only the living

When Pearl killed herself, her soul went into limbo - a nothingness world of shadows and regret. She yearned for her husband and two small children but she could not reach them for the mists are thick between the living and the dead.

On Halloween, the night of the dead, the mists become thin and she found she could push through the veil.

Her soul had not moved from the spot where she had died. There was the living room, where she had taken the fatal mixture of sleeping pills and alcohol. There was the sofa where she had lain, waiting for Roger to come home and find her. But he had stayed out late, and she waited in vain. As the hours passed, she had fallen deeper and deeper into a sleep of death.

Roger was home now, he was sitting in an armchair, his eyes closed, listening to the mournful sound of one of his classical records. How he must miss her. They had been everything to each other - first school friends, then lovers, then newlyweds then teenage parents. He had worked long hours to support his little family, while she had struggled to cope with the demands of motherhood. She kissed him, her lips hovering on his skin, trying to feel his warmth.

They had agreed that they would only have two children but she had grown careless and had become pregnant again. She waited for months, afraid to let him know. Then, in her foolishness, she had pretended to commit suicide so he would feel sorry for her and would not be angry when she told him.

"Oh darling," she breathed. "I'm so sorry I abandoned you and the children. I miss you so much. Do you miss me? Are you lonely? I fear you cannot manage without me."

The front door opened. "Hello darling." A woman's cheerful voice brought Roger to his feet.

The two children came running into the room.

"Look, Daddy, we've got lots and lots of sweets and some money." They were jumping up and down, both talking at once as they described their Trick-or-Treat adventures. Pearl tried to move close to her children but she was whirled away by their energy.

She was disconcerted by their happiness. "Do you not miss me, my darlings?" she sighed. "I miss you, I love you." But her voice was inaudible, for the living know only the living.

Time had passed. But how could her children forget her? She had waited in limbo, unable to leave them behind. She looked at Roger and Helga. They were in each other's arms, kissing. Roger had found love again and a new mother for the children.

Pearl felt sadness and then she understood that there can be no continuity between the dead and the living. Death, like a pebble, might cause a ripple in the stream but soon no trace is left, memory fades, and the stream flows on.

There was nothing in the world for her now. But where should her soul go? She felt herself being drawn back to limbo, but she was no longer content to stay in nothingness wallowing in regret. The mists swirled around her and in the distance she saw a point of light. She drifted towards it and, as it grew larger, she saw it was a gateway to heaven. There, in the golden light was the soul of her unborn child.

He held out his arms. "I've been waiting for you."

She stared at him in astonishment and then blurted out, "I had forgotten all about you."

He smiled gently. "Do I mean so little to you?"

She hurried towards the child who had been as close to her as life itself when he grew within her womb. Grief overwhelmed her. "I let you die," she sobbed.

"But first you created me and now, at last we are together," said the soul of the child.

As Pearl gathered him into her arms, he kissed her on the cheek and she knew she was forgiven. Hand in hand, the two souls walked across the sunny pastures of heaven, leaving the cares of the world far behind them.

Pillage of the Seasons
The world is plunged into eternal winter

In the middle of the eternal forest was a cottage in which lived Mother Nature and her four daughters. Above the trees black clouds were massing, there was going to be a storm.

"Spring, Spring!" Mother called to her youngest child. "Come in, it's going to rain."

A nearby bush rustled and Spring looked over the top. "Can I bring the satyr with me?"

"No, of course you can't."

A young man emerged from the bush and, avoiding Mother's eye, galloped into the forest as fast as his goat legs would carry him.

Spring looked up to the thunderous sky, gave a squeak and rushed into the house.

Inside was warmth and light. Summer took a cake out of the oven and a delicious smell filled the air.

"Give us a slice," said Autumn. She was a buxom woman and hugely pregnant. Russet curls tumbled over her shoulders. By contrast, Summer was a slender blonde, her shining hair tied into a chignon. She cut a large slice of the golden cake for her sister.

"Leave some for me," complained Winter from her seat by the empty grate. She turned a gaunt, white face to her mother. "Autumn never leaves me anything."

Mother shook her head sadly. All the food they had would not save Winter. Soon she would be dead. But a new baby would be born out of Autumn's bounty and the cycle would continue.

The howl of the wind brought her out of her reverie. "Quickly, my daughters, we must secure the cottage." Spurred by the sound of the approaching storm, the three younger seasons leapt to the task of closing shutters, while Mother Nature bolted the door.

The storm hit, shaking the cottage, thunder rolled and rain beat upon the roof. Above the noise came the shattering crash of a something hitting the door. With a chill of fear Mother realised that the black clouds hid a terrible foe.

Another crash and the door splintered open.

Out in the darkness was a man on horseback. He spurred his steed forwards into the cottage. His face was pale and covered in sores.

"Pestilence," gasped Mother, in dreadful recognition of the first Horseman of the Apocalypse. The rider stared at the sisters, who were screaming in panic and trying to hide behind the upturned table.

With a snarl of triumph he seized Summer, the most beautiful of the seasons. She struggled to escape but he was strong and locked her tightly against his chest, before turning his horse and riding out into the storm.

A second horseman entered and Mother saw that it was War. His nostrils flared and his eyes shone with the lust of battle. He scooped up Spring, who nestled against him as if welcoming his embrace, and then he turned the horse and rode away.

The third horseman was Famine. He was cadaverously thin and rode a horse, which showed every rib. Famine licked greedy lips when he saw Autumn and lifted her onto his saddle, as though she were as light as thistledown.

"Save me, Mother, save me," pleaded Autumn, but Mother Nature was powerless against the might of the riders.

A fourth horseman now entered and he was the most dreadful of all. His face was a skull and he sat upon the animated skeleton of a horse. Death smiled at Winter and Winter smiled back, for hers is the season of dying and she is therefore Death's ally. Without a word, Death wheeled his horse around and rode away.

Mother rushed outside and saw Death gallop after his retreating brothers. There was silence. A shaft of sunlight pierced the gloom and lit the body of the satyr. The foolish creature had tried to stop the attack. Gently, Mother carried him into the cottage.

Winter stretched. "I'm feeling much better," she said. "I think I might live after all." She rose to her feet and helped herself to a slice of cake. "Indeed, without my sisters, I could live forever."

Mother Nature bowed her head over the dying satyr. Would her daughters ever be returned to her? She knew that Winter's reign would last for a long, long time.

Pupil Power
Nursery rhymes are ancient spells of great power.

Eric was on playground duty when Dolly Deyton's knickers caught fire. Despite being only eight years old, the resourceful child rushed to the eco-pond and sat in the water, squealing. The other children, who moments before had been chanting, "Liar, liar pants on fire!" at her, crowded around. Eric was helping Dolly from the pond when the headmistress arrived.

"What's all that noise?"

"Dolly Deyton's knickers caught fire," said Eric.

The headmistress turned upon the shivering child. "Were you smoking again, Dolly?"

"Naa, honest, Ma'm."

"Hmmmm." The headmistress took hold of Dolly's hand. "Come on, let's get you to matron, then we must find you some spare underwear."

She strode back indoors, with her usual vigour, while poor Dolly had to run to keep up with her, the charred remains of her knickers dangling around her knees.

The next day, the headmistress summoned Eric to her room. "Something strange is happening in the playground."

"Something strange?"

"Yes!" A flicker of irritation crossed her face. "Don't you think it strange that what the children chant actually takes place? Look what happened last week, when they sang Tell-Tale Tit at Sally Blake? Her tongue started to bleed and all the neighbourhood dogs tried to get into the playground."

Eric nodded, that had been strange. "I thought we agreed that she had bitten her tongue."

"That's what we told her parents, Mister Nielsen, but you don't really believe that do you? There's something supernatural going on. Our school has become home to a pooka, a cuichaun, a mischievous fairy."

"A fairy?"

"Surely you have such things where you come from – Sweden, isn't it?"

"Norway," he corrected her. "We have stories about Loki, but he was a god, not a fairy."

"Gods, fairies, what does it matter? They're all the same," she said with an impatient wave of the hand.

Eric was outraged. How dare the ignorant woman compare a god to a fairy? He opened his mouth to protest, but shut it again. He didn't want to antagonise her, jobs were scarce and he enjoyed teaching at the school.

Over the next few days, the children chanted their rhymes with increased enthusiasm.

"Cowardy, cowardy custard, dip your face in mustard."

The victim was an innocuous child, called Sid, but the sight of his mustard-covered face was so amusing that Eric joined in the laughter. Unfortunately, the mustard got into Sid's eyes, and he rushed to the cloakroom screaming in pain, narrowly missing the headmistress.

Eric was called to her study. "Well, Mr Neilson are you any nearer to identifying the perpetrator?" Eric shook his head. "Too bad. if we can't stop the pooka, we must stop the chanting."

"You want to forbid the children to say nursery rhymes?"

"I do indeed," she said. "Some of those childish rhymes are ancient spells of great power. In future we'll ban all chanting in the playground."

A week later the children were in the playground chanting a rhyme of Eric's own devising.

> "Rabbits skip and donkeys prance,
> Teacher, teach us how to dance.
> First your heel and then your toe
> Lift your skirt and round you go."

The headmistress came rushing out of the building. "Mr Nielsen, I thought I had made the position clear. Will you please ensure that there is no chanting in the playground?"

She came to a halt and started doing heel-toe dance steps. "What's going on?" She stared at her moving feet and then raised her head. Her eyes met Eric's and he could see her sudden suspicion. "Stop this at once!" she bellowed.

She lifted her skirts, revealing black stockings and long pink bloomers. Round and round she twirled, accompanied by the laughter and clapping of the children.

Eric waited until she was panting with exhaustion, her hair dishevelled and her face red and sweating. Then he hurried away and the spell was broken.

He hid behind the bike shed. Another of his adventures had ended badly. Still, the memory of the headmistress capering would brighten the long Norwegian nights.

With a magical wave of his hand, he said goodbye to the mortal world, transformed himself back into the god Loki, and headed home to Valhalla.

Riding the Jellyfish

Can Chai escape from the research department of the Kore Kudasai toy factory?

Chai bent over his workbench and soldered a final layer of metal to a disc the size of a dinner plate. This could be his best invention yet.

A shadow fell across the bench. Chai looked up and saw Supervisor Wontai frowning down at him.

"You're wasting your time on this one, Chai," said Wontai.

"But Mister Wontai, sir, when the disc is set spinning, it will heat up and its five different metals will expand to make it spin indefinitely."

"It'll never work," said the supervisor. "Tomorrow I want you to start on a new project."

Wontai moved to the next bench leaving Chai to stare forlornly at his disc. He picked it up - it felt perfectly balanced. Clearing a space on his worktop, he stood the disc on edge and spun it.

After a few seconds the disc rose into the air. Up and up it went until it bumped against the ceiling. *Bump, bump.*

"Get it down you fool" yelled Wontai. But even when he climbed on the bench Chai couldn't reach it.

The janitor arrived with a step ladder. He climbed the steps, seized the disc and was pulled from his ladder, which toppled to the floor leaving him hanging, rotating in the air.

There was chaos in the research department as people rushed to shout advice at the terrified janitor.

Mister Yamamoto, the managing director, entered the room just as the exhausted janitor crashed to the floor. The MD ignored him and turned to Chai. "I see that you are responsible for another fiasco." He spat the word out then turned to the crowd. "This man created the Teeny Tots Magnetic Building Kit."

The onlookers murmured their interest. The story of the magnetic building kit was known to them all. An unfortunate child had created a wormhole with the kit, which had sucked through not only the building blocks, but also his pet cat. Ten thousand sets of building blocks had been withdrawn at great cost.

"The only reason you're still employed," said Mister Yamamoto, turning back to Chai, "is because you're legally bound to pay the Company back out of your wages. But I warn you, if that thing is there when the chairman visits tomorrow, you're in trouble."

Chai spent the rest of the day soldering together a bowl-like cage. It was of sturdy construction and had a dozen long ropes attached around its rim.

"It'll never work," said his supervisor, with his usual pessimism. But spurred by the thought that Chai's dismissal might also mean his own, Wontai found a long-handled broom and helped push the disc into the cage.

"Now all we have to do is tie weights onto the ropes," Chai said.

But Wontai had had enough. "We?" he said. "It's home time and I'm off. You get it down yourself, you incompetent dog."

Chai worked through the night. First he attached the oxy-acetylene tanks from his welding kit, then the plastic-moulding equipment, then the grinders, presses, band saws, boring machines, compressors and sanders.

It became more difficult to attach things as the sea of churning equipment and broken benches increased. But Chai was a determined man and added the computers, then the printers, the fax machine, the filing cabinets and even the coffee machine.

When Wontai returned early next morning a deafening crashing and grinding noise filled the room as the cage rotated.

"I think it's slowed down a bit," said Chai.

"What the *hell*?" screamed the supervisor. In a panic, he opened a window and used the broom to push the disc out.

The disc, within its covering cage, drifted upwards like a giant jellyfish, taking the contents of the Kore Kudasai research department with it. Long lines of equipment bumped and crashed across the room and out of the window. As the disc rose, they dangled from it like tentacles.

In a kamikaze effort to stop its ascent, Chai leapt onto one of the tentacles and clung there, astride a prototype Dinky Dolly Baby Carriage.

"Let go!" yelled the supervisor. "The chairman will want to see you."

Chai responded by waving goodbye as he rose into the blue. Freedom at last.

<u>Salvation</u>

When survival means murder mankind will never change.

First there was a skirmish, then a war, then the war to end all wars. After Armageddon the world was plunged into the darkness of a nuclear winter. Two survivors stood upon a Scottish island.

"How long must we wait?" said the woman.

"Until the sun shines once more," said the man.

Years passed and children were born. These were not ordinary children for radiation had warped the human genome. The first was a boy with eyes the size of saucers.

"Shall I kill him?" said the father.

"No!" said the mother and she named him Christopher.

The second was a girl whose skin was covered in scales.

"Shall I kill her?" said the father.

"No!" said the mother and she called her Eve.

The third was a blob, with neither arms nor legs.

"I shall kill this one!" said the father.

"No!" said the mother. "For I love him as much as the others."

The man grew fond of his children. Sometimes he would close the shutters, light the kerosene lamp and show them the books that he had saved – great books of art and literature. With his wonderful eyes Christopher could see every brush stroke. With her wonderful memory Eve could memorise great swathes of writing. But Blob's gift was the greatest of all, for he could see into men's hearts.

One day the shutters were not properly closed and on the mainland a band of robbers saw the light. That night, when his parents were asleep, Blob heard the sound of distant oars. He warned his brother. "They are coming!"

Christopher rose from his bed, woke Eve, picked up Blob and the three of them hurried down to the shore.

They saw nothing but Blob could hear the thoughts of the robbers, cruel thoughts of murder and greed.

"They are coming!" he said again.

Christopher peered into the night and at last he could see the boat, a dark shape against the black water.

"They are over there," he said, pointing the boat out to Eve.

She took off her nightgown and slipped, naked, into the chilly sea. The gill slits in Eve's neck opened and she dived and swam like a fish towards the boat. Blob heard shouts and splashing as Eve pulled away the oars and left the boat to drift away. Minutes later Eve returned, climbed shivering from the water, picked up her gown and ran back to the house. Christopher was about to follow with Blob in his arms.

"Wait," said Blob, for he had heard a splash and now he felt the rage of the man who was swimming towards them. "There is one still coming, more evil than the rest."

Christopher hid Blob behind a rock and stood upon the beach, his arms folded. The man staggered up the beach towards him and drew a knife from his belt.

Chris showed no fear. "This is private land."

"You little brat I shall gut you from groin to throat!" The man lunged at Christopher but the boy turned and ran up towards the centre of the island. The robber followed. Through a copse of long-dead trees they ran. Chris nimbly avoided the twisted trunks but the robber crashed through, bouncing from tree to tree in a bruising chase. Christopher was well ahead when he stopped and turned.

Blob sensed the robber's triumph and his bloodlust as he rushed towards his victim, knife at the ready. Then he felt the man's surprise as Christopher dodged and he plunged over the edge of a ravine, then terror and despair and, finally a flash of agony as he hit the jagged rocks below.

"Are they all gone?" asked Christopher when he returned to the beach. Blob listened but could hear nothing but the wind ruffling the surface of the waves.

"Yes," he said. He looked into his brother's heart and was sad to see triumph, rather than remorse, at the killing.

"The darkness is lifting," said Christopher. "The nuclear winter is coming to an end."

He scooped Blob up and carried him back to the house. Blob said nothing, but deep in his heart he knew that mankind would never change.

Snouts in the Trough
When bankers turn into greedy pigs

John Jenkins, hurried along the corridor that led to the boardroom of World Bankers Inc. He glanced at a map his editor had given him and identified the door that led to the anteroom. Adjusting his ill-fitting waiter's uniform he opened the door.

A man laying cups and saucers on a tray looked up. "Are you from the agency?"

"Yes," lied John.

"What happened to Steve?"

Steve was lying bound and gagged in the ground floor broom cupboard.

"He rang in ill, I've come as his replacement. I hear it's an important meeting."

"Yes, head bankers from twenty different countries, so smarten up."

The bankers did not look up as John entered with the coffee, their attention was on the chairman at the head of the conference table.

"Libor, money laundering, sanction breaking, these are all old hat my friends, though not without their value. No, we must set our sights on new horizons." He caught John's eye and continued. "But now we will take a coffee break."

There was much filling of cups and passing round milk and sugar. In attempting to help, John was able to secrete a microphone into one of the sugar bowls.

"Hurry up." His fellow waiter hissed at him. "They don't want us hanging around."

John followed the man out of the room. "What do we do now?" he asked.

"We wait to serve lunch, then wash up the coffee cups." The man sat down and took a crumpled copy of the Racing Post out of his pocket.

John put the receiver into his ear and heard the chairman's voice. "No, not gold, my friends, the next global target is…"

There was a crunching then a gurgle and the sound stopped. Dammit, some stupid person had eaten his microphone.

Time passed slowly until the lunch trolley arrived. John peered at the contents - roast beef, vegetables and bowls of trifle.

"I thought their taste would be a bit more sophisticated," he said.

"Hurry up and serve," said his companion, "I want to get to Newmarket."

They knocked on the doors and wheeled the trolley into the boardroom. Conversation ceased. "Where are the plates? We've forgotten the plates," whispered John.

"No need for plates, help me get the trough." The man knelt down and pulled a long, silver trough out from underneath the table. There were murmurs of appreciation as he and John placed it on the table and poured in gravy, sprouts, roast potatoes, slices of beef, carrots and parsnips. The man picked up one of the bowls of trifle and poured it on top of the mess. John copied him, his stomach heaving as he did so.

All attention was on the trough and, when the waiter wheeled the trolley out of the room, instead of following him, John slipped behind a screen beside the door.

He pulled a camera out of his pocket intending to get a front-page picture.

"Before we eat, my friends, I suggest we make ourselves comfortable," said the chairman. John peered through the latticework of the screen and saw him peel off a latex mask to reveal a porcine face, complete with a flattened snout and protruding tusks. He undid the buttons of his waistcoat, and his stomach bulged out. All copied him except for one, younger than the rest.

"Never mind, Cedric," said the chairman, putting an avuncular arm around his shoulders. "You will soon be one of us."

Click. John took a picture. "What was that?" said the chairman. "I saw a flash from behind the screen."

All eyes were turned in John's direction when the doors burst open and the waiter rushed in, followed by a bevy of security guards.

"They've found Steve in the broom cupboard!" he yelled. "There's a terrorist in our midst."

There was much milling around. The security guards, confused by the appearance of the bankers, were uncertain who to arrest. In the melee John escaped.

As he ran down the corridor he realised he had left his camera behind. What a story he had to tell, but who would believe him? A crestfallen John knew he would have to return to his editor empty handed.

Sometimes it is Better not to Know
What is the secret of Celia's serenity?

Celia had long ceased to worry about her family and it was with a serene heart and a happy soul that she picked sweet peas in the evening sun. The phone rang and she went indoors to answer it.

"Hello?"

"Mrs Morrison? I'm having an affair with your husband."

"I think you must have the wrong number," said Celia, inhaling the scent from the sweet peas. She put the phone down and went to find a vase.

Once, long ago, when she was a young woman, she had let things upset her. Her wayward husband and difficult children had given her enough problems to turn what should have been a good life into a nightmare of stress and worry. She found her mind drifting back to those unhappy days and concentrated instead on arranging the flowers in a vase, grouping their different colours into a harmonious whole.

The phone rang again.

"Mrs Morrison, I must tell you that your husband is going to leave you." It was the same woman but this time the voice held a hint of anger.

"I'm sure you're mistaken."

"Your husband and I are lovers and I'm having his baby."

"I'm sorry," said Celia. "But surely, you realised that he is a married man."

"Of course I did. But he doesn't love you any more."

"I think you are wrong, dear." Celia gently put the phone down.

Geoffrey would be home soon, it was time to put her lasagne into the oven. She went into the kitchen and sprinkled extra parmesan on top.

His key sounded in the lock and she hurried into the hall to greet him. He looked tired as he dumped his briefcase onto the floor and took off his jacket.

"Did you have a good day, dear?" she said, lifting her head for a kiss. He pecked her on the cheek, his lips damp against her skin.

"I could do with a sherry."

She brought a glass out to him and they sat side by side on the swing seat in the garden. It was a beautiful evening. Celia listened to the deep cadences of her husband's voice as he described the winning of a new contract for his welding business. A flock of starlings wheeled above the cedars. It split into two and continued the aerial ballet, forming the shape of a heart against the blushing sky.

From the kitchen came the ting of the timer.

"Supper is ready."

She was taking the lasagne out of the oven when the doorbell rang. She heard her husband's feet cross the hall. The door opened and she heard a female voice.

"You didn't answer my phone calls."

"I told you never to come to my home." Geoffrey sounded angry.

"I must speak to you. We must plan for the future."

Celia tried not to listen. Happiness comes from within, shut out all unpleasantness. She concentrated on the delicious smell of toasted cheese and rich sauce as she lifted the lasagne onto the top of the oven.

"I'm having your baby."

"I thought you were taking precautions."

Celia started to lay the supper tray, feeling the weight of the cutlery and admiring the gleam of newly-polished silver.

"I love you." The woman sounded increasingly desperate.

"My dear Sara, you would be surprised how many young women have fallen in love with me since I became wealthy."

"You bastard. I'll tell your wife."

There was a pause and then Geoffrey's amused voice said. "I suspect you have already told her."

"Bastard," shouted the woman again.

The front door slammed and moments later Geoffrey came into the kitchen. Celia could see by his heightened colour that he was upset. She stood uncertainly and watched his gaze flicker to the laden tray. Then his face cleared.

"Dear Celia," he said, crossing to her and putting an arm around her waist. "What a perfect wife you have become."

She relaxed against him and he stroked a finger along the scar that stretched across the centre of her forehead. "Arranging your visit to the Stepford Clinic was the best thing I ever did."

Survival of the Fattest

Would Anya be one of the chosen ones?

Anya sat at the kitchen table and stirred melted butter into her porridge until it shone with grease. Her mother stood over her and, sensing her reluctance, said, "Come on, eat all of it."

"It was better with milk," sighed Anya.

"Yes, well, there is no milk. Daisy was killed a month ago. You should know. You ate most of her."

Her voice was sharp and Anya felt tears spring into her eyes. She glanced down at her thighs, which had become so fat that they rubbed together when she walked and had to be oiled to stop the chaffing.

"Do I have to, Mother?"

"Of course you have to," said her father, entering the room. He squeezed her shoulder, in a gesture that was part encouragement and part a check on the depth of fat. "You're doing well, Anya."

When her parents left for the temple, Anya sat at the window and stared down the street. The sun-moon was close to the horizon, its light casting long shadows. Soon it would be joining the other suns on the opposite side of the planet where the Sea of Monsters would enjoy the ten-year-long brilliance of an eternal day.

Anya sighed and dreamed of Rupert. She had scarcely seen him since the fattening began. As if her dreams became solid, Rupert appeared, hurrying towards her. Anya shrank back against the curtain, trying to hide her bulk.

"Anya," his voice was deep and husky with emotion. "Don't hide from me, we have so little time."

"I have become fat and ugly," she sighed.

"You are not ugly. You are beautiful. Do you still love me?"

"Yes," she said and leaned forward for a kiss.

"Come away with me. We can survive up in the mountains."

She stared at him in dismay. She would have died with him gladly, but live with him through the terrors of an eternal night? Everyone knew the stories about fighting and cannibalism told by the last survivors.

Anya tried to speak, to tell him how much she loved him, to explain why she was unable to run away, but the tears were flowing too fast.

"I promise I will come for you when the night is over," he said. She drew a juddering breath but when she looked up Rupert had gone.

On Weighing Day, the villagers gathered at the temple to say goodbye to the daylight. Only a sliver of the sun-moon appeared over the horizon and the brief day was little more than dusk. Everyone's face was turned to the disappearance, except for Anya, who searched the crowd for Rupert. Had he gone already? The world was an empty place without him.

Fields had been planted with seed that would lie dormant until the daylight returned. Then the hibernators would wake, their fat reserves having kept them alive through ten long years. The girls would be impregnated and work in the fields, while the Men of Power would guard the knowledge that kept the colonists alive.

Since the terraforming went wrong and the mica-covered moons had wandered from their orbits, only the Men of Power could calculate day lengths and say when to plant and when to harvest.

Anya passed the weighing and was ushered to the side of the stage to join the chosen ones. In the congregation her parents were smiling at her, but she could see the torchlight glinting on her mother's tears. Soon they would be gone, her beloved parents, joining the rest of the village in the fatal paralysis of the death juice.

Already the fattened animals had taken the hibernation draught and were locked in the survival vault. Soon the Anya and her fellow maidens would join them. She looked at the priest, the soothsayer and the headman - fat, middle-aged men, the Men of Power, who would father the next generation. Anya felt stirrings of revolt and then she remembered Rupert's promise.

Was it possible? Would he come for her? Could happiness be waiting for her after all? She managed to return her parents' brave smiles as she was led away. I love you, she mouthed at them, but her heart sang of Rupert.

Tar Babies
What could the tar babies do?

The president stared out at the tar pit that had opened on the White House lawn.

"I thought these things were only appearing in the Southern States."

"They're spreading," said Hank Barfield, his head of security. "But we've found the source of the tar babies that create them." He slotted a disc into the viewer and the screen was filled with a scene from the last century. "This was when they were pumping a bacterial soup into disused oil wells in an attempt to recreate oil. Note this protester, Mr President." He pointed to an aging hippy, who tripped and fell head-first down the shaft.

"Didn't he die?" said the President.

"Oh yes, but his cells lived on and were the basis for these hominids. We've managed to capture one of them. He's under guard in the anteroom, Mr President. Would you like to see him?"

"Hell, yes."

Hank left the room and came back with a tar baby. The creature's legs were shackled, he was manacled to a security guard on either side while a third guard held a cocked gun to his head.

"Welcome to the White House," said the President.

"Love and peace."

"How many of you are there?"

"Love and peace."

The hominid gave the same answer to all questions.

"It's obviously not intelligent," said the President.

"More like an animal," said Hank. "I wonder if it's edible."

"I doubt it, not if it's petroleum-based. Perhaps we could use it as fuel," suggested the President. "Let's set fire to it and see."

They took it out into the garden.

"Hadn't we better kill it first?" said Hank.

The President nodded to one of the security guards who stepped forwards and shot it through the head. *Bang!* The hominid's limbs liquefied and withdrew into its body, slipping out of the shackles. Its head sank down into its neck, its stomach expanded and it ended up as a sphere.

"What the Hell happened there?" asked the President. "Is it dead?"

"It seems to be getting hard," said Hank, prodding it with his finger. "I think we should break it open."

At a nod from the President, a guard hit it with the butt of his gun. The gun bounced off the hardening carapace, which showed no sign of damage.

"I'll try to set fire to it," said the President, clicking his lighter. The carapace glowed under the flame but rapidly returned to normal.

"We could try explosives," suggested Hank.

The President looked at his watch. "We'll do it tomorrow," he said. "Bring whatever it takes."

The next day a tank was standing on the White House lawn. It was surrounded by soldiers, some carrying bazookas, some flame throwers, some water cannon, and some grenades.

A curious crowd gathered outside the railings and watched the ball being rolled out onto the lawn. A cheer went up as the President waved. This had better work.

First the ball was doused with water – nothing.

Then it was bathed in fire – nothing.

Then it was rocked with explosions from the grenades – nothing.

The crowd was becoming restless and cries of derision could be heard. Rockets from the bazookas had no effect. Finally, the turret of the tank turned so the huge gun was trained on the ball.

BOOM!

When the smoke cleared the ball had split open. Everyone watched, open-mouthed, as a dozen black imps scrambled out.

"War, war, war," piped the imps and jumped excitedly up and down.

Flames and bullets shredded the air around them as they turned and ran for the tar pit.

"War, war, war." Occasionally one was hit, and jumped lopsidedly for a while, but quickly recovered. "War, war, war," their tiny voices died away as they jumped into the tar pit and disappeared.

Someone in the crowd laughed and the laughter spread.

"Follow me," snarled the President, and led the way indoors. "The whole thing has made me a laughing stock." The President reached his office and sank down onto his chair. "You don't think they really mean to attack us, do you?"

Hank gave a dismissive laugh.

"What could they do?"

The President relaxed. "You're right."

It was then that the ground started to shake.

The Alien Ambassador

He was attempting to farm a registered colony.

Art stood on the lowest level of the Guantanamo Bay prison. It was his first day on the job and he paused, uncertainly. The door to the corridor clanged shut behind him.

"Get on with it," said his supervisor through the bars. "You're meant to be checking the cells, not composing bloody poetry."

Art moved forwards to the first cell. A familiar smell of rotting eggs assailed his nostrils, it was a Chitaurian. The creature must have heard him coming because it had switched on its hologramatic mask. A flickering facsimile of a human face was projected upwards from the neck of its cloak.

"Release me at once. I am the Chitaurian ambassador and I claim diplomatic protection."

Art did not answer but hurried down the corridor to the next cell, which contained greys.

"Unlock the door," a grey said in a high, reedy voice.

"Yes, master," said Art. The others turned, huge eyes wide with excitement at having been rescued by a slave.

"Is there any way out except past the Chitaurian?" asked a grey as they crowded out of the cell.

"No, master," said Art, with the blank deference of an abductee.

"Perhaps it won't notice us," suggested another. It was wrong. As the group tiptoed past the Chitaurian's cell they were met by a telepathic roar.

"Release me at once." Without its mask, the Chitaurian's head was reptilian with a domed forehead and angry red eyes.

"Yes, Lord." A grey grabbed the keys off Art and struggled with the lock.

"This is all your fault, you useless minions. I sent you to announce my coming but what happened? You terrified the humans with your abductions."

The greys huddled before the huge Chitaurian, gibbering their apologies as it emerged from its cell.

"Oh, get out of my way!" It strode down the corridor towards the door. "Unlock this."

Art obediently unlocked the door. Mick looked up from his desk. His eyes widened with shock as he saw his entire contingent of prisoners crowding through the doorway. Before Art could use his stun beam, the Chitaurian leapt down the corridor and killed Mick with a swipe of its clawed hand. Beyond and above them came the sound of sirens. Mick had hit the alarm button.

"Which way out?" Panicking greys ran in all directions. "This way, masters." Art pointed the way down a side corridor and into a store room. It had been built beyond the lead shielding of the rest of the complex and was the only place a force field could be projected. A shimmering wall ran across the room.

"Oh good, a tractor beam," said one of the greys. In the distance came the sound of shouts and running feet. With little squeaks of fear, the greys rushed into the force field and disappeared.

The Chitaurian held back. "Where have they gone?" it asked.

"They've been conveyed to a transport ship which will take them back to their star system," said Art, dropping all pretence of servility. "The Zeta Reticulan Government has agreed to deal with them."

The lizard frowned. "I thought as much. You're no abductee slave, are you?"

"No, I'm an Arcturian - and you're under arrest for attempting to farm one of our registered colonies."

"We're not part of your Federation. We'll feed where we want."

Art glared at it. "You can put your arguments to the Galactic Council. There's a custodial ship waiting for you."

"Never," snarled the Lizard. "I prefer to stay and fight it out with the cattle."

Art produced a volition gun and bathed the creature in blue light.

"Get into the beam." Reluctantly, the lizard entered the tractor beam and disappeared.

Armed men burst through the door, throwing themselves to the floor and covering Art with their guns. He swung round, bathing the group in the volition ray.

"Don't fire," he said. The men crouched, unable to raise their weapons. Art smiled at them. For all their faults, humans were doing well on their blue-green planet. He raised his hand in a gesture that was part blessing and part farewell, then he stepped into the force field and was gone.

The Autobiography of General Gore
An Armani suit hides a multitude of proportional problems

Chapter One. The Early Days.

I had a happy childhood. We may have been poor in worldly goods but we were rich in nature's bounty.

My education was undertaken by a forest ranger, who supplied books and writing materials to us younger gorillas. Of course, none of us could talk, but I developed a fine copper-plate handwriting.

I wrote a goodbye note to my mother, intending to find success in the urban jungle. Alas, if I had known that I would never see my dear mother again, how differently I would have taken my leave.

Chapter Two. The Journey

I swiftly mastered the skill of riding the moped I borrowed from the forest ranger, and was soon bowling along the rutted track that led out of the jungle.

Having reached town, I entered a shop and tried to ask where I could get a bed for the night.

At that time I was only able to speak in grunts, so I indicated that I needed paper and pen to make my wants known.

The foolish woman behind the counter misinterpreted my gestures and ran screaming out of the shop and into the street, where she attracted a large crowd.

I will not dwell on the indignity of being caught in a net and dragged to the zoo, suffice to say that I was incarcerated with a gorilla, who was strange in every sense of the word.

Chapter Three. The Escape.

Without exception, every human visiting the zoo was clothed. No wonder the sight of a naked male had terrified the shop assistant. The first thing I had to do, upon escaping from the zoo, was to find myself some clothes.

Every day a woman would give my companion bananas and sit on a nearby bench for hours, doing her knitting. Apparently, his glowering countenance reminded her of her late husband.

With my superior intelligence, I hatched an escape plan. The next time the woman visited, I pretended to attack my fellow prisoner. He made a good show of cowering and whimpering and the lovesick woman entered the cage and started hitting me with her handbag. I grabbed her bag and we both escaped, slamming the cage door shut behind us.

"I love you!" she wailed to my companion as we hurried away.

Fortunately, the sight of ready cash, calmed the fears of the man in the clothes shop and we bought ourselves suits, shirts and ties. We stepped out onto the streets of the Urban Jungle with confidence – misplaced confidence, as it turned out.

Chapter Four. Salvation.

We were arrested for stealing the handbag and hauled before the Chief of Police - a man of impressive proportions who glared at us from behind a desk.

"I'll deal with this matter in private," he growled, dismissing the arresting officers.

When we were alone with him, he pointed at our naked feet. "You hillbillies come into town and think you can get away with just wearing a cheap suit. You need shoes, dammit. Shoes, socks, and a decent chiropodist."

I picked up a pen from the desk and wrote "What is a chiropodist?"

"Oh no," he groaned. "Don't tell me you haven't even had the laryngeal operation? How on earth do you guys think you can fit in without being able to talk?" He rolled his eyes to heaven. Then he opened the top drawer of his desk and took out a wad of notes. "Look, get yourselves fixed. Buy decent suits - an Armani hides a multitude of proportional problems. As long as you don't actually knuckle-walk, you should pass as reasonably human. Then, when you are ready, come back to me and I'll see about getting you jobs."

"Why are you helping us?" I wrote.

He looked pleased. "Can't you guess? I'm a gorilla too."

Chapter Five, The Return.

A merciful nature, courage and presence of mind – all were attributes which led to my rapid rise through the ranks of the military. Several years later I visited the tribe in my chauffeur-driven car to receive the accolades of my erstwhile companions and visit my mother's grave. From what low beginnings I have risen.

The Bathroom Mirror
How to save a failing marriage.

I'm a bathroom mirror. The bathroom I reflect was once clean and tidy but the towel rail is now dull, the cabinet dusty and I have to peer through dried toothpaste splatters.

Here comes the master of the house in his monogrammed towelling robe. It was once white and fluffy but, like everything else in this place, it has become grey and flat.

He's peering at me. Take a good look – the greasy pores, the morning stubble, the receding hairline and the scattering of grey hairs. What happened to the young man I once knew? Zilch has happened in his boring life, the years just passed that's all.

What's he doing now? Oh Yuk, he's taking his robe off – this will be more than the usual quick flap with a wet flannel. He's turning sideways, no improvement there, boyo. A white flabby body is a white flabby body, whichever way you look at it. He's sucking his stomach in – now all he has to do is learn not to breathe. Woosh – avalanche! If he does much more of this he'll get a hernia.

He's really pulling out the stops this morning – a careful shave, a thorough tooth brushing, a wash and a rummage in the cabinet to find a deodorant. Get on with it, man – your missus is going to be late for work.

Bang, bang, bang.

There you are – she's banging on the bathroom door. He's hurried out and now she's in front of me. She gives me a perfunctory glance. She's late, she's annoyed and she hurriedly completes her ablutions and departs.

Next day he comes in earlier: He opens the cabinet door. Blimey, it looks like he's been on a spending spree. Out come an aftershave, a moisturiser, a new deodorant, a bottle of comb-in hair dye and some hair gel. Half an hour later he leaves the bathroom in a cloud of conflicting aromas.

She scuttles in, sniffs the air in puzzlement, shrugs and gets on with her rudimentary toilette. A bit of lipstick wouldn't come amiss, dearie.

A week later she's paying me more attention. What a sight she looks. She's been crying - her eyes are red and puffy. Even her nose looks red and puffy and a string of slime runs down to her lip. She splashes cold water onto her face – a slight improvement but not much. She stares at me, raising her chin and curling her thin-lipped mouth into a pitiful attempt at coquettishness.

It's no good dearie, you need to shape those eyebrows and for heaven's sake do something about those roots – it looks as if a giant millipede is crawling over your head.

Another week and things are looking up. She has cleaned the bathroom. I am now sparkling bright. She's preparing to have a bath. She opens the newly-dusted cabinet and takes out the scented bath oil. Mmm, lovely. Armpit time, nice and smooth, not like the jungle that grew there before.

He comes in. "Oh, sorry."

She turns and smiles, her towel slipping. "I'm about to have a bath, darling."

"Oh, right." He averts his eyes. "I'm just on my way out to – er- a meeting."

"See you later, darling." She lets the towel drop to the floor and he shoots out of the door like a startled virgin.

She stares at me, then cups her hands and lifts her breasts. Not bad but don't let go or they will dangle like mittens. I see her take her pills out of the cabinet, click one out of its plastic bubble and flush it down the loo. I've heard of going round the bend but this is ridiculous.

A couple of months later and she is taking a home pregnancy test. A few minutes later she calls him in.

"Darling," she says, waving a little stick at him. "Wonderful news. We're going to have a baby." She holds out her arms to him and, after a moment's hesitation, he embraces her.

She can't see his face but I can and I almost feel sorry for the poor sap. He has the desperate look of a prisoner who has heard the cell door clang shut behind him.

The Closing Circle

There is only a tiny gap between good and evil.

"And shut the bloody door after you," shouted Harold.

"Yes, darling." Cynthia hurried from the house pulling the front door closed behind her. She hoped the neighbours hadn't heard. How embarrassing.

Poor Harold, thought the dutiful Cynthia, he must be in pain from his arthritis. She glanced at her watch. There was just time to visit her mother at the Rosie Rest Home before her church duties.

"I hate it here." Her mother sat slumped in an armchair. "I want to come and live with you."

"Oh, Mother, you know Harold won't allow it."

"It's not fair!" Her mother's expression twisted with spite. "My only daughter is a selfish bitch."

Cynthia kept smiling. She removed a package from her bag. "Look, Mother, I've brought you a present. It's a touch light. You know you were saying how you could never find the switch."

Her mother regarded the gift without enthusiasm. "Is it safe?" she asked. "It looks like something you bought at a charity shop."

"Of course it's safe," said Cynthia with more certainty than she felt. She had actually bought it at a car-boot sale. "I'll come back after church and show you how to plug it in."

"Going already? You've hardly come!"

At church, Cynthia was dusting pews when the vicar approached.

"I hope you don't mind, Cynthia, but I've taken you off the flower rota and given your position to Mrs Leech."

Cynthia nodded and smiled and, not trusting herself to speak, continued with her dusting.

After the vicar had left, Cynthia noticed the eyes. They were reflected in the gleam of polished oak and brass. She spun round, but there was nobody there. Trembling, Cynthia went over to the candle stand and bought a candle. She lit it, put it into one of the holders then knelt down and said the Lord's Prayer.

"Forgive us our trespasses as we forgive those who trespass against us." She lingered over the words. Few were her trespasses but many, oh so many, were those who trespassed against her.

Cynthia had always imagined the graph of righteousness to be a straight line from absolute evil to absolute good. But lately the graph was curving, the two ends striving to unite to form a circle. She had been struggling to keep the ends of the circle apart, knowing that only a tiny gap separated her from wickedness. Under the gaze of the eyes, she felt a release from tension. The circle closed. She didn't have to struggle any more - she was FREE.

She leapt to her feet and accidently knocked against the candle stand. It toppled over and her lighted candle fell close to a kneeler. Cynthia hesitated. Should she pick up the wrought-iron stand? And then her newfound freedom released her from the obligation. It was too heavy, let the vicar pick it up. It was time he made an effort.

On the walk home Cynthia hesitated outside the Rosie Rest Home. Should she go in and help her mother with the touch lamp? No, she was quite capable of plugging it in herself.

Cynthia sighed, perhaps, in future she would visit her mother less often or, perhaps, not at all. Her heart lifted at the thought.

With a howling of sirens and a flashing of lights, a fire-engine sped past, heading towards the church.

Cynthia had almost reached the turning to her road when an ambulance raced past in the direction of the Rosie Rest Home.

Her footsteps quickened as she approached her house. She wondered if she had closed the front door properly. What if an intruder had entered and had attacked her husband with one of her Sabatier knives? On a day like today, when God was answering all her unspoken dreams, anything was possible.

Her heart sank when she entered the house and heard Harold's snores coming from the living room. The vicar's favourite saying came into her mind - the Lord helps those who help themselves. How true. The eyes were still there, watching her from the rippled places between light and shadow. Cynthia would make damned sure they had something to watch.

The Curse of the Celtic Head
Could Chrissie become a guardian without the knowledge?

When Jon and Chrissie decided to move to the country, they found the ideal cottage. It had a thatched roof, roses growing round the door and an ancient church on a nearby hill.

The old lady who owned the cottage informed them that she was the last of the Guardians and would only sell the cottage if Chrissie was prepared to take over the role. Chrissie agreed but the old lady died unexpectedly in her nursing home before she could divulge the ancient knowledge.

Everything seemed to go wrong for the couple. Their vegetables were blighted and the steering failed on Jon's little tractor so he rammed into the garden wall. It was a dry-stone wall and easily demolished. One stone, larger thanthe others, shifted enough for Jon to see that it was a carved head. He telephoned the county archaeologist, who came rushing round.

"This is wonderful, if I'm not mistaken you've found Magog's head."

"Magog?"

"Yes, our local giant. There used to be a huge statue of him – some believed it was the giant himself, turned to stone. When the frightened villagers destroyed it, the torso was buried under the altar in the church but nobody knew what happened to the rest of it."

The archaeologist bent over and patted the head. To Jon's amazement, his body arched and trembled. For several seconds he remained rigid then he fell to the ground. Jon knelt to feel his pulse. Thank God, he was still alive.He looked at the head. Its eyes had swiveled and were staring at him. Sick with fear, Jon saw that the stone had become flesh. The mouth opened.

"Touch me," it rasped.

"No!"

Jon felt his leg gripped. "Touch the head," the archaeologist said, staring with blank eyes.

Jon tore himself away and rushed into the cottage, locking the door behind him. With trembling fingers, he dialled 999.

By the time the police arrived, Jon and Chrissie were so frightened they had locked themselves in the upstairs bedroom. Two policemen entered the garden. "Don't touch the head!" John yelled out of the window.

He was too late. Both policemen were arching their backs and trembling as the head sucked out their life-force.

Now there were three zombies. But worse was to come. From the church on top of the hill came a splintering crash. The zombies staggered up the hill to greet the torso, which had come to life, battered the door open and emerged into the daylight.

Meanwhile another policeman had come into the garden. Jon saw something wriggling in the flowerbed next to him.

"Run!" he screamed.

But he was too late. A giant hand erupted from the soil and seized the policeman's ankle. Once again Jon and Chrissie watched the zombification process.

"What on earth can we do?" asked Jon.

"We can pray," said Chrissie. Jon recited the Lord's prayer. When he finished, he looked outside. The mayhem was unchanged. The torso, with a retinue of zombies, was humping its way downhill. The fourth and newest zombie dragged an arm across the garden and, at the far end of the vegetable patch, a second hand had emerged. A shaft of sunlight illuminated the chimneybreast. A sign! Chrissie tore at the wallpaper and revealed a hidden cupboard containing a book and a phial of purple liquid.

"Oh my God," said Chrissie, looking in the book. "This isn't even in English. What am I meant to do?" Then she heard the old woman's voice.

"Sprinkle the potion in a circle around you." Chrissie did so. "Recite the words in the book." Chrissie obeyed and, beyond the circle the real world faded. Every time she stumbled over a word, demons from the shadows came closer but the old woman corrected her and they moved away. At last the spell was finished and Chrissie hurried to the window.

Everything was back to normal. Four erstwhile zombies were looking around in bewilderment. The giant torso lay petrified beside the garden wall. The stone head, two arms and a foot lay in the garden and the sound of sirens filled the air as several police cars came roaring up the lane.

The curse of the Celtic head had ended.

The Deserted Island
Only the dead can reach the island of Styx

Brett returned to consciousness, aware of the taste of salt and the grit of sand in his mouth. He raised his head and saw that he had been washed up on a beach.

Had he been shipwrecked? Were there other survivors? He turned and noticed a body lying on the sand. Brett got to his feet, rolled the body over and recognised his brother.

"Mick!" he gasped. "Wake up, wake up." But his brother remained unconscious.

Palms fringed the beach and Brett hoped he would find water he could bring back for his brother. He hurried towards the trees, his footsteps the only marks on the pristine sand. When he was deep within the vegetation, he heard a crashing ahead of him and hid behind a palm. A giant lizard passed, waddling on splayed legs. Brett recognised it at once. It was a Komodo dragon – a flesh-eating reptile with saliva so toxic that one bite meant death. He watched in dismay as it flickered its long, forked tongue, then turned and followed Brett's scent trail to the beach.

Brett picked up a branch and ran after it. The dragon emerged from the trees, saw Mick's body, and headed towards its prey. Brett shouted a warning, raced across the sand and hit it again and again until it turned. It lashed out, catching his arm with razor-sharp teeth. Ignoring the pain, Brett punched it in the eye and the animal lumbered back up the beach towards the trees.

When Brett turned back to his brother, he saw that he was sitting up, staring at him.

"Oh Mick, thank God you're alive."

Mick looked at him with troubled eyes. "And you, Brett, must be dead," he said. "For only the dead can reach the island of Styx."

The dragon's poison had reached Brett's brain, he felt floaty and confused. A memory emerged from the mist. Brett saw the cliff-top barrier sliding across his headlights as he steered the car towards it, felt the impact, then the long, stomach-dropping plunge, and the final devastating crash.

He sank to his knees before Mick. Questions whirled around his head but he knew the answers were terrible.

"Don't," he groaned, begging the memories not to rise higher and make him remember what he had died to forget. But his mind had no mercy and he was reliving the past.

He remembered Mick's anxious face mouthing the words. "I'm sorry Brett, but I'm in love with your wife and Alice is in love with me." Brett had snapped. He had picked up a poker and smashed it down on his brother's head. His pitiless memory recreated the bubbling cry as Mick fell to the floor.

"Forgive me," Brett said and stretched out on the sand in front of his brother.

"Oh Brett, you were always the noble one." Mick leaned forwards and raised him from the sand so they were kneeling and facing each other. He stared at him with intense, dark eyes. "By risking your life for mine you have paid the blood price. Besides, I forgive you with all my heart. But the important thing is - can you find it in your heart to forgive me?"

"You want me to forgive you?" Brett stared at his brother. Mick the adulterer, Mick the seducer of his beloved Alice, Mick, who would take away from him all that he held dear. Was it possible to forgive such a betrayal?

Mick waited expectantly and then his eyes filled with tears. He stood up, turned and walked away. With each step he faded more into the haze. The island held its breath, even the sound of the surf faded away.

"No wait," called Brett. "I will try."

Mick turned and, though tears were rolling down his cheeks, he tried to smile. "Good old Brett."

Brett ran after his brother and reached out his arms. "Come on," he said. "Brothers forever."

"Brothers forever." Mick repeated their childhood mantra, and returned the embrace.

Love for his brother filled Brett's heart and with it came the forgiveness that would save his soul. As they hugged, they became one with the eternal light – and the island of Styx was deserted once more.

The Exorcist
Will she set her husband free?

She stood beside the window looking out. Why did her beloved not come home? The empty road stretched far into the dusk with no sign of the man for whom she longed.

She turned to face the darkening room, ears listening for his step upon the path. Silently she drifted round the room, scarcely being, scarcely touching, scarcely there.

She stared at her reflection in the mirror, so pale against the dusk to be invisible, made fragile by her husband's discontent. Her reflection watched her from the broken mirror, still beautiful despite her grieving. She raised her hand to loosen her golden hair; he had once loved her with her tresses down.

A key was turning in the lock. As light as thistledown, she floated to the door, where he stood silently upon the threshold.

She tried to twine her arms around him, to snare him with the desperation of her love, to show him that without him she would die.

He violently responded to her touch and closed his hands around her slender neck. She leant against him, welcoming his passion, and in a few short minutes she was dead.

She stood beside the window looking out, trapped within the cycle of the deed, haunting the location where she died.

Why did her beloved not come home? The empty road stretched far into the dusk with no sign of the man for whom she longed.

The door creaked open letting a gust of air into the empty house, stirring the dust. The ghostly woman ignored the intrusion and continued to stare out of the window.

Two men entered the house.

"Did we have to come to this spooky place at dusk?" said the younger of the two.

"It's the best time for seeing ghosts," said the older man. Their voices were no more than vibrations in the air to the waiting ghost. She ignored them and continued to listen for her husband's step upon the path.

"I think I see her," said the older man. "Look over by the window."

"Shut up, you're frightening me, I can't see anything."

"It's a sort of shimmer and the temperature in the room is dropping – look she's coming towards us. She's by the mirror now – surely you can see her?"

"Oh, for God's sake I don't know." The young man sounded frightened. "You're the expert. That's why I asked you to come here."

Her reflection watched her from the broken mirror, still beautiful despite her grieving. She raised her hand to loosen her golden hair; he had once loved her with her tresses down.

"Get on with it," said the younger man shivering. "I want to get out of here."

"Myrtle Jones?" commanded the older man.

He repeated her name but locked within her death cycle she paid him no heed. Then a shower of cold water distracted her. The man had unscrewed a bottle and was throwing holy water at her. Its blessed coolness penetrated the ether and now she could see him clearly.

"Oh my God," screamed the young man. "That's her. That must be my grandmother."

"Myrtle Jones," said the older man. "I have a message from your husband. I was holding a séance last week and his spirit came through. He begs you to release him."

A key was turning in the lock.

"They hanged him for your murder," said the younger man, coming towards her, his hands held out in supplication. "His last words were to ask for your forgiveness."

As light as thistledown, she floated to the door, where he stood silently upon the threshold.

"Please grandmother, forgive him, and release him from his torment."

"I command you to have mercy on his soul."

She paused. The ether seemed to hold its breath. Her long-dead husband stood waiting for his suffering to continue.

Gently, like settling thistledown she lowered her arms and gently she forgave him. He turned and walked away into the light. Slowly, she drifted after - scarcely being, scarcely touching, scarcely there, until the light engulfed her and she was no more.

The Golden Years Space Cruise

Why were the tickets so cheap?

A long queue of elderly people stood yawning and blinking in the early-morning sunshine.

"I've been up since dawn," complained Myra to her neighbour, a thin patrician-looking woman who ignored her. Further down the queue a commotion was taking place. An elderly man clung to his briefcase while two uniformed couriers tried to take it from him.

"Get off. Leave me alone, this is hand luggage."

"I'm sorry, sir, but all cases must be checked in." One of the couriers managed to pull the case away from him.

"Bring that back," yelled the man at his rapidly-retreating figure.

"There's always one," sniffed Myra's neighbour. The queue slowly shuffled forwards.

"This is my first cruise," confided Myra.

Her neighbour raised a quizzical eyebrow. "Really?" she said. "I've been on dozens." She looked at Myra's downcast face and added kindly. "Of course, this is the first space cruise."

"Yes, they are such a new thing. My son-in-law says they are remarkably good value for money."

"Indeed." Her neighbour looked away as if to end the conversation but Myra ploughed eagerly on.

"My children clubbed together to pay for it. They said it would be worth every penny." Her eyes scanned the balcony of the terminal, where a few desultory figures stood leaning against the railing.

"I thought they might be here to see me off. I can't see them. Perhaps they haven't got here yet." The queue shuffled forwards. "I hope they come soon or we'll be on board."

"They probably aren't coming," said her neighbour. "Mine wanted to come, of course, but I told them not to. What's the point? All that way, just for a wave."

Ahead of them, the man was creating another disturbance.

"I tell you there's something funny going on," he was saying to the surrounding queue. "Have you ever wondered why the tickets are so cheap? It's because they're one-way tickets, that's why. Yeah, and where is the baggage trailer? I bet you anything our luggage won't be put on board."

Myra looked at her neighbour with round eyes. "All my best dresses are in my suitcase. What does he mean, our luggage won't be put on board?"

"He's talking nonsense," said her neighbour with a sniff. The queue had been shuffling forwards and now they could see past the terminal to where the space rocket stood on its launch pad.

"Oh, wow," gasped Myra. "I can hardly believe I'm going on a space cruise. How clever to fit all those cabins into such a small ship."

The man was working his way back through the queue.

"Don't get on that spaceship," he was saying. "They're trying to get rid of us. This isn't a cruise, it's a one-way ticket to oblivion."

He was beside them now. "This is a trick. There are too many old people. They want us out of the way." His bony fingers clutched Myra's arm.

"Quickly," he said. "You look like a sensible woman. Come away with me, we can slip out of the queue and escape."

"But I must go on the cruise. My children bought me the ticket," she wailed.

"Then your children want to get rid of you," he said.

Uniformed couriers were hurrying towards them and, with one final squeeze of her arm, he slipped out of the queue and disappeared round the corner of the terminal.

"What did he say?" asked one of the couriers. Myra felt tears welling into her eyes.

"He said that my children want to get rid of me."

"That's ridiculous," said the courier. "The man is obviously deranged. I must apologise for the inconvenience, Madam, and, on behalf of the company, I would like to upgrade your ticket to Business Class."

"I was upset too," said her neighbour. "Can I be upgraded?"

"Of course," said the courier. "With the compliments of Golden Years Cruises." He felt in his pocket, brought out two tickets and gave them one each. Then he hurried back to the terminal.

"That was a bit of luck," Myra said. "Business Class eh? I can't wait to tell the kids."

"I always prefer to go Business Class," said her neighbour.

And the queue shuffled slowly on.

The Safari

Could time travel change the course of evolution?

Bran Richards, the wealthiest man on the planet, invested a small fortune on research into time travel. It was his intention to increase his wealth by looking into the future. Unfortunately, the future turned out to be a cosmic soup of infinite possibilities.

"You see, the future hasn't happened yet," explained Professor Potter, head of his research team.

"It's a shame you couldn't figure that out before I spent my billions," said Bran. However, it was possible to travel into the past and already Bran's quick brain was thinking of ways to exploit the discovery.

"We'll set up a travel company to take people back in time. We must think of something to hit the headlines. I know! You and I will go on a Jurassic safari."

"Jurassic? I'm not sure. There were some dangerous dinosaurs."

"That's the idea. Think of the pictures we could get."

"We might change the course of evolution."

"Really, Potter, how can we change the course of evolution if we remain in the machine? Get yourself a safari suit. I must go and arrange publicity."

A week later, the world's press was gathered to watch. Bran stood in front of the time machine, splendidly attired in a smart khaki suit complete with a white pith helmet.

"I have floated around the world in a balloon, but this is my greatest project yet, a Jurassic Safari." Cameras flashed, recording machines whirred.

"How do we know you have really gone back in time?" demanded a reporter.

"I will bring back souvenirs to prove the veracity of my journey – living creatures from the Jurassic."

Potter, who was inside the craft, making last-minute adjustments, groaned. So much for his boss's promise to remain in the time machine.

Bran entered, and secured the door. "Quick!" he said, "Pull that lever and let's set off."

There was a swirliness, both inside their bodies and outside the craft where the waters of time could be seen through the window. Then the multicoloured luminescence condensed into a clearing surrounded by fern trees.

The time machine had landed beside a water hole where a huge, bipedal lizard was drinking.

Bran's camera whirred as the startled creature lunged at the craft. The impact was huge but the time machine was incapable of moving and the lizard bounced off with a howl. They watched it limp away.

"They will never believe this back home," said Bran. "I will have to get proof."

"No!" moaned Potter, but the great man ignored him, opened the door and hurried over to the surrounding forest where he tore down an enormous fern leaf.

While he was gone, Potter watched little lizards emerge from their hiding places and gatherer around the time machine pointing and seeming to communicate with each other. They were so absorbed they didn't notice the return of Bran, who was dragging the fern and destroying countless tiny insects in his haste. He stooped down and grabbed a couple of lizards. The others scattered.

"They'll have to believe us now." Bran placed the lizards and the fern leaf on the floor of the machine. "Time to go home. I think we can congratulate ourselves on a successful safari."

The press were still there. They were wandering around aimlessly. Some were jumping up and down on their cameras, others were fighting, others trying to divest themselves of ill-fitting clothes.

Potter stared out of the window. He had been right. Time travel had altered the future. Mankind had not yet evolved from apes.

Bran was struggling to open the door. "I can't remember how this thing goes," he said, his words were slurring into grunts. Potter managed to help him and they joined the crowd of apes milling around the laboratory.

"What happened there?" asked one of the lizards.

"I don't know," said the other one. "We seem to have been captured by hairy aliens, though I can't believe they have the intelligence to make this craft we are in."

"I suppose it could be time travel," said the first lizard. "But who would be foolish enough to do that?"

Hand in hand the two Jurassic lizards skirted around the milling apes and emerged into a brave new world.

The Last Druid Priest
An explanation for global warming

Caedmon, the last Druid priest of Ancient Britton, lifted a golden cup. A hush fell upon the congregation. Around them the pillars of Stone Henge stood black against the pre-dawn sky. The inner circle was lit by flickering torches, giving an intimate feel to the huge monument.

The priest looked down at the goat spread-eagled on the altar stone. It gazed back at him blearily, subdued by a heavy draft of mistletoe juice. Caedmon frowned at the animal, it was an unworthy offering but virgins were impossible to find.

He glared round at the village maidens, all of them sporting bumps beneath their coarsely-woven dresses. Even the 12-year-old daughter of the blacksmith had a bulge beneath her tunic. The priest was sure it was a cushion but it was beneath his dignity to investigate. Virgins should offer themselves for sacrifice willingly. It was a great honour and this would probably be their last opportunity.

"Arbraaaaa," intoned Ceadmon and took a drink from the cup.

"Carda Arbraaaaa," responded the congregation and waved bunches of oak twigs.

The priest felt the familiar tendrils of mistletoe juice entwine in his brain as he turned to face the eastern horizon. The disc of the sun had broken over the distant hills. The time had come. The priest turned back to the goat, picked up the sacrificial knife and with a dramatic flourish slit the animal's throat.

"Aaaaah," breathed the congregation and watched the goat's blood trickle down the altar stone. The silence that followed was broken by the distant sound of a ram's horn. The Romans were on their way. The congregation shuffled uneasily but the priest quelled them with a stern look. The ceremony must go on.

He turned to face the rising sun. Already the glare made him close his eyes. "Welcome Belenos, greatest god of the heavens."

"Hello," said the sun.

"May your beneficence pour upon the earth as the blood of our sacrifice soaks the ground."

The sun swivelled to peer down at the altar. "A goat?" It was disappointed. "Did none of your maidens think highly enough of me to offer themselves?"

"Oh my lord, you know how things are, it's impossible to find a virgin nowadays. But we have given you a particularly fine goat and I am sure he thought it a great honour to be selected."

"Oh very well," sighed the sun.

"Er…" The priest wrung his hands in anguish as he prepared to break the bad news to the sun. "I'm afraid this will be the last sacrifice for a while. The Romans are taking over."

"Let's hope they are more efficient with their ceremonies," said the sun.

"Actually," the priest was in an agony of embarrassment. "they don't realise that you are a person. They think of you as a fiery chariot."

"A chariot?" bellowed Belenos. The priest risked a squint at the sun and saw that it had turned red and was whirling on its axis – it was seriously displeased.

"B-but I've been told that there's also a religion that worships God the Sun. Perhaps they will take over your ceremonies."

"With a goat?" sneered the sun.

"Oh no, my Lord. They make a great feature of devouring human flesh and blood."

"Really? Very well, I will give them a chance. But you know what will happen if I'm not properly worshipped?"

"Oh no," cried the priest. "Have mercy great golden one. Please do not punish us with global warming."

Belenos looked down at his aging priest and had pity on him.

"Don't worry old man," he said. "It will not be in your lifetime, which may be shorter than you think. But people had better watch out in the future."

"Oh, thank you, thank you, magnificent and merciful god." The priest scrambled to his feet and turned to give the congregation the good news - but they had gone. The Henge was deserted, apart from a few scattered cushions.

A ram's horn sounded, much closer this time and over the brow of a hill marched a phalanx of Roman soldiers. The early-morning sun glinted on their spears.

"Awwwk," squeaked Caedmon, and he hitched up his robes and ran.

The Lion's Den
Will Milly's time machine get a roar of approval from the judges?

James leant forward and stared through the window of the viewing gallery as the final contestant entered the studio.

"Welcome to The Lion's Den," he boomed into the intercom.

The girl sashayed forwards on three-inch heels, carrying a large black box. As she deposited her box on the table in front of the judges. James instructed Camera One to zoom in on the sight of a miniskirt stretched over rounded buttocks and a pleasing length of upper thigh.

"Good evening, Miss – er." Reginald Kaye, the presenter, glanced at his prompt sheet. "Miss Millicent Thackeray. Can I call you Milly?" His smile was vulpine. "What have you brought for us to evaluate, Milly?"

"A time machine," she said.

"Impossible!" said Professor Penfold, the senior of the three judges.

"The machine transfers time from other people to me," she said, indicating the handles attached to the box. "I hold these handles, the donor holds those handles, and the wormholes in the box suck time across from the donor's life to mine."

"Are you saying that you can take an hour of time from somebody's life and add it to your own?" said the professor in disbelief.

"An hour?" The girl gave a sharp laugh. "An hour would hardly be worthwhile. I like to take a year, at least."

"I wouldn't give anyone a year from my life," said Reginald Kaye.

"There's plenty who will," said the girl. "Last week I bought a year from a homeless guy for the price of a pint of beer."

The judges stared at her, shocked.

James glanced at the clock. This was a live programme, and they had to finish before the ad break. He felt his ulcer twinge.

"Ten minutes," he said into Reg's ear piece.

Reg gave a forced laugh. "Perhaps you'd like to demonstrate, my dear."

"Okay," she said, and plugged the machine into a socket on the table. She grasped one pair of handles. "Who'd like to offer me a year of their life?"

There was a pause.

"This whole thing is nonsense," said the Professor and, with an audible sigh, he seized the handles of the box.

A few seconds later, he writhed violently and collapsed across the table. James's ulcer went into spasms.

"You've killed him," yelled Reg.

"No I haven't," said Milly. "He didn't have a year to give - he was going to die anyway. And now the old fool has fused my machine." A wisp of smoke emerged from the box. "Help! The polarity's been reversed - it's sucking the time out of me!" She tried to let go of the handles, but her hands were stuck.

All eyes turned to Milly who was aging rapidly. Her breasts shrivelled and sagged, her legs lost their muscle and swelled at the knees and ankles. Her waist thickened, her back curved and her once-shapely buttocks sagged below the level of the miniskirt.

The sight of pitted flesh filled the monitor. "Cut to Camera Three," yelled James.

A shocked Reginald Kaye managed to smile. "Well, thank you very much for your demonstration, Miss – er – Thackeray, I think we are ready to make our judgement."

He looked at the two remaining judges, who were staring in horror at the crone who had taken Milly's place. "Does the time machine have your roar of approval or your snarl of rejection?"

"What?"

"The producer is ready for your verdict."

They hesitated, then glanced at the prostrated Professor, and hit the snarl button.

"There it is," said Reginald. "I'm afraid you have been rejected from The Lion's Den. Goodbye."

The camera zoomed in as Milly's wrinkled face registered disappointment. She pulled her time machine away from the death grip of the professor but, as she turned to go, she lost her balance on her stiletto heels and toppled to the floor, still holding the box.

"Oh bugger," she said.

Bleep. James hurriedly pushed the delete button.

As the music of an advertisement filled the viewing gallery, he dissolved an Alka Seltzer into a glass of water. His job was over for another week. On the whole, he felt, the programme had gone rather well.

The Lost Child
Would he ever find his daughter?

Simon was dozing on the bench on which he had spent the night, when he was woken by the sound of laughter as children tumbled out of the school and into the playground beside the park.

At once alert, Simon got to his feet and walked towards the chain-link fence that surrounded the school. He paused half-hidden by a bush and stared at the children as they ran around the playground, playing games, letting off energy, full of life.

One of them sat apart from the rest, not joining in the fun. He recognized Jennifer at once. Her hair was styled differently and she had lost weight but the way the light caught her cheekbones and the tilt of her mouth were unmistakable. Simon clutched the fence, feeling the links hard against his fingers.

"Jenny," he called.

Children were looking towards him, their eyes wide and frightened, and he realized that he must look a sight, with his dishevelled clothes and stubbled chin.

"Jenny," he called again, but she continued to stare at the ground, as if in a dream.

A teacher came up to him, glaring suspiciously. "Can I help you?"

Simon showed her his identification card. Lance Ercott, private detective. "I'm looking for a missing child," he said.

She stared at the card for so long that he became concerned that she would recognise it as a fake. At last, she handed it back.

"You can't hang around out here," she said. "I suggest you make an appointment to see the headmistress."

"Can you tell me the name that blond girl?"

"No, I cannot. Leave or I'll call the police."

He left slowly, looking back over his shoulder at the child, but seeing only the woman glaring at him.

Simon rang the headmistress in his role as Lance Ercott and was surprised to be given an interview that afternoon. He bought a razor and spent time in the public toilet making himself presentable.

"We're always happy to co-operate with the authorities, Mister Ercott," said the headmistress as she shook his hand. "What exactly do you want with the school?"

"I have reason to believe that one of your children might be a kidnap victim," he said.

The headmistress nodded. "Her form mistress informed me that you were taking an interest in the girl. I can assure you that she lives with her natural parents and has been a pupil at the school for many years."

"She looked so sad," he said, feeling depression closing over him. He had really thought, really thought that this time... There was the sound of an approaching siren.

"I'm sorry Mister Ercott, or should I say Simon Stainton," she said. He looked up at her, startled by the sound of his name. How did she know? "I was asked to contact the police if you showed up," she said.

He got to his feet just as the door opened and two policemen came in.

"Mister Stainton? Please accompany us to the police station." They were kind, in their way. They held onto his arms, but more to support him and stop him from falling than to prevent him escaping.

Helen was waiting for him at the police station. At the sight of his wife he started to cry. Huge, uncontrollable tears welled out of his eyes and his body was racked with sobs. Helen ran and put her arms around him. "Darling, are you all right?"

"I couldn't find her," he said, and he could feel hot tears trickling down his cheeks.

"Of course you couldn't," she said. "You mustn't keep looking like this. Please understand. Jenny is dead."

For a moment he remembered - the rain, the darkness, the bump as he backed his car into the driveway. For a moment he remembered, and then his tortured brain shied away from the memory. A cry escaped his lips, echoing the anguish within. One day he would have the strength to remember – but not yet, not when his darling daughter might be lost and waiting for her daddy to find her.

With a bowed head he let Helen drive him back to their empty home.

The Manna Plant
Symbiosis could solve the world's food problem

His wife was still asleep when it was time for Richard to go to work. He went up to the bedroom and touched her shoulder.

Her eyes opened "Good morning, darling." Her voice sounded husky and deep within her throat something flickered.

A terrible thought struck him. "You didn't eat any of the manna plant, did you?"

"Oh, Richard," she looked at him through tear-filled eyes. "I'm so sorry. Laura picked one of the fruits. She had already taken a bite out of it before she showed it to me. So I took a bite too, just to check it was okay."

Oh no, not their daughter as well. He should never have brought that damned plant home before it had been fully tested.

When Richard arrived at the Foundation, he was greeted by Dave, a fellow scientist. "We've been feeding mice your manna plants."

Richard groaned when he saw the mice. They stood on their hind legs, holding up their forelegs, which were covered with green, leaf-like flaps. From the mouth, of every mouse bloomed huge, sweet-smelling flowers.

"How do they breathe, or eat?"

"They don't need to," said Dave. "They make food by photosynthesis and absorb gases through those leaf-like flaps. As for drinking the feet are sprouting roots, which can bury themselves in soil."

"No," cried Richard.

"Yes, I'm sorry, Rick, old friend, but it looks as if your hopes of a Nobel Prize have gone AWOL. There is some talk of shipping the fruit out to crisis areas, but strictly top secret."

Richard raced home and entered the house. Silence.

Terrified of what he might find, he looked in the kitchen. It was empty. The debris of breakfast was still on the table. He looked out through the window and saw a figure lying on the lawn. It was Laura. Her eyes were closed and, although her body was covered with a towel, Richard could see that the skin of her face and limbs was green and disfigured by flap-like growths.

There was only one way to save his beloved daughter from her fate. He rushed into the garden and seized her by the throat. Her mouth opened and her tongue protruded. It bulged outwards further and further until it became impossibly large. Then it opened into a scarlet flower.

Thud! There was a blow on the back of his skull and he blacked out.

When Richard came to, he was on his back on the grass. Laura lay across his feet and Helen across his chest, pinning him to the ground. Something was being pushed between his lips and he clamped his mouth shut.

"I'm sorry, darling, but you must eat the fruit," said Helen. He pressed his lips tightly together and shook his head. "If you don't become one of us, you will be against us."

She pushed a finger between his lips, it was slender and hard like a twig. He gritted his teeth but it prized his jaws apart and the manna fruit was pushed in. He tried not to chew or swallow, but it was no use, he coughed and choked and swallowed and it was gone, sliding down to his stomach.

Once she was certain that the fruit had been eaten, Helen rolled off him. He sat up and buried his face in his hands.

"What have you done to me?" he sobbed.

"You tried to kill Laura," she said.

"I tried to save her."

"Now you must save us all."

He had difficulty getting to his feet and knew that the fruit was already taking effect.

"We must hurry," he said and led the way to a fence that separated the garden from the wood beyond. He helped Helen over the fence and together they managed to lift Laura over. In the depths of the wood they found a sunny slope beside a steam.

"Nobody will find us here," said Laura. She did not speak but her words came clearly into Richard's head.

"It's beautiful," said Helen and he realised that they had all become telepathic.

Richard spread out his arms and felt his skin tingle deliciously in the sun. His mouth was blocked by a growing flower bud and he thought a message to his family.

"I love you."

The Norton Hole

Recognition, however short-lived, is always gratifying.

Professor Norton staggered up the hill towards the main building of the cyclotron, chased by distant shouts. He reached a window through which came a voice he recognised. McNab was inside, pontificating. He knocked on the window so hard he could feel the glass tremble beneath his fist.

"Stop the experiment!" he shouted. Inside the room there was confusion and surprise. All eyes turned to him. "Stop the experiment!"

With a startled yelp, the professor felt rough hands seize him and wrestle him to the ground. When the two security guards lifted him up his spectacles were awry and he could feel blood trickling from his nose.

Pressmen were running out of the building, cameras at the ready. *Flash, flash, flash.*

"Stop the experiment!" Professor Norton yelled. "It could destroy the world!"

"Why good afternoon, Professor." McNab emerged from the building. "Did you lose your invitation? No need to stand outside knocking. Come in. You're just in time."

Professor Norton allowed himself to be led into the control room, a guard on either side.

"Let me introduce you all to Professor Norton," said McNab. "I used to be his assistant many years ago. As you probably know, his life's work on cold fusion has led to nothing, zero, a big non-starter. I'm very sorry professor that your disappointment has led you to attack the development of hot fusion."

Did McNab really believe that it was jealousy that brought him here? Had he not read his papers on creating mini black holes? Professor Norton made a desperate plea. "You must stop the experiment. It's too dangerous. It could create a black hole, which will destroy the Earth."

"Nonsense," purred McNab. "Every precaution has been taken. I can assure you that there is absolutely no possibility of anything going wrong." He looked at the piece of paper in his hand. "Now where was I?" He found the right place and continued with his speech. "I would like to thank the European Union for the use of this magnificent new cyclotron. The world can now look forward to unlimited supplies of free and unpolluting energy." He moved towards a bank of control panels and monitors.

"No!" yelled Professor Norton bursting free from the guards and rushing towards him.

With a triumphant grin his nemesis pulled the switch.

Cameras flashed, recording the moment. They flashed again, recording the professor's humiliation as he was tackled to the ground and held in a painful arm lock.

Deep in the heart of the cyclotron, hydrogen atoms were hurled together at unimaginable speed. Millions of them fused, releasing energy.

.McNab pointed to a dial as its pointer moved from zero up a scale of kilowatts. "Energy is being created - the world's first nuclear-fusion power. And I would like to assure Professor Norton that the planet still exists." There was a smattering of laughter and a round of applause. "Perhaps an apology is due, Professor?"

Professor Norton stared at the dial as it flickered and went back to zero. It was as his calculations had predicted.

"A small glitch," said McNab.

Inside the cyclotron, a mass had formed with enough gravitational pull to suck back energy released by further impacts. The mass of atomic nuclei ate its way down through the metal floor of the compression chamber making a hole the size of a pin head. When it started eating through the basement of the building, it had added enough matter to make a hole the size of a golf ball. As it passed through the soil, a startled worm passed over the event horizon and was distorted into a long brown thread before being sucked into what had now become a black hole.

The next day, the story made headline news. It was given extra punch by contrasting the triumph of McNab with the humiliation of Professor Norton.

By the time the world discovered the black hole, it had reached the centre of the Earth. It was several miles across and swallowing matter at a huge and increasing rate.

It was some consolation to Professor Norton that they named it after him. Recognition, however short-lived, is always gratifying.

The Perfect Pot
Fire makes love strong

Once, at the dawn of time, there were two lovers. People had no names in those far off times, so he called her Beauty and she called him Strength.

He built a hut from woven branches, beside a river which ran through a wood. In the day they would make love on the banks of the river and at night they would make love in the hut. The earth responded to their love making and all around them the trees were laden with fruit and the waters of the river teamed with fish.

One day, a chill wind blew the leaves from the trees and chopped the smooth waters of the river into little waves. As if blown by the wind, a woman appeared on the opposite bank of the river. Her hair was as black as a raven's wing and her skin was as white as milk. When she bathed naked in the river, Strength could not take his eyes off her. He called her Desire.

Beauty woke one morning and found Strength had gone. With anguish in her heart, she left the hut and saw her man on the other side of the river with Desire in his arms.

Beauty was abandoned, and yet she was not alone for she had a child growing within her. The wind dried her tears and the wind was the wind of change. Down by the riverside Beauty knelt, where she and Strength had made love. She plunged her hands into the thick, red clay and she made a pot – round as eternity, deep as devotion and curved like a heart.

All her love for Strength went into creating a pot so perfect that even the restless wind paused to admire it. But the pot was delicate and easily broken, so Beauty placed it high on a shelf in the hut.

In the depths of winter, when all was still, Beauty's child was born. She held him close and suckled him and called him Purpose, for he had given her life new meaning.

In spring, when the woods were bursting with fresh life, she had visitors. Strength and Desire stood outside the hut.

"You must leave the hut," said Desire. "Strength built it and we want to live in it."

"Please let me stay," begged Beauty. "I have a baby to look after."

But Desire was without mercy and forced her out of the hut, while Strength hung his head in shame.

"Look at your son," Beauty said to Strength. He looked and, when she saw the torment in his eyes, she pitied him. Before she disappeared into the woods, she looked back at him and smiled.

Beauty's smile melted the ice Desire had placed in his heart. That night, Strength waited till Desire was asleep then crept out of the hut and went into the woods to find Beauty and the baby.

Desire woke shortly after and found that he had gone. Her rage knew no bounds. She set the hut on fire with embers from the hearth. But the fire was justice, the fire was vengeance, as she reached up to smash the perfect pot, the fire caught Desire and burnt her to ashes.

Far away, in the darkness of the woods, Beauty saw the fire. She hurried towards it and, when she saw the burning hut, she gave a cry of distress, thinking that Strength might be inside.

"Beauty." She heard her name and turned to see Strength running out of the woods towards her. She was so relieved to see him that she let him gather her into his arms.

"Oh Beauty, I am so sorry," he wept as he kissed her and then the baby. "Please let me stay and look after you."

Beauty kissed his damp cheeks and assured him that he was forgiven and that her love was as strong as ever.

In the morning, rain fell upon the embers of the hut, making them sizzle and cool. Strength saw Beauty's perfect pot among the ashes.

"This is magnificent," he said.

"Be careful," said Beauty, "it's very fragile." But the lovely, heart-shaped pot wasn't fragile any more – the fire had made it strong.

The Priest and the Wicca

Is being burnt alive a just punishment?

Agnes Dyer's cat was sitting on the dresser, watching its mistress grind hibiscus seeds in a mortar. It withdrew into the shadows as the village priest burst in.

"The door has a knocker," said Agnes, feeling her cheeks flush. She still found his presence exciting, even after all those years.

"I don't knock on the door of Evil," he said.

"Oh? You go right in, eh, Charles?" She cackled at her own wit.

The priest was not amused. "You weren't in church on Sunday, Agnes."

"I had to help Mrs Fletcher deliver a child."

"You put worldly needs above the worship of God?"

"Yes, verily I do, the woman could have died without me. Are you really here because you missed me in church?"

"No, I'm here about Squire Gilbert. You healed the battle wound from which he was dying and now he is paying his tithe to you, instead of to the church."

"Yes," agreed Agnes. "He's a very generous man, the Squire, and so grateful for my humble talents."

"Humble talents? Works of the Devil, you mean. I demand the money which rightfully belongs to the church."

Agnes shook her head. "Sorry, I need the money to buy medicines for the poor. Herbs don't grow on trees you know."

The priest rallied to his argument. "The Lord sends sickness to punish evildoers. If people wish to become well, they must come to church to do penance." His eyes rested upon the cat. "Look, a Familiar!"

The cat snarled as the priest's finger pointed at it.

"Don't be too familiar with the cat," warned Agnes. "It might bite."

"It's a demon in disguise," said the priest, "What's its name?"

"Blackie."

"Belaqui – a demon from the tenth ring of Hell. That proves it."

"Proves what?"

"It proves you are a witch."

"Oh nonsense," said Agnes.

"What about that, and that?" he said pointing around the room.

"A cooking pot and a broom? Everyone has those."

"A cauldron and a besom," corrected the priest. He peered at Agnes. "You've got a wart on your nose."

Agnes reached up a hand, removed the wart and looked at it. "It's not a wart, it's a hibiscus seed."

"I bet there's a witch's mark somewhere on your body," he said.

"Well, you're not going to start looking for it," she said archly,

"I won't have to," he said, dropping his bombshell with a smirk. "The Witch Finder General is coming to the village tomorrow and I'll make sure that you are the first witch he finds."

Agnes sank down onto a chair, her face white. "Please, Charles, forget this nonsense."

He shook his head. "It's not I who shall judge you but the Lord."

"Do you feel nothing for me? After the love we once had for each other?"

He frowned. "I've forbidden you ever to mention it."

"I loved you, Charles, truly I did. I thought you felt the same."

"How dare you, woman. I am a priest vowed to celibacy. You seduced me by witchcraft. That's what it was. You cast an evil spell over me and made me weak."

"But don't you understand, Charles? If you deliver me to the Witch Finder General, I will be tortured and burnt alive."

The priest looked down at her without pity. "Thou shalt not suffer a witch to live." He moved towards the door.

"Please, Charles. Do you honestly believe that it is a just punishment to burn someone alive?" she asked.

He turned "If they have transgressed against the laws of God." Then he left the cottage, slamming the door behind him.

The priest had not gone far down the road when a bolt of lightning came out of the sky and struck him down. The cat joined Agnes at the window to watch a spiral of smoke rise from the blackened remains.

"Congratulations," said Belaqui.

"It seems a little harsh," said Agnes. "But he broke his vow of celibacy and agreed that being burnt alive is a just punishment." She put the wand back into the drawer beside her book of spells and sighed, "Poor Charles, I'm going to miss our little talks."

The Schisombuphrenic
Two individuals sharing a body

Simon Seale switched on in a police cell lit by a high, barred window. His watch had been removed, but he knew what the time would be – eight o'clock. He always switched on at eight in the morning.

Last night had been the worst yet. For years his dreams had become more vivid and disagreeable, swirling lights, loud music, women and brawling. Last night he dreamt he had been in a lap-dancing club. A huge pair of pink buttocks had been gyrating inches from his face.

By concentrating hard he had managed to levitate a toothpick from the table. It was the first time he had been able to influence a dream but things ended badly. His attempted jab coincided with a gyration which made the toothpick sink several millimetres into the girl's flesh. Her screams reverberated through the club, police were called and Simon's alter-ego was arrested.

It took an hour for him to be released. The sergeant ploughed through the paperwork with the slow thoroughness of the semi-literate.

Simon was late for work.

"Where were you?" asked Adrian. "I thought I was going to have to make the presentation without you."

You wish, thought Simon.

They entered the room, where half a dozen suited men were sitting facing a screen. The clients had been enjoying coffee and biscuits, the tantalising smell of rich-roast hung in the air.

Adrian took his place at the projector, the lights dimmed and upon the screen appeared a woodland scene.

"This is to emphasise the green credentials of the new Rapier Excel," said Simon.

The camera zeroed in on a bolt, sitting on a rosette of leaves. The bolt was picked up by a fairy who cradled it lovingly before joining a multitude of other fairies, assembling the car.

"There's nothing fairy about our car," complained a client.

"Oh no," said Simon. "This is the clever part. When they have built the car, the fairies fuse to form a dragon."

The dragon and car played together then raced away - the car in front. The lights came up and Simon stood before a sceptical audience.

"I don't like the bolt, It looks like litter."

"We could change that," said Simon. He was aware that everyone was staring at his tie and looked down to see that its end had risen and was weaving around like a cobra. Desperately, Simon flattened it.

"What about pixies instead of fairies?" A client was talking but his eyes were fixed on Simon's chest where his handkerchief was slowly emerging from his breast pocket.

"Thank you very much, Mr Seale," said the manager rising to his feet and indicating that Simon should leave the room. "Adrian will take over now." He beckoned to Adrian who leapt forward to take Simon's place.

Simon sat at his desk staring into space. Tears of self-pity trickled down his cheeks. He longed to go to a concert or an opera, but his alter-ego made his nights unbearable. Now his days would be unbearable too.

Simon got up and walked to the lifts. There was only one way out. He took a lift to the top floor, where there was access to the roof.

One step, that's all it would take. One step, a few seconds of falling, and then his miserable life would be finished. He stood on the parapet took a deep breath and blacked out.

Simon awoke at home on the sofa. It must be morning, but why was it still dark? There was an envelope beside him on the coffee table. He opened it. Inside was a ticket to tomorrow's opera and a sheet of paper on which was written the single word TRUCE?

With a sudden surge of hope Simon switched on the television. It was eight o'clock in the evening. He and his alter ego had switched! What did it mean? For a start, it meant he could go to the opera.

He wondered how his alter-ego would cope with life in the advertising agency. Rather well, he reckoned. He would certainly be more than a match for Adrian.

He leant over, picked up a pen, and wrote YES.

The Swatting of Barnaby
An innocent misunderstanding

I admit, m'lud, that me and my mate Barnaby were three sheets to the wind, in fact we were pretty legless.

We were rolling home after a night on the tiles and I invited my mate in to have coffee. It was after midnight and the street lights were out and search as I may I could not find my keys.

I says to Barnaby, "Come on, there must be a way in."

Well, we tried all the doors and all the windows and we even tried the garage, but the house was locked as tight as a nun's nasty.

It became a bit of a challenge and Barnaby saw a tree that overhung the roof. I suppose the light should have dawned then m'lud, but, what with being pie eyed and a tad hysterical, I let the poor bastard climb onto the roof. The next thing I know he gave a cheery wave and disappeared down the chimney.

Well, it seemed like a fine plan and I waited in happy anticipation that soon I would be sipping a mug of the hot stuff. There was much scumbling and scraping and then a muffled voice said, "I'm stuck!"

Bloody Barnaby, I might have known he would get into trouble. I could hardly leave him stuck in my chimney and so I broke a window and got into the house.

I knew something was amiss at once. Unless someone had replaced my kitchen with luxury oak cabinets I had got into the wrong house.

"Help!" That stupid git, Barnaby, was still yelling from the chimney so I hurried into the living room. His booted foot was hanging down the middle of the inglenook fireplace like an out-of-season Santa. I gave it a yank and, crash, he landed in the hearth amid a shower of soot and brick dust.

Did I mention the living room had white carpets? The owners of the house must have read too many home décor magazines, the whole place was like a Shah's palace.

Anyway, along with Barnaby came the thing that had blocked his descent - a box. It crashed onto the fender, broke open and spilt out its contents in a glittering pile of gold and jewels. We looked at each other in astonishment. Who on earth would hide their valuables up a chimney?

We couldn't leave all that bling getting covered in soot so we picked up as much as we could and stuffed it into our pockets, intending to deposit it in a safe place.

The room looked as if it had been hit by a soot bomb. We decided to write a note of apology about the state the place was in. I left Barnaby rummaging in the bureau for a pen and paper, while I went into the kitchen to get him a glass of water. The poor sap was feeling a bit faint after all the excitement.

I noticed some fresh lemons in one of those fancy, wire baskets so I picked up a knife to cut a slice. I reckoned it would make the water more refreshing for poor old Barnaby.

It was then that I heard him yell so I went running back into the living room. He had discovered a gun in the bureau and was holding it up high.

"Look what I've found!"

He had barely finished speaking when the front door burst open and an armed swat team rushed into the house. Some interfering... I mean, alert neighbour must have rung the police.

Poor Barnaby swung round and, in his shock, it appeared as if he pointed the gun at the policemen. The unfortunate bastard was cut down in a hail of bullets.

I flung myself to the floor and begged for mercy. They handcuffed me in a rough way, and showed no sympathy for my grief at the loss of my friend. Nor did they believe my explanation of why we were in a stranger's house in the middle of the night.

I admit, it doesn't look good. The broken window , the gun, the knife, the pockets stuffed with jewels. But I can assure you m'lud, it has all been an innocent misunderstanding.

The Thirteenth Planet
He should never have let the rat get at the supplements.

Bruce finished writing his report on the twelfth planet on his list. Acid rain and flesh-eating fungi made it unsuitable for colonisation.

The body of the experimental rat he had placed on the surface lay on the table beside him. It had died horribly and he silently asked its forgiveness before crossing over to the disposal chute and ejecting it into space. The rats had been his only companions on the long voyage and he had become fond of them.

Twelve planets, twelve dead rats, so far this expedition had failed to find a single colonisable planet.

"It's just you and me pal," he said as he placed some food pellets into the thirteenth cage. He expected a little pink nose to come waffling out of the straw but nothing happened.

"One more planet to go and then I can go home. So can you – if you survive." He filled the water bowl but there was still no sign of the rat.

"Where are you, Lucky?" he asked. He called the rat Lucky because it was the last to die.

He poked at the straw and revealed a hole in the side of the cage. Lucky had escaped!

Bruce glanced around the untidy cabin. Clothes and equipment were strewn everywhere, there were dozens of places a rat might hide.

Bruce tidied up and found a hole in the cupboard where he stored his food. Lucky had been at the concentrates. Oh dear, a rat fed on pellets was one thing. A rat fed on concentrated vitamin and mineral supplements was another. The dratted creatures were already too intelligent for comfort.

Bruce was late to bed. The cabin was neater than it had been all journey but there was still no sign of Lucky. He was tired when he woke the next morning. A strong coffee would wake him up and then he must prepare for the final landing.

He frowned. His computer was on, surely he remembered switching it off. Such carelessness would drain the ship's battery. A wild thought came – it couldn't have been the rat -could it? No, that would be impossible.

All the settings for the landing were automatic, as was the setting for the return home. Although Bruce was officially the ship's captain, he was a scientist and not a navigator, such intricate calculations were beyond him.

Through the porthole the thirteenth planet grew bigger. Soon Bruce could see the surface. It was green - that was a good sign, where there was photosynthesis there would be oxygen. The spaceship landed in a small valley beside a stream. The vegetation that surrounded it was unlike anything Bruce had seen before – more like giant lichens than terrestrial trees and plants.

This was the moment to put a rat out to test for viability, but there was still no sign of Lucky. Bruce sighed. He would have to suit up and go onto the surface of the planet to gather air, soil and water samples.

Bruce put on his suit and moved to the air lock. Damn that thirteenth rat, it had certainly not been lucky for him. He emerged into a strange world. There was no birdsong but far away came the roar of a mighty animal. They would have to kill off any predators, he thought, if the planet proved suitable for colonisation.

He gathered his samples and made his way back to the spaceship. The door was locked! Desperately he tugged at the handle, discarding his precious samples and treading them underfoot in his panic. There were only a few minutes left before the automatic systems triggered the return home.

He was still struggling with the door when he saw a face at the porthole - a white, pointed face with a pink nose and long whiskers. It was Lucky! The rat stared at him and then raised a paw in farewell as the engine kicked into life.

Stunned, Bruce flung himself back, out of the way of the tongue of flame that carried the craft upwards until it was lost in the blue of the sky. The roar of a mighty beast sounded again, and this time it was nearer.

The Time Pipe

Get the pest controller, the time pipe is leaking.

Walter Budd sat in his office cubicle, copying information onto the computer. It was a tedious job. He glanced at his watch: quarter past three. Another two hours and fifteen minutes before he could return home to an empty flat and his dirty breakfast dishes.

He sighed and paused to stretch his back then saw the vortex – a swirling hole in the air beside him. Puzzled, Walter reached out a finger, touched it and was sucked through. He felt the air whizzing past him as he plummeted downwards at an ever-increasing rate.

"Aaaargh, something's dropped out of the time pipe!" shrieked a female voice, as the terrified Walter fell through the air.

For long seconds the fall continued, then Walter hit a shagpile carpet of such dimensions that the pile completely enveloped him. He was winded, but amazed to be still alive.

"What was it?" the female voice said.

"A human," boomed a male voice.

"Kill it."

Walter looked around. Behind him was a long, low cave.

"There it is!" screamed the female. Walter hurled himself into the cave just as something came sweeping down behind him, so close that he could feel the wind of it.

"It's got under the sofa. Get it out!"

"I'm not lifting heavy furniture," said the male. "We'll have to get the pest controller."

"Typical," she sneered. "You try to save money by doing the plumbing yourself and end up paying for a pest controller. The garden is still infested by dinosaurs after the last leak." Their voices faded into the distance.

Hours passed and Walter grew hungry. He emerged from the cave, his body tense, ready for any warning of attack. The room was in darkness, illuminated only by moonlight. Walter pushed his way through the carpet to a huge patio door overlooking a moonlit garden. It was a wondrous place, with flowers as big as trees and a shining lake.

Then he saw the woman. She was standing up to her waist in the carpet, gazing out at the garden, just as he had done. His heart missed a beat. She too must have fallen through a hole in the time pipe.

He hurried towards her. She was beautiful, with long dark hair and a slender figure. They must be the only two humans in this strange other-world. She would be Eve to his Adam; together they would face the challenges of the garden and perhaps even start a new tribe. What an adventure – humans and dinosaurs, living together like in The Lost World. His heart filled with happiness.

"Hello," he said. "Don't be frightened, I'm human, like you."

He approached slowly, not wanting to frighten her. It wasn't until he was close that he saw that something was wrong. Her profile was strange – her nose too pointed and her chin too flat. He reached out and touched her hair. It was a solid block, not individual strands.

Walter turned to run, but his touch had triggered a mechanism. With a whooshing sound, a transparent cage descended from above and enclosed him.

The lights of the room came on and he flung up his hands to protect his eyes from the glare.

"Got the bugger." The female voice was triumphant. "Well done pest controller. Bung it back in the time pipe."

Walter fell head-over-heels as the cage was picked up and inverted. He felt himself being tipped out and tumbled back into his office.

He lay on the floor in a swirl of emotions. Hope, disappointment, shock and fear – Walter felt them all. Gradually he recovered, sat up and looked around. Everything appeared normal - there was no whirling vortex, his computer was on and the pile of papers he had been working on lay undisturbed on the desk.

Walter got to his feet, sat back on his chair and looked at his watch. The time was a quarter past three: he had been replaced into the time pipe at the moment he had left it. He waited for a while but nothing happened, so he started copying data into his computer.

Slowly the happiness ebbed out of his soul. Walter Budd's adventure was over.

The Time Switch
Would Sandra fail her second chance?

Sandra looked at the electrician as he pulled a tangle of wires out of the socket and stared at them. He was very young, scarcely old enough to be a qualified electrician. He coloured under her gaze.

"I'll soon have them sorted out," he said.

She nodded and left him to it. For some reason the electricity in her flat had been behaving oddly. Appliances she thought had been switched off turned themselves on and lights flickered.

She had complained to the landlord and he had sent round this lad. Sandra shrugged. At least it wasn't her responsibility. If it didn't get sorted out she would move. Foot loose and fancy free that was her life now. A merry widow – what an oxymoron. The misery of losing Roger still weighed her down. The memory of their last day had not dimmed with the passing of time. She had argued with him over breakfast and made him late for his bus. He had rushed out of the house and ran straight across the road into the path of a refuse lorry. She felt tears prickle and longed for redemption.

"Right, ma'am. I've finished."

Sandra hurriedly wiped her eyes and turned to the electrician. "Did you manage to fix it?"

He looked at her with compassion and Sandra was embarrassed that he had seen her grief. "Yes, ma'am, I've fixed it. Good luck."

Good luck? What an extraordinary thing to say. Sandra watched the lad leave then went to try the switch.

CLICK.

At first she thought nothing had happened for the light did not switch on. She was about to call the electrician back when she realised that she was no longer in the flat. She looked round in a amazement at the little living room with chintz curtains and a beamed ceiling. She was back in the cottage – the home she had shared with Roger.

As if in a dream she went into the kitchen. Breakfast was laid on the table, boiled eggs and toast. The kettle whistled and she walked over to the counter and made two cups of coffee. She was slipping back into her old life. Memories of widowhood were fading fast.

Someone was coming down the stairs, she looked up expectantly and through the kitchen door came Roger.

"Darling!" Her heart filled with happiness at the sight of her husband. She put her arms around him and raised her head for a kiss. He hesitated and then kissed her briefly, his lips scarcely brushing hers.

"This is a change from last night," he said.

"Last night?" Her brain was a jumble of old and new memories. Did they quarrel last night? Yes, perhaps they did.

"I'm not giving up smoking," he said. "Nor my Saturday night out with the boys." He was defiant, inviting her to continue the argument.

For a moment she was annoyed by his selfishness. They had so little money, paying the mortgage was a struggle and yet he was happy to squander cash on his own pleasures. She was tempted to respond but a fading memory told her that she must not.

"Whatever you think best, dear," she said and put a cup of coffee on the table in front of him.

He looked at her sideways, wondering if she was about to attack him from a different angle, but she merely smiled and got on with her breakfast.

Gradually the tension between them relaxed and they sat in companionable silence.

"Actually," he said at last. "I am trying to cut down."

"That's good," she said.

He looked at his watch. "Time to go, the bus is due."

He rose to his feet and went into the hall to pick up his briefcase.

"See you tonight," she said and stood in the doorway to watch him look left and right before safely crossing the road.

She frowned. A different memory was struggling to remain in her mind but it didn't belong there, it belonged in an alternative life, a life of rented flats and loneliness. As it blinked out of existence she was left with a vision of a young electrician with a smiling face and a halo around his head.

The Wiccan Study Group.

Is the U3A group a coven of witches?

Mr Ambridge was paying a courtesy visit to the Wiccan Study Group and had become lost in a maze of roads. Arriving late, he knocked on the door of a neat little bungalow. There was a pause and the door was opened by a woman whose amiable face lit with a smile.

"Oh Mr Ambridge, we're so glad you could come. I'm the leader of our little group." She led him through the hall. "I'm afraid we've started without you."

His apologies for lateness were cut short when the leader flung open the living room door to reveal an elderly woman spread-eagled on the floor. She lay, naked, within a pentacle chalked on the parquet flooring.

Mr Ambridge tore his gaze away from the horrid sight and saw half a dozen women seated around the walls.

"A big welcome for the chairman of our U3A." The leader was saying. "Mr Ambridge is the first man to visit our little group and we're hoping to take advantage of his presence by asking him to perform the Penetration Ceremony on Mrs Prendergast." She turned to Mr Ambrose. "We would have preferred a virgin but Mrs Prendergast is the next best thing, she has been widowed for many years."

"Are you suggesting," Mr Ambridge spluttered, "that I should have –er- sex with that – er- woman?"

The leader frowned. "We don't like to think of it as sex, Mr Ambridge, we think of it as a fertility rite to appease Mother Earth. There's no need for foreplay, a simple penetration will suffice."

"I absolutely refuse."

There were murmurs of disappointment. Mrs Prendergast moaned and threshed about on the floor. The others rose from their chairs and rushed towards her with clucks of dismay like a flock of bantams.

"Poor Mrs Prendergast has a dodgy hip," the leader explained. "It took her ages to get ready for the ceremony."

Mr Ambridge stood well back while Mrs Prendergast was helped to her feet and ushered solicitously out of the room. When the group had re-gathered, the leader announced that rather than waste the pentacle, they would try a summoning spell instead.

Mr Ambridge watched while the leader put a casserole dish in the centre of the pentacle and sprinkled wood chippings into it.

"I really don't think this sort of thing is suitable for the U3A," he muttered.

"Amaymon, amaymon," chanted the leader. After bowing to all four corners of the compass, she lit a black candle, waved it around and threw it into the casserole dish. Whoosh! The wood chippings caught fire and billowing smoke filled the air.

"Fire!" yelled Mr Ambridge. He was about to rush from the room when he saw that the smoke had formed a column within the pentacle.

He watched in amazement as it coalesced into the form of a demon, which snarled and threw itself at the invisible confines of the pentacle. Mr Ambridge screamed - a shrill, terrified sound, which caught the attention of the demon. It snarled, exposing long, yellow fangs then attacked, lunging and clawing at the air as it tried to reach him.

"George Sebastian Prendergast. How dare you resurrect yourself in my presence?" Mrs Prendergast had returned to the room, now dressed in a pink jump suit. She stood at the edge of the pentacle, her tight, grey curls wobbling as she shook her fists.

The creature stopped and turned to stare at her. A look of horrified recognition crossed its face. Then, with a whimper, it shrivelled away, leaving a faint smell of sulphur.

The leader was all apologies. "Oh my dear, I'm so sorry. What a dreadful experience, and after all you've been through. I'd no idea you had married a demon."

"Haven't we all?" said a bitter voice.

It was the end of the meeting. The leader turned to Mr Ambridge.

"Thank you so much for coming. I do hope you found it informative."

"He says that he doesn't think our group is suitable for the U3A," piped up one of the women.

"Is that true?" The leader's face was no longer amiable. She reached out and removed a fallen hair from his shoulder.

"Oh no, no, a m-m-misunderstanding," stammered Mr Ambridge. "I'm very impressed, very. An excellent group."

He made a hurried exit. Was it his imagination, or did the sound of cackling laughter speed him on his way?

The Wig Man
Her old professor was behaving strangely

"My life is a sham," said Professor Pragnell and lay back on the couch, dislodging his bushy, red wig so it sat at a rakish angle.

Lucy stared at him in consternation. What on earth was her professor doing in her consultation room? It had been five years since she had graduated, but she recognised him instantly, despite his disguise. She decided to play it by the book.

"How does that make you feel?" she said.

He stared at the ceiling for long seconds and then turned his watery, blue eyes on her. "Clever," he said.

She frowned. "Professor Pragnell, I must ask why you are wearing that ludicrous wig."

"Ludicrous?" He looked affronted and reached up to adjust it. "My dear Lucy, I have discovered that if a person's attention is drawn to a single feature, they will not remember the rest of the face. Your receptionist, for example, will only remember the wig and nothing more."

"But why have you come to see me?" asked Lucy.

"I need your help, my dear. You always showed such – promise." He pronounced the word strangely and Lucy felt a tingle of nervousness. She glanced at the alarm button on her desk, and then looked hurriedly away.

"You say that you feel your life is a sham," she said. "Why is that?"

"I live the life of a successful academic. Ha! If people only knew…" His voice trailed off and a wolfish smile spread across his face.

Lucy bent over her notebook. This must be a test of her technique and she was determined to conduct the session correctly.

"Did you have a happy childhood?" she asked. "What was your relationship with your mother?"

"Happy? Yes, I suppose I was happy and my relationship with my mother was good – at first."

"At first?" queried Lucy.

"Yes. She became more distant."

"Do you know why that was?"

"She didn't like the things I did."

"What sort of things?" said Lucy, trying to hide her apprehension.

Professor Pragnell sat up and stared at her. "Let me ask you a hypothetical question, Lucy. Why should it be worse to pluck a cat than to pluck a flower? They are both living things, are they not?"

Lucy stared at him. "What do you mean – pluck a cat."

"Pluck, you know, take bits off."

She felt sick with disgust. "Is that what you did?"

"Not exactly." He leant back, relishing the effect his words had on her. "It was a hypothetical question, Lucy, and one that my mother couldn't answer either."

Lucy stood up. "I must ask you to leave, Professor."

He looked at her in mock astonishment. "Why?"

"I don't think I can help you," she said, anxious to get him out of the room. "I'll make sure your money is refunded."

"Oh no, Lucy, I know that you will be able to help me. You will help me very much." He smiled that ghastly smile again and she reached for the alarm bell. He was too quick for her. He leapt to his feet, a knife flashed in his hand and sliced down on the desk, severing the wire, so her frantic pressing produced no sound.

He seized her wrist. "You wanted to know how to pluck a cat," he said. "I will show you, Lucy." She tried to scream but he pressed his hand against her mouth. "This is how you do it, Lucy."

His breath was hot in her ear and she felt the blade of the knife slide against her skin. She stopped struggling then and sat very still as he used the razor-sharp blade to cut away her hair.

"Ooh, lovely blonde hair," he said, gathering it into his hands and pressing it against his face. "I've been dreaming of your hair, Lucy, ever since you sat in my class and the sun turned it to glistering gold. Yes." He seemed to be in a state of ecstasy as he inhaled deeply, savouring the scent of her tresses. "This will make a magnificent wig, my dear."

He took a plastic bag out of his pocket and carefully folded the hair into it, then he left the room and she collapsed into tears.

The Wrong Handbag.
A final gift rejected

Julia stood beside the manager and looked around the forlorn little room where her mother had spent the last two years of her life.

"I'm sorry for your loss, but we must clear the room for our next resident," said the manager, indicating the belongings that were piled upon the bed.

Julia looked at the remnants of her mother's life, at the yellowing photographs in their cheap wooden frames. Images of her father and mother stared back at her with she, their only child, smiling at the camera. Later her mother on her own, with Julia older and no longer smiling. The memories hurt and she said to the manager. "Give everything to charity."

"Wait!" The manager stepped forwards and searched through the pile. "She wanted you to have her handbag. She was very insistent. She would have given it to you earlier but you hardly ever came to visit." There was a hint of reproach in her voice.

"I'm busy," said Julia. And it was true, life was hard and she had to work all hours to stay afloat. Besides she had little to say to the old woman who had been her mother.

The manager found the handbag. It was made from hog skin and had gold-plated fittings. It had once been expensive – a gift from her father, but was now battered and worn. Julia took it from the manager and glanced inside – it was empty. She threw it back onto the bed.

"You can get rid of this as well."

The manager was shocked. "Surely you want a memento of your mother."

Julia stared at the bed. There was a small, black patent-leather bag she had given her mother one Christmas. It was unused, tissue paper still wrapped around the handle.

"I'll have this," she said, picking it out of the pile.

A few weeks later she saw her mother's old handbag again. It was on the front page of the local paper, being held aloft by a triumphant young woman, while in her other hand she waved a scratch card. Above the picture was the headline BAGGING A BARGAIN!

With trembling hands Julia picked the paper from the pile at the newsagents and scanned the story. The scratch card had been hidden in a pocket of the bag, which had been bought at a charity shop. It was worth half a million pounds. With it was a message from the unknown benefactor. *"I am too old to enjoy these winnings, may they bring happiness to your life."*

The awful realisation dawned on Julia that for her there was no hope, no salvation – she had taken the wrong handbag.

Tiger Alert!
An encounter with a shape-changing tiger

"*Varanus Komodoensis*," said Stephen, reading from the sign posted beside the Komodo dragon's cage. He turned to Celia. "People thought its saliva was poisonous, but it's just full of bacteria."

The light glinted on his spectacles. Celia used to think that wearing spectacles indicated her fiancé's intelligence. Now, she realised they just showed that he was a short-sighted nerd.

"Poison dart frog *Dendrobates leacomelas*." He had moved to a nearby tank. "Observe its bright yellow and black colouring. What does this tell you, Celia?"

"If the dragon doesn't get you the frog will," observed Celia brightly.

Stephen showed not a glimmer of amusement. "It is a warning sign to predators that the frog secretes a poisonous alkaloid."

Celia sighed. What was meant to be a romantic day at London Zoo was turning out to be an opportunity for Stephen to impress her with his knowledge.

"Can we go outside while the sun is still shining?" she said.

Outside she took a deep breath and faintly on the breeze came the musky scent of big cats. "Let's go this way," she said.

They arrived at a tiger cage. The great beast lay on a rocky ledge dozing in the sun. It opened its deep green eyes and gazed at Celia.

"Siberian tiger *Panthera tigris altaica (abeo)*" read Stephen. He frowned. "Why is that last word in brackets?"

Celia gazed at the tiger and fell in love with its power and beauty while Stephen fretted about the Latin,

"Abeo, it means change." He gave a superior little laugh. "Are they implying that the tiger is a shape changer?"

How Celia wished the tiger stood beside her instead of Stephen. And then it happened! Stephen and the tiger changed places. To the outside observer nothing had altered, but Celia knew the tiger stood beside her. He regarded her with deep green eyes. She took his arm and felt the powerful muscles beneath her hand. His musky scent wafted around her. He was gorgeous.

She looked into the cage. Even as a tiger Stephen was less than impressive, skinny and without the feeling of power that made her tigerman so attractive.

"Goodbye, Stephen," she said and strolled off arm in arm with her tigerman. What a wonderful afternoon they had. They watched the chimpanzees tea party and the feeding of the seals. They went for a ride on the elephant and would have gone into the petting zoo but for Celia's concern that the tigerman might be tempted to snack. Best of all, he never said a word but was content to follow where she led.

It was near closing time when an announcement came over the loud speaker that a tiger had escaped. "Please evacuate the zoo," said the voice of the announcer. "Proceed as quickly as possible to the nearest exit."

As they hurried towards the exit Celia saw a keeper with a gun running towards them.

"Please don't shoot the tiger, it's my fiancé, Stephen." Even as she spoke, Celia realized how ridiculous she must sound. To her surprise the keeper nodded and turned to the tigerman.

"Been up to your old tricks again, eh?"

The tigerman snarled revealing tiger's teeth. The keeper raised his gun. "You've had a lucky escape young lady."

"Don't shoot him!" cried Celia.

"Shoot him? Don't be ridiculous he's one of the last of his kind. He's going back to his cage and woe betide him if he pulls this stunt again." The keeper gestured with his gun and a dejected tigerman slunk back into captivity.

There was a rustle in the bushes. "Is it safe to come out?" It was Stephen.

"I suppose so."

He emerged as a tiger but swiftly morphed into a man. "I've lost my specs," he said, blinking at her short-sightedly.

"You've lost more than that," she said averting her eyes from his nakedness.

"Yes, I've lost faith in you, Celia. You knew this had happened. Goodbye Stephen, you said as you walked away with that creature."

She could think of no excuse. "Sorry," she muttered.

"Consider our engagement terminated," he said and, with as much dignity as his naked butt would allow, he strode away towards the exit.

Toads Like Hairy Pets

When gorgeous hair means everything

Chrissie admired herself in the mirror. Never had her hair looked thicker and more glossy.

"Here, Chrissie, come and look at this!" Her husband called to her from the living room.

She gave a sigh of irritation and went to see what he was watching. The television showed an earnest-looking scientist holding a bottle of Andromeda shampoo.

"Despite our best efforts we have been unable to identify the mysterious substance contained in the shampoo."

The scene changed to Downing Street where a reporter was standing in the rain. "As a precaution the Government has decided to withdraw Andromeda shampoo from sale."

"What a fuss about nothing," her husband said.

Chrissie glared. It was alright for him, he refused to try the new shampoo even though it might make his hair grow back.

"I'm going to the shops while there's still some left," she said but she was too late, the shelf was empty.

Over the following weeks Chrissie eked out her supply of shampoo. It became an obsession with her. She thought of little else but Andromeda shampoo and the picture of Stone Henge on the label. The label seemed to speak to her, but what was it saying?

"I've always wanted to visit Stone Henge," she told her husband.

"No you haven't," he replied and remained lying on the sofa.

She drove down on her own. Hundreds of women were staging a sit-down strike in front of a police cordon. The few men in the crowd were also tossing magnificent heads of hair.

"Hair, hair, hair, hair. We want to have glossy hair!" they chanted. Chrissie sat down and joined in.

A policeman lifted his mobile phone. Was he going to call for reinforcements? This was the moment for action. A woman, who looked like a Viking with flowing red hair, leapt to her feet. "Charge!" she yelled. With screams of excitement the crowd charged.

What happened to the policemen? Chrissie did not know or care. Borne on a wave of exhilaration she rushed towards the standing stones. Now what? Chrissie paused uncertainly and everyone else did the same. Their goal had been achieved and it was empty.

"What do we do now?" she asked a man who was standing beside her.

"I don't know." He smiled and brushed a lock of shining, golden hair back from his forehead. "All I know is that I want to keep my gorgeous new hair."

Chrissie's heart beat faster, what a handsome man and with the right priorities too.

"Look!" Someone pointed upwards to a giant saucer-shaped spaceship, which descended from the clouds and hovered beside the Henge.

"Humans," came a booming voice from the alien craft. "You are the privileged few who have been chosen as exotic pets by the people of Andromeda."

Wow! What an honour! Chrissie watched in excitement as a bridge was lowered from the craft and a group of aliens descended. She blinked, disconcerted by their ugliness. They looked like ten-foot high, bipedal toads with long legs and bulging bellies.

"Please come forward to be fitted with collars and leads," boomed the voice. The chosen ones hesitated. "As you see, your owners are amphibians," continued the voice. "Mammalian hair is a precious rarity. I can assure you that you will be well looked after and your hair will be washed regularly with the very best shampoo."

"Hurrah," yelled the Viking and rushed forwards, followed by the crowd.

Chrissie's new friend pushed her aside in his desperation to be at the front of the queue and she fell. Many feet trampled over her and by the time she had picked herself up it was too late. The lucky ones had been collared and led into the spaceship.

Those few remaining watched in dismay as the bridge was raised and the spaceship disappeared into the clouds.

Chrissie collapsed sobbing onto the grass. Soon her Andromeda shampoo would be finished, soon her life would be a barren waste of mousy brown locks and a bald husband. She felt bruised and rejected but somewhere in the depths of her mind a seed of sanity started to grow. Perhaps, one day, she might be grateful for her escape.

Uncle Angus's Origami Boat/Tent
A great inventor has had enough

I was excited when my Uncle Angus offered to take me on an expedition through the Grand Canyon.

"It will be an opportunity for me to try out my new invention," he said.

When I discovered that his invention was an origami boat/tent I should have said, "No!" But I was young and foolish and on a long college vacation so I agreed to accompany him.

When folded flat the origami boat/tent was three yards long and took up most of the interior car space. I had to crouch down in the foot well.

"Couldn't you put another fold in it," I complained.

Uncle Angus explained at great length about exponential increases in the size of the hinges and the structural difficulties in having too many folds. I was fond of the eccentric old man and nodded my head politely.

We reached the riverbank and unfolded the boat/tent once then twice so it lay flat on the grass measuring approximately six yards by two. A curious crowd gathered.

"What's that? A dance floor?" asked a man.

"It's a boat/tent," said my Uncle. We folded it in two lengthwise – that was the easy part. We then had to fold the joints for ends. Most of the crowd had got bored and disappeared by the time we launched our canoe into the river.

"Good luck," said the man. "You're going to need it."

We ignored the insult and paddled away. We soon became caught in the current and were carried down the Colorado river at great speed. High above us loomed the great walls of the Canyon. It was a spectacular sight and if I hadn't had to struggle so hard to hold the canoe steady, I might have enjoyed it. After a while we came to a grassy bank.

"We'll camp here," said Uncle Angus.

It was late afternoon and clouds were gathering. By the time we had unfolded the boat and folded it in half crosswise to form the tent, it had started to rain.

We sat on a tarpaulin underneath the tent which had once been our boat and listened to the rain drumming on the roof.

"So far it has been a great success," said Uncle Angus.

We ate our sandwiches in companionable silence and settled down in our sleeping bags.

We were woken several hours later by a man who shouted into our tent, "A flash flood is coming. Get in your boat."

We sleepily emerged from the tent into a moon-lit night.

"Where is your boat?" said the man, who appeared to be some sort of official.

"This is our boat," said my Uncle, indicating the tent. "It's a convertible."

The man blinked. "Well hurry up and convert it then, or you'll be washed away."

He paused to watch the start of the elaborate system of transformation.

"Forget it," he said. "You had better come with me."

I obediently followed the man to his boat – a powerful looking inflatable motorboat. When I looked round my uncle was still struggling to convert the tent. He had got it down and in its folded flat position. I was about to jump down and help him when the flood hit.

My poor uncle was lifted by the wave, still standing on the folded boat/tent and went hurtling down the river ahead of us. Over the rapids he sailed, still standing – and that was how Uncle Angus invented the surf board.

"What the hell is he doing?" said the man.

But more was to come. My uncle had been holding onto the tarpaulin and now the speed of his journey made it billow out behind him. Desperate not to lose it he clung on and was lifted up into the air.

"What is he doing now?" yelled the man.

My heart was bursting with excitement and admiration. My uncle had just invented kite surfing.

We rescued him in the end. The poor man was bruised, bedraggled and exhausted.

I tried to encourage him to develop his exciting new inventions but he had had enough. History has credited his inventions to others and as for the origami boat/tent? It was taken to the city dump.

We Have a Message
Important information from the ants

Lately, the ants had been up to something. Major McNab looked down from the back-bedroom window and saw that they were on his garden path again. Down the length of the path were the words **WE HAVE A MESSAGE.** The brown, shimmering letters were made from hundreds of ants.

"Well, I have a message for you, you bloody little insects," growled the major. He hurried downstairs and boiled a kettle then swooshed the boiling water over the concrete path. The carnage was terrible. All the ants in **W, E** and **H** were destroyed, the rest fled back to their colonies. The major returned to the house with the satisfaction of a job well done. Bloody insects. He knew what their message would be – SURRENDER OR DIE, or something like that.

He rang the local paper and told them how he had stopped the uprising of the ants.

A sardonic-looking photographer arrived and the major led him into the garden. He stood pointing to where the letters had been while the photographer busied himself with lenses and light meters.

"Ready?"

The major heard a gasp. He looked up and saw that the photographer had stiffened and was pointing with a trembling finger to of the garden.

There, half-hidden under the shade of an overhanging willow tree, was a brown figure. It had the same strange shimmering quality as the letters and the major realised that the ants had had the bloody cheek to form themselves into the facsimile of a human. The figure spoke in a voice so soft and distorted that it was unintelligible.

"What did it say?" asked the photographer, who had got over his shock and was clicking away, taking picture after picture with frenzied speed.

"It's probably saying it has a message for us," suggested the major. "But don't trust the blighter – it's only those bloody ants in disguise."

"Ants?" gasped the photographer and, as if on cue, the column collapsed and thousands of ants scuttled away.

At last the major was taken seriously. The picture of the ant-man was in all the national papers and the next day there was a ring on the Major's doorbell. The Prime Minister was on his doorstep, surrounded by a retinue of bodyguards and civil servants, while dozens of cameramen and reporters crowded the road behind them.

"This is a great moment for mankind," announced the PM. "I look forward to communicating with the ant-man and bringing his message to the world." He waved at the crowd, pushed past the major and entered the house.

Major McNab was in awe of the Prime Minister. He stood aside as his house was taken over by marksmen, cameramen, advisers, scientists and politicians. Eventually he was invited to join the Prime Minister on the garden path.

A breeze lifted the PM's boyish fringe, revealing the tell-tale plugs of a hair implant. "Where does this figure usually appear?" he asked.

The major's fascinated gaze travelled beyond the hair plugs to the surrounding buildings. Every window was crammed with people and cameras. Heads peered over the garden fence like coconuts on a shy. His gaze travelled back to the PM, who was waiting for an answer.

"Oh-er-yes. It appears over there." The major pointed to the shadow below the tree where a pair of feet was starting to grow.

A myriad cameras clicked as the feet grew into legs and then the body could be seen. At first it was transparent and ghost-like, a fragile structure, formed by a network of soldier ants. As worker ants plugged the gaps it became more solid until, after several minutes the familiar brown, shimmering figure stood at the bottom of the garden.

"Greetings," said the PM in a resonant voice. "I believe you have a message for us."

The man-shape swayed. The head turned blindly towards the breeze and the mouth opened. Across the hole that formed the mouth, a bridge of ants quivered in the wind. Their changing vibrations created a strange humming whisper.

"Boiling water is dangerous."

Their message delivered, the column of ants collapsed and disappeared, happy in the hope that the world was now a safer place.

Weighing the Hearts
Thus are extinguished the undistinguished

Frank and Doris Stencil had always been Church of England so they were surprised to be greeted by Anubis in the afterlife.

"I know who you are," said Doris. "You're that dog-headed god from Egypt."

"Jackal-headed," corrected Anubis, but he looked pleased. "I see you are acquainted with the Book of the Dead."

"No, you were in that film, you know – The Mummy Returns."

Frank, meanwhile, was looking around at what appeared to be a pillared hall. "What's going on?" he said. "What are we doing here? We were on the A259."

"Ah, yes," said Anubis, checking the clipboard he was carrying. "Did you see the articulated lorry, which had pulled out to overtake you?"

"No."

"Ah, that would explain why you moved into its path. It clipped you and sent you spinning into a tree."

"Oh!" They both looked disconcerted, then Frank pointed to a set of scales on a table in front of Anubis.

"What's that?"

"These are the scales I use for weighing hearts. In your case I will weigh both your hearts together. They are very small."

"Are those our hearts?" Frank pointed, with distaste, at two meaty lumps on a scale.

"Yes, they are weighed against the feather of truth." Despite the difference in weights between the feather and the hearts, the scales were even.

Anubis consulted the paper on his clipboard. "I see you are from England and have therefore consumed ten times more of the earth's resources than is your rightful share. This isn't your fault, of course, and I'm sure you have contributed ten times more to the benefit of mankind. Have you created any great works of art? Novels? Poetry? Music? Paintings?"

The couple shook their heads and the scales tilted.

"Have you contributed to the sum of human knowledge? Quantum mechanics? Astronomy? Technology?"

"No, we're just ordinary people," said Frank.

"I'm sure you must have done something," said Anubis, consulting his paper once more. "Have you enlarged your minds? Have you studied history? Geography? Philosophy? Have you travelled?"

"We don't read books much – but we like to go to Eastbourne," said Doris, looking worriedly at the scales which had tilted still further. In the shadows something moved – a strange looking animal with the head of a crocodile.

"Aaargh, what's that?" screamed Doris.

"Never mind him," said Anubis, gesturing the creature back into hiding. "I'm sure Ammit won't be needed. There must be something that interests you?"

"Well, I like watching football," said Frank.

"I sometimes go to Bingo," said Doris.

The scale containing their hearts was almost as low as it could go. The couple wracked their brains.

"We had a cat once," said Doris. Slowly the scale rose again.

"Ah, a sacred cat chose to live with you, that's wonderful," said Anubis. "I'm sure he will supplicate on your behalf so you can enter paradise."

He turned to the huge gilded doors behind him and waved his arms to command them to open. They parted just far enough to allow a cat-headed man through. Behind the man was a glorious light and the sound of heavenly music. The man minced towards them. He was fat, dressed in a tunic and had a shoulder bag.

"Timothy?" said Doris uncertainly.

"Will you supplicate on behalf of this couple?" asked Anubis.

Timothy looked his former owners up and down. "Well, I didn't expect to see you here so soon. I expect you're sorry now at the way you treated me." His voice was high and peevish.

"We fed you," said Frank.

"And stroked you," said Doris.

"And castrated me," he interjected.

"Well, yes," agreed Frank. "Sorry about that. Doris was worried that you might be smelly."

"It was Frank who had you de-clawed," said Doris. "When you scratched the furniture."

"I think the weighing is over," said Anubis.

"Can I stay and watch?" asked Timothy. Anubis bowed in agreement and they watched as Ammit emerged once more from the shadows and gobbled the two hearts down.

Frank and Doris, who had turned to run from the demon, disappeared as swiftly as if a switch had been flicked off.

Anubis nodded his head and pronounced, "Thus are extinguished the undistinguished."

What Women Want
Could the simple pleasures of life become chores?

Betsie Brown hummed happily while she dusted the photo frames on her mantelpiece. Fifteen grandchildren and another on the way – she would soon be running out of space for all the pictures. She looked around her neat little living room. Tomorrow she would beeswax the furniture but today she didn't have time, she had to go and see the doctor. Betsie took off her apron, checked her tightly-curled grey hair in the mirror, put on her coat and set off.

As she walked down the street, she noted with approval the houses where the nets were white and the windows shone. Knockers polished, doorsteps scrubbed, gardens weeded – there was nothing like good housekeeping to make a nice neighbourhood. Sometimes, like a bad tooth in a smiling mouth, there was an uncared-for house belonging to a Working Woman. Betsie regarded Working Women with contempt.

A young woman drove past in a silver sports car, her loose blonde hair blowing in the wind. For a moment Betsie wondered what it would be like to experience such freedom. She shook her head, worried by the strange thoughts she had been having lately, that, and the sharp pain at the top of her nose.

Betsie sat in the surgery and surveyed the doctor – a Working Woman. The doctor's blouse was creased, her collar un-starched, her shoes unpolished. The doctor looked up from her notes.

"What can I do for you Mrs Brown?"

"I have a pain in my nose."

"Tilt your head back please, let's have a look." The doctor picked up a penlight torch and shone it up Betsie's nostril. "Ah yes, there seems to be something blocking your nasal passage. Have you been poking things up your nose Mrs Brown?"

"No I have not." Betsie was affronted. The doctor rummaged in a drawer and brought out a pair of long, slender tweezers.

"It should be easy enough to remove," she said, and gently slid the tweezers up Betsie's nose. "Ah, got it." She gave a tug. "It seems to be attached."

"Ouch," said Betsie. The obstruction came away. The doctor pulled it out and held it up triumphantly. It looked like a small, square cornflake.

"What is it?" asked Betsie, dabbing with a clean, white handkerchief at the blood and mucus dripping out of her nose.

"It's a Stepford chip." The doctor stared at it in fascination. "It must have been put into you when you were young."

"Who would do such a thing?"

"The Government. They chipped a whole generation of women to make them stay at home."

"But why?"

"In those days the population was plummeting and children were running wild. Something had to be done."

"Have you got a chip?" Betsie asked the doctor.

"Of course not." The doctor dismissed the thought impatiently and returned to her exposition.

"The problem was solved, but by a gross violation of human rights. The Stepford project had to be hushed up."

For a moment the doctor looked angry, and then she turned to Betsie with a bright smile.

"But never mind Mrs Brown, your body has rejected the chip – you are free."

Betsie realised that the pleasure she had taken in little acts of creativity had been misplaced. The cakes and jam and hand-knitted jerseys that had been so appreciated by family and friends could more easily have been bought. Instead of caring for her possessions she could have been replacing them, if only she had been a Working Woman. The doctor was about to throw the Stepford chip into the disposal bin, when Betsie stopped her.

"Wait!" Betsie thought of the delicious, home-made steak-and-kidney pudding waiting in the oven at home. How could she bear to lose the simple pleasures of life - cooking, sewing and maintaining a perfect house? Without a chip these might become chores to be avoided.

"What are you having for dinner tonight, doctor?" Betsie asked. The doctor ran a distracted hand across her forehead. "I hadn't thought," she said. "I might buy a takeaway or take a pizza out of the freezer. Why?"

Betsie held her head high. "Please doctor, I want you to put the chip back in again."

- The end -

Printed in Great Britain
by Amazon